THE ORDER OF CHAOS

THE NINE WORLDS RISING BOOK 2

LYRA WOLF

RAVENWELL PRESS

Cover design by Dominic Forbes

Ravenwell Press

eBook ISBN: 978-1-944912-31-4
Paperback ISBN: 978-1-944912-35-2
First Edition

To Hannah, who always believed in this story...except for that bit about the cat. You really crushed my dreams with that one.

If I cannot bend heaven, I will raise hell.

— Virgil, *The Aeneid*

PROLOGUE, OR HOW SPENCER AND MOLLY OF ST. GEORGE UNIVERSITY WERE ABOUT TO LEARN YOU JUST DON'T GO AROUND RELEASING STRANGE MEN IN CAVES

(SERIOUSLY. IT'S NEVER A GOOD IDEA.)

Present Day

Basel, Switzerland

"This is Stephen King level shit." Spencer clutched the EMS meter in a death grip. "It keeps spiking. The energy in this place is insane."

The EMS meter buzzed and whirred, ricocheting off the tight cavern walls we squeezed between. Its high tones pierced my eardrums.

I ignored the building pressure tightening and twisting in my head.

No one dared step foot in this cave tucked away in the forest outside Basel for five hundred years. Not since the legend of the "Screaming Man" first began.

Those who claimed to have heard the wailing were always found the same way. Shivering. Weeping. Begging God for mercy on their souls because their reckoning was coming.

We would be the first to record this "dark" supernatural

force that supposedly haunted *Dornach Hollows*. And then our Youtube channel, *GhostsGoneWild*, would finally go viral. I'd waited years for quality content like this, and no banshee or ghoul would make me quit.

"I don't want to go any farther, Molly." Mud and grit smeared Spencer's forehead and checkered Vans sneakers. "The meter's never behaved so wildly."

"We can't stop now," I said. "Just think of the views and the subs and keep going."

Spencer replied with grumbles. About how he gave up his summer break in California to be mauled by a ghost in the mud. Or worse, a clown. He always freaked out. It's what made him a fan favorite.

I pushed my tortoiseshell glasses higher up my stubby nose slick with sweat and held out our camera. I filmed, taking in the cave as we ventured deeper.

Stalagmites and stalactites glistened in the light of our flashlights before plunging back into darkness once we passed. A colony of bats clung to the pale limestone.

Pressing out of the narrow passage, we emptied into a chamber and finally could take a deep breath of damp and rock. The EMS meter's constant whirr rose into the vault that swelled at least a 150 feet over our heads.

"Wow, I've never experienced such a place. It's so..."

"Angry?" Spencer finished.

A growl of chilled air swept across my neck. Over my arms.

And with it a heaviness.

A rage.

The EMF meter's needle shot to the right, squealing and buzzing. My head pounded now.

"I don't like this," Spencer said. "Something bad is here. Something pissed off."

I rolled my eyes.

"You need to calm down." I jerked the camera from one stretch of the chamber to the other. "I have too much riding on this to quit now. We've dealt with angry spirits before."

The meter continued to wail. It thundered in my ears along with that force weighing down my shoulders. My insides.

"But none that's so...threatening," he said. "We need to leave. Now."

I opened my mouth to tell him just where he could go.

A throat cleared somewhere in the darkness.

"Excuse me, sorry to interrupt your argument, but I'd be greatly appreciative if you could loosen these bonds for me?" a voice asked. It dripped with honey and danger.

I jumped a good two feet back. The EMS meter flew out of Spencer's hand. It struck the stone and an explosion of AA batteries burst out of the plastic casing.

It continued to screech with no power source, bristling my stomach from the impossibility.

"Who said that?" I asked, forcing out the words. "Are you...Are you who haunts this cave?"

Our flashlight beams flickered off the stone walls and ceiling as we searched for the voice's owner. The camera shook in my hand, but I wouldn't stop filming. This is what we'd come for.

"Trust me, if I was a spirit I'd haunt somewhere exceedingly less damp," it said. "If you could just turn a little to the left. Yes, like that. I'm over here."

We caught a flash of bare skin. A shock of red hair.

It was a man.

My heart hammered against my ribs as we raced to him, my heels sliding on shards and fragments of stone.

I never expected what we saw.

Horror.

Black cords tied him tight against a slab of rock, and burns covered his body in a savage mix of crisp skin and wet scars. Patches of red hair peppered the gnarled topography of his scalp.

But his face...

I clapped my hand over my mouth, trying to keep down what threatened to come up.

"What happened to you?" I asked.

Something grim settled behind his clouded eyes. Something terrible...

In a second it vanished.

He gave a crooked smile. Well, he tried to smile with what lips remained. I wished he wouldn't have. It made him more unnerving.

"That is a long story, and I'm afraid I'm a bit pressed for time. Massive to-do list," he said. "Now, if you'd be a dear and untie me, I'd be much obliged."

Though he spoke with all the ease of a relaxed cat, it couldn't mask the timbre of desperation running beneath his friendly words.

It was perfectly understandable given the state of him.

Thin, black cords tugged at his wrists and ankles, pulling him taut. I shuddered at how deep they split into the man's flesh from him wrenching against them.

How was he still alive?

I reached out to undo the jungle of knots and ties binding him rigid.

Spencer gripped my forearm and tugged me away.

"Don't," he said. "I don't think this is human."

I tore myself free.

"What's wrong with you?" I snapped. "He's not some ghost. He's seriously injured and needs our help."

The man held Spencer's gaze and his grizzled eyes flashed. Spencer swallowed his dread.

"He's not like us either," Spencer said. "Normal people don't survive injuries like these."

The man gave a funny sort of grin. Like when you know the answer to a riddle and refuse to share the secret.

The EMS meter kept buzzing and whistling. As if the energy surrounding us powered it.

I didn't care.

"I'm not leaving him here," I said. "We have to get him to a hospital."

I pushed Spencer back and set to work untying the black cords from around the man's seared body. He winced as I peeled them away from his flesh. Out of his flesh. Unwinding and breaking and tearing.

Putrid tissue filled my quick breaths.

Death.

Decay.

I tried not to think about his blood cramming beneath my fingernails.

Or how the odd material of the cords made me want to recoil. There was something that felt oddly...*organic*...about them.

This poor, poor man.

One arm free. Then the other.

What reason would there be to do this to anyone?

A leg next.

I snapped the final cord.

He slipped his last ankle free from his bonds.

I smiled releasing him, anticipating the same flood of warmth I experienced when I'd released a sparrow caught in a mess of wire on my grandmother's farm.

A feeling like a vacuum sucked the air from my lungs instead.

I felt only cold.

Frigid.

The EMS meter's plastic casing cracked, and the whine dwindled into a moan and into silence. Almost as if the force powering it was now too great. As if I'd released something powerful.

Deadly.

For two seconds, I believed Spencer right.

No. I'd done a good thing.

The decent thing.

The man stood off the rock and lengthened his stance. He rolled his shoulders and stretched his neck left and then right enjoying the prize of movement.

How could he stand at all?

Adrenaline. That was the answer. The same thing that allowed mothers to lift cars off of their children.

I took a step towards him to offer him my shoulder to lean against. He looked at it. His right eye twitched.

"Let's get you to a doctor before you finally collapse," I said.

He put out his arm, stopping me. He tried to screw his face into something I could only assume he meant to be pleasant.

It only made me shudder harder.

"Unnecessary," he said. "If you'd excuse me a moment, there's something I've been dying to do."

He walked into the darkness, faltering only once before strengthening into an almost feline stride.

I moved my flashlight with him.

My breath hitched.

A twisting body of scales squirmed beneath a pile of

rubble. A snake. A snake at least twelve feet from nose to tip with yellow eyes and white fangs so sharp I could feel them pierce my flesh.

He walked to the snake, his toes stretching against the rock with each solid step. The snake hissed and flicked its pink tongue. It thrashed harder, trying to free itself. Trying to strike his heels.

"Took ages of screaming to shake this place hard enough to loosen the rock," he said. "One lucky stone was all I needed to break its back."

A glint of pleasure lifted the man's features as he stared down at the serpent. Laughter followed, a wild rush of it that made my stomach churn.

He bent and gripped the snake with both hands beneath its head. The animal writhed as the man's face reflected in the storm of its yellow eyes that wanted to kill...

He twisted.

He smiled when a clear snap echoed and darted against the cave walls.

"I endured scalding venom eating into my flesh for centuries from that son of a bitch." He grimaced, looking down at his charred arms. Raw stomach. "You wouldn't have any aloe vera?" he asked. "No? No matter."

He stood, seeming even taller than earlier.

He flickered. A wash of images flashed in and out and over him, through him, until one popped to the surface, hiding the mangled man beneath absolute divinity.

Very naked divinity.

Thick, copper red hair waved like flames around a sharp and beautiful face and fell just past a set of strong shoulders. His body was lean and hard, defined in all the right places.

His eyes shot to my own. Striking green that bore into

my depths, promising me my every secret desire to completion.

Spencer and I didn't say a word. Didn't move. We couldn't. I didn't know if it was more from fear, shock, or the shock of finally finding the truth we always wanted.

The supernatural existed, and I stared right at him.

And I kept filming.

The man held out his hands and inspected them. His perfect hands I couldn't stop imagining running down the length of my spine.

"That's much better," he said. "Feeling back to my old self already."

"What the hell are you?" I asked.

Laughter lit behind his eyes.

"Mortals like you can't usually handle what I am. But seeing as it's the end of the worlds and all..."

"Wait, what?"

He looked at us and smiled. Wry. Devastating.

I dared a step closer to get a better shot.

A wave of heat rolled off of him and struck me in the chest.

His eyes erupted with fire. A blaze that broiled my cheeks.

And I knew.

This was not a man or a spirit. This was something worse.

A god.

Reckoning.

He pulled my camera out of my grasp and squeezed until it glowed as red as the fire burning within his eyes. Molten glass and plastic ran between his fingers to my feet.

"I am Loki, the Destroyer and Breaker of Worlds—and Ragnarok is here."

1

BACK IN BUSINESS AGAIN

I was back.

As if the gods could keep me down.

Bitch, please. It would take more than a little scalding snake venom to stop me.

The gods only achieved making me angrier with their pathetic attempt to trap me. To torture me. Every drop of liquid fire that slipped from that snake's fangs branded my purpose deeper into my chest. Every second I endured lost in that darkness hardened my resolve to take their lives as they took the lives of my family.

A pure and exquisite wrath filled me. I starved for blood. For judgement.

For Ragnarok. The end of everything.

And I loved it.

I was going to burn them all to the ground for what they did.

This would be such fun.

As eager for the show as I was, I unfortunately had a to-do list a mile long. It didn't help the world was nothing how I left it in 1526.

After narrowly avoiding getting struck by a growling block of metal on wheels, and then by something I later learned was a bus, and by an old woman riding a bee-cycle, I realized it was far more interesting.

Car engines roared and trams rattled along metal tracks. Music blared out of white buds in ears, and people spoke into enchanted rectangles while other larger rectangles yelled back from shop windows and inside apartments.

Lives were no longer simple. They were much more complicated. Faster. Louder. Chaotic.

Perfect.

I even ate something marvelous called an ice cream cone.

I found it a shame to destroy this new world, really. But what can one do?

I took another bite of my pistachio ice cream and looked down at my plain black suit and grimaced.

The man in the Münster Cathedral, my first stop on my grand tour of the cosmos, did his best giving me some clothes after I'd shown up naked at the altar. But I couldn't destroy the worlds in a poly-blend suit.

That would be the true tragedy.

I needed something new. Something fabulous.

I would make Ragnarok look good.

I caught humans chattering about a place called a "department store," which seemed the very thing I required. And the best apparently was on Marktplatz, the main square in Basel's city center. I headed there at once.

Doors of glass slid open and I walked across polished, white tiles that reflected the glaring lights from the ceiling. An odd place stuffed with clothes on metal racks, bins filled with merino wool scarves, and perfume bottles lining back-lit shelves.

I felt eyes on me. I turned. A woman stared at me from behind a glass counter. Perfect painted red lips. Legs for days. She twirled her brunette hair around a manicured finger. I understood. I had a certain effect on women. And men. And everyone.

I flashed her my most devastating smile. After a few words back and forth brimming with euphemisms, Elena offered to help me navigate these new Midgardian fashions.

She picked out a pair of black, tight-fitting trousers and insisted helping me put on a black t-shirt. She said it really showed off the hard definition of my chest. I enjoyed her perfume of jasmine as she clasped silver chains around my neck that matched the silver rings she stacked on my fingers.

To complete the look, an extravagant jacquard tuxedo jacket with red stitched floral embroidery caught my eye. Elena tried to talk me out of it for something more subdued. I never was one for anything subdued. Besides, the jacket reminded me of the heavy patterned fabrics I had adored in the sixteenth century. I was a sucker for embroidery.

Total damage amounted to 2,340.09 francs.

Oh.

Now, this was embarrassing.

I had no money. Elena bit her bottom lip. What to do? Her eyes darkened and roved down my chest. Then lower.

I brushed the side of her hand with my fingertips. I could feel her quiver beneath my touch.

Perhaps an arrangement could be made?

The dressing room walls shook and clothes fell off hangers. We got quite carried away. Unspeakable acts.

She muffled her cries into a wool coat.

Can I be blamed? Five hundred years was a lengthy time to go without sex. Without food. Without light.

Hope.

I pushed the dark and damp of the cave from my mind, forcing myself to focus only on the heat and sweat and pleasure of the dressing room.

Once finished, she stuffed a hundred franc note in my back pocket and whispered a "thank you" in my ear. A pink flush of complete satisfaction brightened her cheeks.

Leaving the store, I straightened my aviator sunglasses and walked out into the wind that howled through Marktplatz. Heavy flakes of snow fell from a gray sky, catching in the waves of my copper hair.

Winter in July. Fimbulwinter.

The first sign of Ragnarok.

My fault, I'm afraid.

I breathed in the rush of the cold and what I as the Destroyer promised. I held the fates of all living creatures in my hand like a small bird.

Such a thought sickened me when I learned what Odin had kept from me. The truth of what I was. What my destiny meant.

But certain events changed all that.

I took off across the cobblestones, dodging the green trams that slithered through the city like snakes. The massive red Rathaus spread the length of the square, looking the same as the last time I walked here.

Looking the same as the first time I caught sight of her.

Sigyn.

Memories rose around me as I started up the steep alley of Totengässlein. I stretched out my arm and ran my fingers along the lime plaster homes as I climbed the steps. I could almost feel her beside me again. Her warmth. Her fidelity...

The noise of Marktplatz dissolved into stillness as I kept on, as if I stepped into the past. Into a hush where I could pretend I'd see her running to me after her day working at her father's printing press.

I sauntered on, out of one memory and into another.

Into Herr Burgi's apothecary, where she bought all her ingredients for the salves and medicines she made. To help others. To share her passion for medicine and science.

Gods I missed her.

I missed them.

I chased the ghosts I conjured through the streets that remained untouched by modernity. And in those seconds, the ghosts were real.

I had them back.

I had my family back.

I stopped. Clouds of hot breath rolled out from my lungs.

Sigyn's home stood before me.

Nothing was straight about the house anymore, as if the entire structure had sighed and relaxed into the city.

I pulled out a votive candle I'd bought (*bought*, because Sigyn didn't approve of petty theft) at a grocery store and placed it in front of the green door. Snapping my fingers, I ignited the wick. It burst into a beautiful flame. She loved prayer candles, and now I lit one for her as she had once done for me in the Münster Cathedral. When I knew I loved her.

I closed my eyes, thinking of Sigyn. Thinking of Narfi and Nari, our twin boys.

They had been born in this house. I thought my life whole.

And then everything shattered.

The gods believed our children the instigators of Ragnarok. All because some stupid prophecy said so. And

Odin believed it. They all believed it. They would kill my family to stop my destiny. I couldn't allow that.

I gave my life for theirs. What better deal could the gods hope for than the Destroyer himself? But they betrayed me. They murdered Sigyn. They killed my sons and ripped out their guts and used them to tie me to that rock.

Then there was only darkness. Suffocating pain.

That's when I became what I never wanted to become. And it was their fault.

I made a fist and leaned my forehead against the chilled door.

"They promised you'd all be safe," I whispered, as if this inch of oak was all that separated her from hearing me. "It should have only been me."

I tightened my fist and cinders cracked between my fingers. Heavy snow melted against my cheeks and steam rose off my shoulders and arms.

"I will make them pay for their betrayal. And then, I can be with you. We will be a family again."

I took in a shivery breath and stepped backward and into something solid.

No.

Some*one*.

"Watch it, asshole."

Asshole? No one called me an asshole.

I swung around and stared down at a sniveling thirteen-year-old boy. He wore a slouchy knit cap that unfortunately didn't hide enough of his scrunched, mean face. I would fix that problem.

I reached for his scrawny neck, but stopped.

He held a thin booklet jam-packed with colors and figures wearing winged helmets and red capes. At the top, written in bright, big, bold letters was the word *THOR*.

What the f—

I ripped it out of the boy's grubby hands, ignoring his rampage of threats and curses. I flipped through glossed pages covered in images of Thor and Odin, of all the gods, fighting enemies and vanquishing foes with one mighty strike of Thor's hammer, Mjolnir.

Of course, their likenesses weren't exactly accurate, but where was…

…oh gods.

A snarly looking figure clad in tights and wearing an impractical horned helmet stared back at me.

The villain.

Me.

While Thor and Odin and the rest were hailed as heroes, they made me the monster of the story? After what they did?

A voice whispered in my mind.

Burn them. Kill them. Destroy them.

The boy and the street dissolved into a field of dead grass that stretched for miles around me. Hot wind blew through my hair, and that familiar stench of ash and death filled my lungs. I was no longer in Basel. I was on Vigridr, the battlefield of Ragnarok.

Twirling sparks snapped within the red haze, smothering this place. And there it stood. As always.

A figure covered in a shroud of white linen. The spirit of this place. At least, that's what I assumed it was. I honestly didn't know, and I didn't care. Our tête-à-têtes offered me momentary escapes from the horror the gods had trapped me within.

"This is shameful fodder." I pointed at the comic book. "I refuse to wait a second more for their blood."

"Patience. You shall have your war." Brimstone saturated

its voice.

"Patience?" I snapped. "I've done five hundred years of patience."

"Have I failed you yet?" it asked. "During your bondage, your suffering, I gave you purpose. I made you what you are. Ragnarok is here and you walk free because of me."

This spirit never failed at being cocky.

I walked towards it, a fan of heat exploding beneath my every step.

"You? You seem to forget I'm the Destroyer. I've ignited Ragnarok, and it's mine to command."

It laughed. I wasn't sure with me, or at me.

"Your position is quite precarious," it said. "The gods will discover you've escaped. They will hunt you down and throw you back into that darkness and pain. Until you secure an army, you remain vulnerable."

That thought sliced through my guts. I wouldn't return there.

I couldn't.

But only one army was formidable enough against Odin's precious warriors of Valhalla.

Odin collected their souls like a miser collected gold coins. He cut down healthy men. Let the better side lose. Did worse to get what he wanted. All for a gambit to stop little ol' me.

"I guess acquiring an unbeatable army just made my to-do list."

I sensed it grin.

"Once the army is yours, once you are untouchable, you will complete your most important task."

Now this part I liked.

My fire spiraled hot and wicked in my veins. It wanted

out, and I would let it out in the most cataclysmic way. It was going to be amazing.

"I will wake Surtr." Embers crackled within my words. "And the final battle will begin."

Surtr. Fire giant. Pure darkness spat out of the bowels of Muspelheim itself. Paired with my chaos...my heart somersaulted imagining the carnage we would unleash together.

The spirit took a step closer to me. Molten points of orange and yellow light swept around us.

"And when Surtr drives its flaming sword into the heart of Vigridr, it will finish Ragnarok," it said. "All will end and your destiny as the Destroyer will be fulfilled."

Fire erupted behind my eyes. They were only fire, and soon would be all the Nine Worlds.

"Now go burn them. Kill them. Destroy them."

Each word swelled in my bones with the beautiful carnage I was about to unleash.

The figure vanished.

Vigridr shifted beneath my feet. The dried grass blurred within the crimson fog.

A jerk and a shove.

Another shove.

Something was shoving me.

No.

Some*one*.

"Give it back asshole, or I'm going to break your nose."

I was back in front of Sigyn's house and the teenager obviously wasn't finished with me yet.

As I wasn't with him.

I twisted my lips slowly into a smile as I met the boy's gaze. His nostrils flared and his glare was pure menace. I loved it when humans challenged me. As if they stood a chance.

"Some kindly advice from me to you," I said. "I'd start preparing that nasty, greasy soul of yours, because in a matter of days, you won't be worrying over such trivial possessions as this drivel anymore."

I fluttered his book just out of his reach.

He jumped for it, only an inch short of grazing the smooth pages. Pity.

I laughed and sent a rush of flames down the cover. Thor and Odin's images blistered and peeled. The colors blackened into ash. It was all extremely poetic.

The menace in the boy's eyes iced into fear.

A shrill scream burst out of his lungs and he took off running, his heels sliding across the slick cobblestone and arms waving to keep his balance. He resembled a very flabbergasted penguin.

Humans never could keep their wits when faced with divinity.

And I never could keep to a schedule.

With one final glance back at the house, I turned and left into the blowing snow. I had an army to obtain, after all.

But why did it have to be hers?

2

ISLE OF THE DEAD

I shoved the last bite of a strawberry ice cream cone in my mouth and stepped off the tram onto the cement platform of Dreispitz. Drab didn't even begin to describe this South-East scab of Basel languishing in smoke and industry.

Crisscrossing wires jostled over my head as the tram left the platform. Cars snarled along the roads lined with aluminum street lamps and ugly homes. My nostrils burned from the diesel and other acrid chemicals.

I already regretted this visit.

I crossed the street and strode towards a gateway made of limestone and arches and wrought iron bars.

Wolfgottesacker Cemetery. One of the few remaining cemeteries in the city. The Swiss were too pragmatic to cherish a bunch of slacking skeletons eternally. The dead took up an awful lot of space, contributing nothing. Cold? True. But it was better than when they buried them beneath cathedrals. Summers were quite ripe.

Entering the cemetery, the pavement split into several paths that cut through grass coated in gray frost. Robins huddled against the cold in tree branches above me as I kept to a trail that edged a wall lined with massive headstones. Bushes and wilting wild flowers crammed around the stones, each more ornate than the last.

I almost felt back in the eras I remembered. When marble and heavy architecture were favored to glass and steel.

Drinking songs from raucous feasts pulsed inside my ears, while mead bursting with honey and orange tingled my tongue. The scratch of wool pricked my fingertips and wood smoke filled my breaths from a spitting fire.

It was all so warm. Inviting...

The screech of a train from the train yard behind the cemetery plunged me into a frigid truth. The world moved on leaving the old world behind.

Leaving *me* behind.

Pain bit into my palms. I forced my fingers out of fists I hadn't realized I'd made and glanced down. Eight red, crescent moons marked my skin from my own nails.

This is why I hated cemeteries. It always brought out the glummest of sentiments in me.

Glum was so boring.

And it would only get worse where I headed.

Hel.

The realm of the dishonorable dead. A catch-all for those who died cowards, or behaved a touch too naughty.

It also happened to be ruled by my daughter, Hel. Because if you're given your own realm to rule, you might as well name it after yourself. Narcissistic? Perhaps. But a little self-confidence never hurt anyone. Although, it did make things dreadfully confusing at times.

I stood in front of the doors of an immense mausoleum and gripped the doorknob. The grit of the tarnished brass scratched my palm as I forced the door open. The rusted hinges squealed.

I walked inside the crypt and into swirling dust and dirt. Ten alcoves lined the walls in neat rows, each stuffed with a wooden coffin in varying stages of decay.

I guess one was as good as any.

I pulled out a coffin from the bottom row, splintering the wood against the stone as I slid it into the center of the room.

I flung open the lid. A leathered corpse looked back at me with empty eye sockets and a yawning mouth. Kneeling, I lowered my hands into the coffin and clasped its upper arms. I tried not to think how my fingers plunged through its brittle, silk tuxedo.

"My apologies," I said to the corpse. "But I need this more than you."

I tossed the shriveled thing out of the coffin and brushed away the wood shavings from the bottom.

I was not looking forward to this reunion.

Taking in a breath, I rapped my knuckles against the bottom.

Knock. Knock. Knock.

The stone floor shook beneath my knees. I shot up and skipped back as the entire mausoleum quaked. Coffins rattled out of their alcoves and cracked open, striking the marble. Corpses and skeletons burst out in gray clouds of dust that covered my shoulders and shoes.

Of course.

The bottom of the coffin shifted and gave way, revealing a narrow staircase inside.

All graves were the gateway to Hel, you see.

I snapped my fingers and ignited a small flame in my palm and descended the steps. Cobwebs clung to my clothes and silverfish skittered away from the light, retreating into the gloom.

The air cooled.

Damp and rot filled my every breath.

A light suction and a pop.

A bit of a tickle.

And I stepped out of one realm and into another.

My heels sank into black sand as I plodded along a beach littered with swords and human skulls. The Shore of Corpses. As lovely a place as it sounded.

The Veiled Sea thundered against sharp rocks and mounds of rusted armor, coating me in a fine mist that cut a shiver down to my bones.

Gods I hated this realm. I just prayed my brand new Louboutin Chelsea boots survived. If they got scuffed...

I shook the mummy dust out of my clothes and trudged up a hill and onto a path strewn with rocks and pebbles that led directly to Hel's palace, Eljudnir.

I could already make out its pointed spires rising above a layer of fog. A hundred windows of halls and wings reflected the blood reds and bruised purples of the darkening sky. The entire palace looked simultaneously cruel and melancholy, much like its mistress.

I stepped onto a bridge that spanned the Gjoll River, which separated the living from the dead. The planks bowed and cracked beneath my feet, the wood as rotten as the woman standing at the far end waiting for me.

Modgud. The guardian of this bridge who possessed all the charm of a pissed off wasp.

"Hello Modgud," I said. "My, are you using a new stitching pattern to keep your head sewn on your neck? It's done wonders for your whole, uhhh, *thing*, you have going on here. Very fetching."

She eyed me, which was a problem. I never knew which eye actually looked at me. I decided it was the blue one.

"She's not pleased with you being here," Modgud growled.

"That makes two of us."

Hel could always sense when a new soul crossed into her realm. And the fact I was still alive was like a foghorn. She always said the living gave her a headache.

I made to pass Modgud, but she put out a withered arm and stopped me.

"You cannot pass until I know your business," she said.

I rolled my eyes. The dead were always sticklers for rules. I guess rules were all they had left to worry about.

"As lovely as this little interrogation is, I'm in a bit of a rush."

"No business, no entrance."

It took everything in me not to tear off her leg and shove it up her—

"Let him in." A voice with all the sweetness of a razor called from a window. Hel's voice. "The quicker we let him in, the quicker we get him out."

A warm welcome, as always.

* * *

A SERVANT that looked held together more by the starch in his clothes than his own decaying skin escorted me down a long hall of checkered tiles.

Chandeliers made from ribs and pelvises lined the vaulted ceiling. I preferred them to the marble busts of faces frozen in various expressions of torment lining the black walls.

She always loved to collect the macabre, and this entire place was like a poem dedicated to the grotesque.

The servant pushed open an oak door with his good shoulder—I'm sorry, his *only* shoulder.

"My mistress will be with you momentarily," he said wearily.

He shuffled away as I walked across the gleaming black marble floors of her private quarters. Sparsely decorated. A heavy mahogany desk. A divan of good velvet. Very practical. Very boring.

A roar of cheers and the strike of steel flooded the room, coming from the terrace.

But it was a plasticized human body that took my attention. Neatly filleted and positioned with a racket in its hand, as if playing a game of badminton.

"One of my newest pieces," Hel spoke behind me. "Imported from Midgard. They use only the finest criminals to make these."

I turned and faced her. The plasticized human was more serene.

She wore an elegant black pantsuit with diamonds and Elven crystals encrusting the tops of her shoulders and running the length of the right lapel. Pointed silver finger cuffs capped her fingers. But her face...The right side was blue and withered. The left was divine.

I could see the strong features of her mother in her brow and ebony hair, but her eyes were mine. Green, sly, and quick.

"Have you ever considered taking up watercolors?" I said. "You might consider branching out into less morbid hobbies."

She narrowed her eyes and walked towards me. Her black heels clicked against the marble floor.

Another burst of cheers rocked through the terrace.

"Why have you come, Father?" she asked. "Is my kingdom all you have left to go to now you're a fugitive?"

She always had all the pleasantness of a hurricane. That was all her mother.

"So you know where I've been?"

She turned away and walked out onto the terrace. I followed.

"Yes. Odin came to me shortly after it happened," she said over the clang of metal.

I tensed hearing his name. My betrayer. The man I gave everything to.

I hungered to plunge my hand into his chest and rip out his beating heart and crush it like he did my own.

But all in good time.

An arena erupted beneath us packed with her subjects. Thousands cheered her and cheered the dozen warriors battling each other with axes and swords and maces. They were brutal as they sliced open necks and stirred bowels with spears.

I couldn't help a smile pull on my lips.

While Odin's warriors matched Hel's in bloodlust and skill, they all died honorable men. Honor is weakness, and fairness has no place in war. Only dishonesty gets results.

And Hel's legions of thieves and thugs were as dishonest as they come.

Hel braced her hands on the railing and stared over her empire of death and gore.

"He told me all about the tragedy. The girl. The cave. The torture." She paused and smiled, as if enjoying thinking of the beautiful horror of it all. "You really embroil yourself in the worst situations."

I grated my teeth.

"It was not my fault," I said. Warned.

Laughter burst out of her lungs.

"Of course not. It never is." Sarcasm dripped from each word. "I'd never seen Odin so distant. Like his mind was elsewhere. I suspect it was still in that cave with you."

I crushed my nails against my palms in perfect unison as a muscle bound gladiator cut his axe into the shoulder of his foe. And then straight between his eyes. A lovely spray of blood soaked into the dirt floor of the arena.

"Why did Odin come to you?"

Hel grinned, watching the fallen soldier be dragged away along with four others. It was only temporary, of course. Tomorrow they'd pop back up and be battle ready again. You couldn't die twice, after all.

"He told me that if you ever miraculously escaped your prison, if you ever stepped foot in my kingdom, I was to send him word."

Did he now?

"And are you?"

She stiffened and scraped her silver finger cuffs against the stone rail.

"I will not be commanded," she said.

I smiled.

Now that sentiment was all me.

She released the tension from her shoulders.

"If you've come to bargain for Sigyn's soul, she isn't here," she said, changing the subject.

My stomach roiled thinking of Sigyn in this place. Of her light being smothered by the damp and cold and shadows...

"Of course she isn't here," I said. "She died honorably protecting our children. She wouldn't be stuck in this pit."

Hel's eyes snapped to mine.

"You speak very freely for someone whose freedom rests

on me keeping my mouth shut," she said. "If you've not come for Sigyn, then why have you come?"

I looked below at two gladiators swinging maces and swords, a storm of sweat and steel. They were the storm I needed to finish the gods.

"Ragnarok."

She lengthened her spine.

"The end of everything," she said. "Death."

"Death," I repeated, my skin prickling with the rush of exquisite wrath.

The gladiator ran his sword through the stomach of his opponent. He fell to his knees. Blood and foam bubbled out of his lips and ran down his chin.

Applause filled the arena with thunder.

Hel faced me.

"And what have you to do with Ragnarok?" she asked.

I chuckled.

"So, Odin didn't tell you everything, then?"

"Such as?"

"I'm the Destroyer—The Breaker of Worlds—and I've ignited Ragnarok."

She tilted her head. A mixture of disbelief and wonder softened her features.

"They broke their promise to me. Frigg murdered Sigyn and our sons..." My voice cracked. I had to remain above the surface of the grief threatening to pull me under. "They've taken too much for too long. I'm bringing the gods' reckoning."

Burn them. Kill them. Destroy them.

The voice whispered in my ear again. Louder than before.

Her mouth parted.

"But you'll die, too," she breathed.

So she did have some slice of concern for her father's well-being, after all. It warmed my heart.

I shrugged.

"Comes with the job, I'm afraid."

"I've never pegged you as the suicidal type."

I smiled.

"And miss the chance to watch all my dear old friends go down in flames courtesy of me? It's like you don't know me at all."

And just like that, her concern hardened into her usual ice.

"You're right. I don't."

She gave a signal to her men below. They nodded and lifted a gate. A rush of lions and tigers exploded out onto the dirt and ripped their claws through the gladiators' armor like paper.

"This is your quarrel with the gods, not mine," she said.

"Is it not? They've harmed our entire family. It's time they pay."

She arched her eyebrow.

"Family?" Scorn filled the word. "You dare speak of family to me? You've not exactly been the model father. And when the gods came for my brothers and me…"

This I would not be blamed for.

I reached out and clasped her upper arm and stroked my thumb over her sleeve.

"Your mother and I thought we were protecting you—"

She stepped back, throwing me off her.

"The gods took me from my home in Ironwood," she shot back, each word a strike across my cheek.

"I didn't know it was all a grand con by Odin—"

"They took me from my brothers. From all I had known and loved."

Pain speared the back of my throat.

"Of course they did," I said, raising my voice above hers. "Because they wanted to tear our family apart. Because they believed you, *all* my children, their undoing."

Her lips tightened. She stared out into the distance.

"They keep trying to control me..."

"That's what they do. They take. They rip apart. They rule. They need to be taught that we are not to be ruled."

I took her hand as I used to when she was a child. When I'd explain to her the constellations and the stories behind them. Of course, she only wanted to know the most gruesome ones.

"You've still not given me a good reason why to join forces with you," she said. "I owe you nothing."

"Because, for once, our ambitions align."

Her skin prickled beneath my fingertips.

"What do you know of my ambitions?"

Voices boiled in my head again as I leaned in to her ear.

"Can you not hear the call?" I whispered.

Burn them. Kill them. Destroy them.

The words rippled down my spine. Beautiful. Caressing. Consuming.

I gripped her upper arms.

"Can you not feel it?"

Her eyes rolled back in her head and she closed them and inhaled deeply.

"I hear Ragnarok," she whispered. "I feel its hunger. I admit it's rooted a want deep within me these last days."

Soldiers dropped like flies as the lions and tigers tore off arms and sank teeth into heads, bursting them open like pomegranate seeds.

"And what do you want, Daughter?"

A smile tugged at the decaying corner of her mouth.

"I want the worlds to be quiet. I want their lives to end. I want their souls to fill my kingdom and be mine. And then I will answer to no one."

Everything rode on this moment.

"This is what I'm offering you. All will be yours," I said. "I only need your army and we will end them."

Her eyes flashed open, and she pulled away.

"No," she said.

My heart plummeted into my stomach.

No?

She walked back inside and to a black lacquered table shoved hard beside a crackling fireplace. She tried to pour herself a drink. She ended up missing the glass entirely and splattering her fingers instead with port.

"Odin's wrath is not worth the risk. I'm already outside his favor simply because I exist. It was a blessing he let me be banished here, with a purpose, unlike my brothers' fates to spend eternity toiling away. The thought of him taking my kingdom away from me..."

I shook my head and poured the port into the glass for her.

"What is Odin to us when he falls at our feet?"

I handed her the glass. She only stared at it.

"And if he doesn't?" she asked. "If you fail?"

Now that was insulting.

"I won't," I said. "I can't."

Her eyes searched mine. She wanted to believe me.

"Pretty sentiment, but you've already fallen once to Odin in trying to protect what was yours," she said.

Anger rushed in me from her brazen words. More so from the truth contained within their thorns.

"It's different now. I am the Destroyer. It is my fate. I really don't see the problem here."

She shook her head.

"The problem is I just don't trust you."

Ah. That old chestnut.

"The army of Hel is the only one that can match Odin's of Valhalla," I said.

She raised her head, as if proud of that fact.

"Yes, my warriors are quite formidable...but..."

"Your army ensures the victory Ragnarok promises," I said. And here it came. The begging. Sincere begging. The worst kind.

"Hel, I need you."

"And I need assurance," she snapped back.

I ran my fingers through my hair, ready to pull it out. Why couldn't she see? There was no risk if she gave me what I needed.

And if she didn't...

My skin burned with the memory of the snake's venom pouring over me.

"We aren't speaking of toy soldiers and war games," I said. "This is Ragnarok. Inevitability. And it is ours."

I held out the glass of port to her again.

She paused. She thought. A glint flashed in her eyes. The same glint I got when struck by an idea of genius.

Oh. This could get dicey.

"If I would agree, and that's a big if, you'd need to prove you can come through."

Now we were getting somewhere.

"Name it."

She took the glass from me and drained the port.

"Balder."

I choked.

"What?"

3

BENEATH THE MISTLETOE

Hel pulled out a brass key and unlocked a door. She led me into a small chamber.

"No one has ever seen what I'm about to show you. Not one snide remark."

"What kind of father do you think I am? Give me a little credit."

The entire room was empty except for the arched alcove at the far end. Candles flickered wild and dim, scattered across a table covered in velvet and crammed with trinkets and baubles.

No.

Gods no.

In the center, surrounded by freshly cut roses and prayer beads, stood a grinning portrait of Balder.

I never knew I could be this disappointed in any person.

"Is this...an altar?"

She let out an irritated sigh.

"I knew you wouldn't understand." She lit a stick of incense. "He's the most amazing man in all the Nine Worlds."

"Amazing is not the word I would choose."

I would have gone with "dick."

She placed the incense in front of his portrait, letting the smoke curl around its edges and over his smug face that always begged me to punch him and break his flawless nose.

"When you took me to Asgard as a child, the other children pointed and laughed at my appearance. But not him." Her eyes glazed, seeing into a dream. "He stopped them and then spent the afternoon speaking to me of pretty things."

She pointed at a smooth stone placed reverently on a silk pillow.

"He gave me this. He said whenever I touched this stone, it would always let me remember goodness."

"I can't believe you made him an altar," I whispered beneath my breath.

"This is my bargain," she said. "Give me Balder, send his soul directly to me, prove you won't muck something up, and I will give you the army you desire."

Hold on...

"Are you saying all I have to do is kill Balder?"

Her mouth, one half pristine, the other half decayed, twisted into a smile.

"That's exactly what I'm saying."

Excitement washed through me. I knew this sweet, sweet day would come.

Although the fact I had to go right into the heart of Asgard didn't thrill me.

I hated the spark of fear chewing at my edges. I hated how my skin burned with the thought of that venom again.

That darkness.

And there was another itsy, bitsy problem.

I had no suitable weapons capable of killing a god.

"If I'm to risk going back to Asgard and kill Balder for you, I'm going to need more than just my good looks."

She extended her finger and waved it at me, her silver cuff catching the pale light.

"Quite right."

Hel knelt before the altar and pushed aside the velvet table covering. She pulled out a red leather box with gold fittings from a shelf and balanced it on her lap. The hinges groaned as she opened the box to me.

I lost my breath.

They were such beautiful things.

I removed a pair of exquisite daggers from their silk lining and admired their perfect balance. Their lethal double edges.

I gripped the leather-wrapped hilts in each hand and squeezed. Delight raced in my veins. I'd missed the sensation of steel against my palms.

"Andvari himself forged these daggers for me. They are the strongest Dwarven steel Svartalfheim offers."

Dwarven steel. The only metal that could end a god's life.

That could end Balder's life.

"I will enjoy cutting these through his throat," I said, running my thumb over the bevel.

She chuckled.

"Unfortunately, they won't even sever a blonde hair on his head."

My heart fell.

"Is this some kind of twisted joke?"

"After the gods tied you to that rock, they became oddly nervous," she said. "They flooded Balder with every single protective spell and charm they could find."

Balder was the biggest prick in all the Nine Worlds, and

now the gods made him invincible to boot? That was bullshit.

"Nervous?" I said. "You'd think after throwing me in that pit they would have felt some security. False as it may have been."

I suppose I had promised them their total and utter ruin before they...*well.* I just loved knowing my threats got beneath their skin for all these centuries.

She shrugged.

"One would think, but there must be some reason they'd bother going to such lengths with Balder. He must be important, but why, I cannot say."

"Then how am I supposed to accomplish this 'impossible' task you've set me? You can't toy with my hopes like this."

Mischief sparked behind her eyes.

She lifted the box's velvet lining and pulled out a paltry sprig of mistletoe. One end was stuffed with white berries and green leaves, but the other side was sharpened into a lovely little point.

Hel looked at the dart as if a lover.

"Nothing can hurt him. Nothing can kill him. Except for this."

I laughed.

"That puny thing? You've got to be kidding me."

She raised her right brow.

"You doubt? You're not the only one that can pull a trick," she said. "Frigg collected oaths from every living creature that it would not harm her son. I was horrified. I'd be parted from Balder forever. I couldn't allow that. I cast a spell and hid this darling sprig of mistletoe within a shadow. Frigg walked right by, never realizing she missed the only thing that could take her son's life."

I went rigid at hearing that bitch's name. The one that had torn her knife into...That had...had...

Hel handed the fragile dart to me, freeing me from the beasts and monsters in my head.

It wouldn't produce the gruesome arc of blood I wanted, but it would have to do. Besides, the satisfaction of killing Odin and Frigg's dear son with something so harmless would more than make up for it.

"Do we have a deal?" she asked. "Will you kill Balder in exchange for my army?"

I continued to stare at the dart of mistletoe in my hand and what it meant.

All I wanted.

Or losing it all.

4

HOME, SWEET HOME

Asgard

Dirt pushed beneath my fingernails as I surged my hand up and out of the earth. I clawed at the grass, heaving myself out of a grave and onto a hill.

Clumps of mud and clay rained off my shoulders as I stood and stared out over Asgard.

The sun sank behind the Asgardian Sea, glazing the land in pinks and twilight blues. A flash of green lit that hard line where ocean met sky. The sun disappeared and night closed in as I closed in on the gods.

I sucked in that familiar salt and pine and smiled.

I was home.

And killing Balder was going to be glorious.

Twigs split behind me. Voices of men neared coming up the hill.

I ducked behind an oak and pressed my back against its trunk. I held my breath and gripped the hilts of my daggers on my belt.

A group of farmers walked by, their lanterns bobbing at their hips as they returned from their barley fields.

If some random yokel discovered me before I buried this mistletoe into Balder's heart, I would be thoroughly put out.

Something always tried to spoil the fun.

I'd have to play this game carefully.

I snapped my fingers. The muscles in my arms and legs curved and softened as my hips widened in proportion with my new magnificent breasts. I ran my fingers through my black hair that now reached past my waist, loving how my curls sprang when I released them.

Most importantly, my gown of canary yellow silks and vibrant teals was to die for.

I walked back around the oak and looked out over the city, tapping my red painted nails against the bark.

Now, where to find Balder...

My full lips pulled into a devious smile.

It was a Tuesday.

And I knew exactly where he'd be.

* * *

I SLUNK THROUGH THE CITY, avoiding the crush of men and women bustling across streets and squeezing down alleys.

The heat of the day still radiated off the fine limestone buildings and pointed arches, all decorated with color and patterns.

Nothing had changed. The same olive trees in clay pots crowded the balconies. The same bakers produced the same loaves stuffed with grains and herbs. The same fishmonger charged double than the one on Gretha Street.

I didn't know why this surprised me. Asgard was not a place of change, but of continuity. It's what kept it strong, and exceedingly dull. It still beat the cold of Jotunheim or the snobbishness of Alfheim. Elves always acted like they powdered their own arseholes.

I stopped at a corner of a street and stood in the shadows behind a barrel. The windows of *The Black Raven* glowed, spreading heated memories down to my toes. The best brothel in the city. I'd lost entire weeks in the embraces of the women and men inside.

A figure stopped in front of the open door, breaking me from my sweet recollections. The light outlined his trim silhouette in gold.

Balder the Beautiful. God of goodness and light.

Disgusting.

He clasped his hands together in prayer, making me grind my teeth harder. No doubt praying to be led to some poor soul in need of his glory.

Tuesdays were when he went "fishing," as he coined it. Casting out his line in sinful places and reeling in the wretch he hoped to rescue from wickedness.

At least, that's the lie he told everyone.

He paid those he bedded handsomely to keep his secret, especially from his wife, Nanna.

Balder squared his shoulders and straightened his fur-lined cloak. Looked right, looked left, and slipped inside.

I crept around the back and entered through the servant's door. A mixture of laughter and moans filled the high ceilings. I padded across erotic mosaics, weaving between marble pillars and floor vases of etched brass.

The air was heavy with cinnamon, cardamom, and the tang of sex.

I peeked through a sheer curtain into the main room.

Balder sat on a pile of brightly colored cushions surrounded by three women and a man, their eyes lined with coal. They fed him fresh oysters and ran their fingers stacked with rings of gold and pearls through his blonde hair.

I never understood all the fuss. His blue eyes were average, though everyone else said they sparkled. His angled face was nothing compared to mine. He did have a strong jaw, I'd give him that. But then he'd speak and ruin everything.

Balder freed his perfectly manicured hand from their groping and lifted it to order a pint of mead.

I smiled.

I loved when opportunities presented themselves like this.

I grabbed a silver tray from the bar and stacked it full with tankards of mead. If I was going to play the part...

No one noticed the new girl walking into the room stuffed with men and women reclining on silk pillows, smoking pipes and eating candied fruit out of silver bowls.

"Fortitude is one of the greatest of virtues," Balder's voice carried over the din of chatter and flirtations.

One of the girls yawned.

"Without courage, what are you, really?" he said. "And don't get me started on temperance. Show me a man who can't control himself and I'll show you a wretch."

He leaned back, letting a woman with chestnut hair bound in plaits slip another oyster into his mouth.

Enough of this.

I "tripped" over the foot of a man with his head lost up the skirts of a smiling woman and spilled five tankards of mead into Balder's lap.

I knew I shouldn't have done that, but I just couldn't help myself.

He cursed and stood, sheets of mead running off his trousers and splashing the floor and his polished boots.

"What's the matter with you?" He shook his hands, sending droplets of sticky mead flying into the eyes and cheeks of the other patrons.

I fell to my knees and laced my fingers together and pleaded.

"A thousand apologies, my lord." I squeezed my breasts so tight together they nearly popped out of my gown. "I've often heard of your beauty and charm, but I never thought I'd be blessed to see it in person. I was taken by shock."

I dared to look up at his horrible face and batted my eyelashes.

His tight lips slackened, and he cleared the anger from his throat.

"That's quite alright. Accidents do happen, and I'm starting to feel grateful this one did." He put his finger beneath my chin and bid me to rise. "What's your name? I thought I knew everyone here."

"Leda, your grace," I said. "I've just moved to the city all the way from Bretha."

He raised an eyebrow and smoothed his short hair.

"And how do you find city life?"

"I find it awfully lonely." I held his gaze and skated my teeth over my bottom lip. "Especially in my bed."

A spark of hunger lit behind his eyes. I had him. Not that I ever doubted. I was irresistible.

"If you permit me, *Leda*, I'd be more than willing to give you company this evening."

I smiled and reached out my hand and traced the gold embroidery of his tunic across his collar bone. He shivered and forced a dry swallow.

"I've been told how great your *stamina* is for mercy." I tangled my fingers within the laces of his green tunic and unraveled one. And then one more. "And how *big* your heart."

He shifted in his boots.

"I always help those in need," he rasped.

I dug into his tunic and furs and pulled him against my breasts. Wonder and lust settled into his expression.

The women and men behind him scowled at me for losing them their business. Terse whispers followed. No doubt questioning *who is this new girl*? Questions were never good.

"I am in need," I breathed into his ear. "Great need. Right. Now."

I turned on my heel and tugged him down the hallway. I couldn't stop myself from smiling as I led him exactly where I wanted to go.

This was almost too easy.

I took him into a room in the back and flung him onto a bed of feather mattresses and clean sheets. A fire crackled in the hearth, perfect for warming naked skin.

"Most aren't so forceful," he said, struggling to unbuckle his belt. "You're magnificent!"

"I know," I said, shutting the door. "And the night has only begun."

He freed himself from his belt, only to get his head stuck in his own tunic as he tried to pull it off. Gods he was useless.

I heaved him to his feet and tossed the tunic to the floor and threw him into a solid chair. I needed something sturdy for this.

Blood rushed to his cheeks.

"My, you're a strong one!" he said. "What other surprises do you have in store for me?"

I straddled him, skating my hands over and down his naked shoulders.

"A few, I'd imagine."

I tried to dig into my bodice for the dart I had wedged between my breasts, but he grabbed my right wrist and jerked me against his chest covered in fine hair. Rapture flushed his cheeks and darkened his eyes.

"I need to touch every inch of you," he said. "None have heated my blood like you before."

"You flatter."

I squirmed my wrist free only to have him grasp my left one and skate his thumb over my palm. Was he an octopus? How many hands did he have? My patience ran thin.

"Are you ready to be sent to the realms of pleasure?" he asked.

I rolled my eyes inward and crushed my lips against his to shut him up. He was like kissing a suffocating goldfish. Wet and blubbing.

The things I did for murder.

Lost in his passion, he released my wrist and slid his hands down my back, finally allowing me to pull out the little spear of mistletoe from my bodice.

I gripped it in my hand that was no longer a woman's, but my own hand, and hovered it inches from his larynx.

I couldn't resist shifting back into my devilishly handsome self for this.

I wanted Balder to see my face in those split seconds before death claimed him. To know it was I who killed him.

I broke our kiss and leaned against his ear, ready to plunge the dart into his thrashing artery.

"I'm afraid the only one being sent anywhere is you," I said in my own voice.

His entire body tensed and gooseflesh raised the hairs on his arms.

I rammed the dart towards his pulse.

He was faster.

Balder shoved me off him and tumbled heel over head backwards out of his chair.

He looked up at me, his face a storm of emotions. Fear. Terror.

Childlike wonder.

"You," he forced out between trembling lips.

I took a step towards him. He scrambled backwards along the floorboards.

"Me."

He shook his head, continuing to scuttle away. Sweat beaded at his temples.

"This is impossible."

"I never much adhered to that word."

I kicked the chair out of the way, launching it into splinters against the fireplace.

He hit the wall. There was nowhere else for him to go. Poor dear.

His eyes flashed to the dart of mistletoe I clasped.

"What...what are you going to do to me with that?"

"I thought that obvious. Kill you, of course."

He stood, sliding his back against the wall. I neared him still, savoring his panic as he struggled to free his knife sheathed around his upper leg.

This was so worth it.

"You have no idea how long I've fantasized about killing you," I said. "All the ways. All the fantastical ways. But in none of them did I ever kill the god of goodness in the back of a whorehouse. This is far better."

Balder pulled out his knife and pointed it at my chest.

I chuckled.

Now we could really start having some fun.

"You can't hurt me," he said. "Not anymore."

"Then why do you cower?"

"Because I'm facing a ghost."

I shrugged.

"I guess it is shocking to see someone you thought you trapped in a cave forever. That would probably create all kinds of concerns for one's wellbeing."

I took one step closer, letting the tip of his blade touch the fiber of my shirt directly over my heart. The feel of it excited me further.

He straightened, as if waking from a dream.

"There's nothing you can do to me," he said, again. "Mother collected oaths from every creature and plant in the Nine Worlds to not hurt me. I'm untouchable."

Mother.

Frigg.

My blood boiled.

"I'd like to know why you necessitated such measures. What are you to them?"

A smile cracked his face.

"Salvation."

Gods. I couldn't take him anymore.

I shoved his knife away and lunged at him with the mistletoe dart. He jumped to the right of my attack, making me only graze his cheek.

He was sprightlier than I remembered.

Balder touched a clean line of blood trailing from his ear to chin.

"What the?" he said, looking at his fingertips shining with his own blood.

"Apparently she forgot something." I held out the

mistletoe and gave it a small shake.

Shock stiffened his lips.

"This is going to be great," I said. "I'm going to murder you with a sprig of mistletoe."

I pulled out one of my daggers in my left hand, keeping the dart ready for his heart in my right.

I attacked him again. He blocked my blow, crossing our blades and keeping all of his vital organs sadly just out of my reach.

He pushed me back and leapt onto the bed, slashing wildly at me with his knife and trying to keep his balance as his boots sank into layers of feather and wool.

One solid kick to the bed frame and down he fell. I gripped his ankles and dragged him towards me, his constant flailing and thrashing and whining making it extremely difficult.

"Stop being such a baby about this!" I yelled, trying to grab hold of his bouncing calf.

He struck me in the chest with his heel.

He threw two pillows at me.

Feathers burst out of them and drifted through the air making it like feel like Yule.

Slipping out of my grip, he bolted for the door.

I kicked him in the back of the leg and he fell, his knees and palms striking the floorboards. His knife spun beneath the bed. He scrambled for it, but pulled out a painted periwinkle chamber pot instead.

I stood over him and laughed.

"It's over."

The door swung open.

"What's going on in here?" A man asked. Ivar. His soft brown eyes met mine and his mouth I remembered kissing dropped open in recognition. He had always been my favorite. I considered him a friend.

Balder looked at him. I didn't like that look.

"Get out!" I warned Ivar.

I raced to him, but Balder already wrapped his arm around his chest and held Ivar in front of him. He smashed the chamber pot against the doorframe and held a sharp shard of porcelain against Ivar's throat.

"Let him go," I said.

His face tightened.

"No closer, or I swear I will spill all his blood," he rasped. "Do you want that sin on your conscience?"

I stopped. I hated how my heart hammered against my chest.

Balder's death ensured Hel's army. Ensured my safety.

My vengeance.

I met Ivar's terrified gaze again. The irony wasn't lost on me I worried over someone's life that was destined to die anyway, but he didn't deserve to die like this.

I put up my hands.

Balder shoved him towards me and into my arms and fled down the hall.

I would make Balder bleed out slowly, *painfully*, for this.

I stalked after him. He collided with two women locked in an embrace only to stumble into a girl carrying a tray of grapes.

"Watch it!"

Grapes popped as he trampled across them, grinding their flesh into the mosaics.

Women and men cracked open their doors, checking on the commotion. They all gasped and shouted and cheered my name as I sprinted by. I knew they'd miss me.

At least someone did.

"Please, go about your business and keep up your noble work," I said to them. "Sorry I couldn't stay longer to satisfy you all today. A raincheck for next time."

Balder exploded out of the front door and I followed him into the warm, summer night air. Gravel crunched beneath us.

He headed towards the palace.

I stopped.

Bollocks.

He went right into the belly of the beast, and he would raise the alarm of my return.

They'd know I was back, and they'd all come looking for me.

And that made this all exceedingly more thrilling.

I loved it when the stakes raised.

5

BEST SERVED COLD

Near a hundred warriors thundered out of the palace gates, their chainmail rattling against their breastplates and broadswords. They split off into patrols of ten men each and spread through the city and surrounding fields and forests. One band even marched towards the cliffs lining the ocean's edge.

I felt honored that my return encouraged a small army to search for me.

So many armed soldiers would make it impossible to get inside the palace walls.

If it were anybody else.

Dodging the patrols, I snuck behind topiaries and shuffled along the massive walls towards the Southern side. I ran my hands over the bumps and ruts of the stone. Where was it? Ah! There.

I traced the curve of a simple, harmless circle with my fingertip I'd chiseled into the rock eons ago.

They still hadn't discovered it.

When the wall was being built, I had the foresight to bribe the builder to make a small addition to the gods' design. A tunnel for my personal and exclusive use. It led straight to my rooms, allowing me to come and go as I pleased. Anything to avoid Odin's bloody raven spies.

Exceptionally handy, and now it would prove useful once again.

I pressed the stone, and it slid back about an inch. A puff of dust. The grind of rock and screech of metal. A hidden entry swung open, and I squeezed inside, closing it behind me.

I felt my way along the tunnel, ignoring the memories snapping at my heels with every familiar echo of my footsteps. I touched the smooth oak of the door that led directly into my rooms and stopped as dread drenched me.

My rooms had been some of the finest in the palace, with views of the ocean and a good breeze. They wouldn't have let them go to waste once they ensured I wasn't ever returning to them. I didn't know if I could stomach them being redecorated into something fit for a prudish grandmother.

I grasped the handle, now brittle with rust, and twisted.

I hoped they at least installed a sauna or something worthwhile...

The door opened.

My breath caught in my throat.

I walked into the past. Into a slice of time preserved, perfect and clear. Chilling.

The clothes I'd tossed out of my wardrobe when Odin told me the truth remained crumpled on the floor. Thick layers of dust and dirt coated the bright silks in gray, same as it covered the tangled sheets of my bed making everything appear as stone.

Wine bottles were left open, stuck in shelves and lying

beneath the divan. Cobwebs stretched across the glass, gluing the bottles in place.

I stepped into the hush and picked up a tarnished silver knife, dust sloughing off the blade and handle. Odin had handed it to me to cut my lips free after Frigg had sewn them shut. The bits of thread I'd pulled out of my flesh remained scattered across the table, resting like burial mounds beneath the grime.

Cold stung my spine.

It was like I had never left.

Nothing had been touched since that night when I lost everything.

When they took everything.

And I understood. They tried to make it like I never existed. They tried to forget me and locked it all away as they had locked me away.

I slammed the knife onto the table, triggering a fresh thirst for their lives.

I would not be forgotten.

Walking across marble and disintegrating fur rugs, I grasped the main door handle, pushing away the familiarity of it against my skin. I cracked the door open. A chorus of metal clattered down the hallway as a patrol marched past. Damn. I closed it again.

No matter.

I snapped my fingers and shifted my form once again. The muscles in my arms expanded and my chest grew at least a dozen inches across. I scratched my heavy beard with the iron hook that was now my right hand.

I stood before my old mirror and admired Tyr, god of nobility and justice, staring back at me in the dull and flaking surface. I combed my now blonde hair out of my kind eyes and tucked it neatly behind my ear as Tyr always wore it. Gods forbid he give it any style.

I smiled at myself.

Turning on my heel, I walked out the door and whistled a Jotun folk tune as I strolled past a group of guards. They saluted me and I threw them a wink back. Any servant I crossed bowed their heads. I'd forgotten what this was like.

This was going to be even more delicious when I found Balder. Wherever that little rat was hiding. The palace was a maze of rooms, halls, and passageways. A very long night waited ahead of me. I just needed to find an opportunity.

"Tyr! Wait!" a familiar voice called behind me.

Sometimes opportunities found you.

I stopped, turned, and stared directly into Thor's small eyes. His fiery beard hid most of his windburned face beneath a jungle of wild whiskers. And though he had all the sense of a dodo, he had the temper of a lion dunked in a pond.

I did not expect the violence with how my muscles clamped me rigid seeing him again. Seeing him for the first time since...

...everything in me screamed to ram my hook into that thick skull of his.

Burn them. Kill them. Destroy them...

But I'd probably only hit air given the limited size of his brain. Besides, it wasn't worth him missing the party I was bringing them.

"Tyr?" he said again. "You alright? You seem...*off*."

I took a steady breath, shaking the ringing from my ears, and forced a smile. I couldn't let this opportunity slip. If anyone knew where Balder hid, it would be Thor.

"Never better," I said. "Just a little distracted by the news. Terrible this."

Thor's face sank and he crisscrossed his arms, stretching his simple wool shirt to its breaking point across his biceps.

"So you think..." He whispered now. "So you think Loki is really back? That Balder really saw him?"

Laughter threatened to jump out of my throat. I pounded it back down. If only he knew to whom he actually spoke, he'd surely piss himself.

I considered revealing myself just to see it.

"I don't doubt it. This is Loki we are talking about."

"He always was weaselly."

I did my best to hide my scorn at that.

"Yes, *well*, I would feel much more settled if I could speak to Balder about what he saw. Where is he being hidden?"

Eagerness sparked my skin.

A crack of laughter boomed from Thor's lungs as he clapped me on the back. I thanked all manner of holy beings for my new, larger size. I only fell an inch forward instead of being flung halfway across the room.

"You really must be distracted to have so easily forgotten where he is," he said. "Especially as it was your idea where to hide him. You're so silly sometimes, Tyr."

Damn.

"Yes. Of course. This Loki business has me quite upset. I can't seem to remember a blasted thing. Perhaps if you refreshed my memory—"

"I don't understand how this has happened," he interrupted. "We took every precaution."

I rubbed my wrists where they tied my son's guts into my flesh to arrest my powers. Their *precautions*.

"I know," I forced between my teeth.

Thor shifted in his boots.

"If he gets Balder..."

My ears perked and I let my arms fall to my sides. I burned to know the reason he had become so oddly precious to them.

"It will be quite the calamity," I said.

Thor's brows shot to his hairline. I hoped his two brain cells wouldn't figure out the reason for his confusion. Luckily, they'd probably burst into flames before that happened.

"Calamity? What's wrong with you? It will spell our doom," he said. "If Loki is truly back...if he wakes Surtr...Balder is our only hope to stop it. You must get your head checked."

So, Balder really was their salvation? Blast. I didn't see that coming.

I really would have to kill him now. I couldn't allow any further little snags getting in the way of my scheduled mass death and destruction.

Thor put his hand on my shoulder. I hoped he didn't feel me go rigid beneath him as I fought from throwing him off of me.

"Loki is out for blood," he said. "We have to protect Balder. We have to get Loki back in chains if we stand a chance of surviving him."

As if.

He scrubbed his face. He wasn't so sure. I loved how they didn't underestimate me.

"At least I feel better knowing Balder is tucked away in my own rooms. Loki wouldn't dare step a foot in there."

And there it was. I always could count on Thor to slip.

I guess his wife still hadn't ever spilled about the time I snuck into his rooms and indulged in the nighttime naughties with Sif, while he drank the entire mead stores dry.

"You make a sound point. He wouldn't ever, *ever* dare go in there."

* * *

Two burly guards stood on either side of the doors to Thor's rooms. Egil and Haldor. They were quite the pair of champions. One dim, the other shit.

I walked up to them, mimicking Tyr's muscle bound stride. This would be a performance for the ages.

"I bring news for Balder," I said. "Open the doors."

Egil and Haldor shot each other a nervous glance.

"Lord Tyr," Haldor pushed out. "We are under strict orders to not let anyone in or out."

Of course. Why would any of this ever be easy?

I bared my teeth and enjoyed the shiver it sent racing down their strapping frames.

"But I'm not *anyone*, am I?" I growled. "I'm Lord Tyr. I command Asgard's forces. I command you. And you dare deny me entry?"

"I'm sorry, my Lord."

"We'd never deny you anything, but—"

"But what?" I straightened my shoulders, making myself even taller. Even more intimidating.

Egil gulped.

"Our orders come direct from Odin."

My eye twitched hearing that name again.

"As are mine."

I handed them a piece of parchment. Confusion twisted the lines of their faces as they read Odin granting me permission to pass in his own hand. Well, it was really my hand, but a simple illusion hid my large loops beneath Odin's chicken scratch.

"Odin doesn't trust the life of his beloved son, most beloved in all the Nine Worlds, to the protection of only two guards," I said. "Loki is no regular foe. He'd gut you both in five seconds flat."

"Our instructions were to only accept verbal orders from Odin himself."

They were annoyingly stubborn. I guess I had to pull out the threats.

Wonderful!

"If you deny me entry, it will be Balder's blood on your hands. And you will face Odin's wrath for having ignored his direct orders. Do you want the same fate as Sven, the deserter? I believe it took five days for him to die in that cage attached to the ocean cliffs."

Sweat coated their foreheads and wet their hair.

"It is in Odin's hand," Haldor said to Eiger, holding out the parchment to him.

"And it is Lord Tyr," Eiger replied.

They nodded and unlatched the door.

"Good lads," I said. "I'll make sure Odin learns of your accommodation here tonight."

Poor dears didn't stand a chance. They didn't call me the god of lies and tricks for no reason.

I walked in and they shut the doors behind me. I loved the echo of the iron bolt flooding the tense silence with finality.

Balder was mine.

I sauntered through Thor's rooms stuffed with weapons, heavy furniture, and drinking horns on every shelf. Only a handful of candles were lit. Everything else was shadow and moonlight.

"Father? Is that you?" Balder's voice carried in from the terrace.

"Afraid it's only me," I said, walking towards him. Salt and candle wax filled my lungs.

He braced his hands against the railing, staring out over the Asgardian Sea. He turned and looked at me over his shoulder. A sad smile tugged at his lips. His face etched with worry.

I'd never seen him so hollow. Grave.

"I'm glad you're here, Tyr," he said. "I don't want to be alone when...when it happens."

He returned his gaze to the ocean and rubbed his thumbs against the stone.

I shifted out of Tyr's form and back into my true self. I took out the dart of mistletoe from inside my coat pocket and walked slowly to him across the tile.

"When what happens?" I asked, keeping Tyr's voice.

Bursts of foam and surf coated the rocky beach below with every strike of the waves.

"We deserve this," he said, not answering.

Another step closer. Then one more.

"We deserve to die at Ragnarok."

I stopped. That sentiment I did not expect.

"You're silent, Tyr," he said. "Do I shock you?"

"A little," I said.

I raised the dart in my hand, aiming for his liver.

"After what we did to him, we deserve what he promised."

We were inches apart. It would only take one thrust...

"That night still haunts me," he murmured. "Same as you told me it haunts you. And Father...He's never been the same."

Burn them. Kill them. Destroy them.

"Now Loki's come for me, and I'm resigned to my fate," he said. "It's the only way we can ever atone."

I gripped the dart tighter, but something kept me from stabbing it into his side. Why couldn't I kill him?

The doors exploded open behind us.

I snatched Balder and locked his head in the crook of my arm and squeezed the point of mistletoe against his thrashing pulse. Spinning us around, we faced Thor, Tyr, and Odin.

The ocean roared, and a surge broke against the rocks in a spray of froth. Wind tore through my hair, rippling the strands like flames around my chin and cheeks.

Odin and my eyes locked, his dark russet hair whipping over the angles of his face and silk eyepatch.

Friend. Lover. Liar. Traitor. Brother. Deceiver.

Enemy.

Ice rushed down my spine and I believed myself plunged into the roiling depths of the sea behind me.

Odin turned gaunt.

"It's true," he whispered. "You really are back."

He stared at me as if I were a specter from a nightmare. In a way, I suppose I was to him.

I liked that thought.

"I am delighted you could join us on this festive night," I said. "It would be a great pity to not have an audience to witness the start of the end."

Balder struggled within my hold. I dug the dart further into Balder's throat, making him produce a nice, high-pitched yelp.

Odin's gaze dropped from mine to his son in my arms.

"Let him go," he warned.

I laughed.

"You dare have the balls to ask me to spare your son when you wouldn't show me the same mercy?"

"I tried—"

"*Tried* is as useless as pig shit."

A deep tone hummed in my ears, waking that thirst again to drink their souls.

I forced a calming breath. I couldn't break now.

"I'm afraid there's only one way this is going to end. I promise Balder won't feel a thing, unlike what I've endured."

Odin took a step towards us. Thor and Tyr took one each.

I tutted my tongue and pressed the dart deeper into Balder's flesh. A drop of blood coursed down his neck and soaked into his tunic.

They stopped.

"You can't expect to come out on top," Tyr said.

Tyr, always the voice of reason. Always the one to ruin the fun.

"But I already have," I said. "I've made a deal with Hel, you see."

"What deal?" Thor growled.

"Oh, just that I'd give her Balder's soul in exchange for her army. You know how these bargains go," I said. "Once I dispatch his miserable, excruciating life to Hel, her army marches toward's Vigridr and the final battle will begin and you cannot stop it."

I couldn't help a wicked smile pull on my lips as I gorged on their fear. Fed on their surprise.

Odin's face tightened, delicious and peppered with angst.

And then his face relaxed. Calmed. Something lit behind his gaze, like he knew something I didn't. Like *he* had won...

"Perhaps we can come to an arrangement?" he said.

I snorted.

"You have nothing I want."

"I think you'd be surprised."

I narrowed my eyes.

"Do you really flatter yourself thinking I even have a choice? You took that choice from me when you broke your oath that you'd protect my family."

His shoulders tightened, and he glared at me.

"That wasn't the only oath broken that day."

The ocean thundered, same as my heart.

That oath.

Blood brothers. More.

The scar still marked my arm as it did his own where we had mixed our blood, binding us together.

We had meant everything to each other.

And he knew me.

Truly knew me.

We were supposed to have forever.

I bristled.

And there it was again. That odd sensation stopping me from driving the mistletoe into Balder's pulse and ending him.

My grip loosened.

"You," Frigg spat.

Frigg pushed her way between Thor and Tyr, the moonlight casting her pointed cheeks and blonde hair in silver. She glowered at me, her brown eyes brimming with the same poison that flowed through her veins.

Everything vanished into a tempest of black except for her and I.

Frigg's face lit with glee, ramming her dagger into Sigyn's gut.

As she murdered my sons.

Tore out their guts.

Burn them. Kill them. Destroy them.

I hardened my grip and stabbed the mistletoe into

Balder's neck, thrusting through his flesh and tendons and into his artery. Hot blood laced between my fingers and splattered the tiles.

I loved how they all screamed.

I tugged the mistletoe from his neck and let the blood stream out of him. He collapsed to the floor and clasped his hand against the wound, but the blood still flowed. It drenched his tunic and spread out in a glistening lake towards his mother's feet.

The breeze grew colder.

Frigg collapsed to her knees. She pulled him into her arms, and cradled his face in shaking hands.

"Stay with me," she told him. "You can't leave."

Balder gurgled, choking on his own blood. It soaked into her purple gown. Covered her boney fingers and wrists.

The others only watched. What could they do now that it was finished?

Frigg looked up at me, eyes red and burning with hate. She held him tighter against her chest.

Still the blood continued to flow.

"Fix it," she forced through hot tears. "Don't take my son from me."

A frigid gust of wind tore between us.

I smiled, looking down at her kneeling before me. At her begging me for the same thing she had once refused me.

"And why would I do that when his death gives me exactly what I want?"

She ground her teeth, her cheeks flushed with grief and hands stained in her child's blood.

"This will not go unavenged. Don't think this is over..."

I laughed.

"But it is."

Balder's eyes emptied and his body fell slack in her arms.

Snow fell.

Fimbulwinter arrived in Asgard.

And they knew what it meant.

"Ragnarok is here," I said, loving the fear stiffening their faces. "And you're going to love it."

I met Odin's gaze, wanting to feast on his loss. On his fantastic failure at preventing all he wanted to stop.

Bastard only crossed his arms and sighed, as if only slightly annoyed.

What did he know?

6

ALL FALL DOWN

We stood on the beach, tucked away between the cliffs and pine. Surf washed over the shore, scuttling stones and pulling sand into the sea.

My skin prickled being back in this place.

Because it had been ours.

Every private discussion, every soft spoken secret, it was all shared here.

I forced the memories tugging at me extinguished.

"You always were a sucker for sentimental rot," I said.

I picked up a stone and threw it into the ocean. It's what we always used to do.

Odin stepped next to me and looked out at the summer snow falling into the churning water.

"Don't fool yourself," he said. "Any sentiment we shared is dead."

I sneered.

"You took the words right out of my mouth."

Night shrouded his broad shoulders in blues and grays,

and the shadows hardened the striking lines of his jaw and cheekbones. Pensive. Relentless. He was a storm of a man.

And I had him by the throat.

Although, he remained annoyingly calm. What was the point of murder if I couldn't enjoy his outrage?

"Are you going to petition me to bring back Balder's soul?" I said. "I do hope so. I am eager to tell you no."

He faced me, and a gust of frigid air rustled his navy tunic and gray furs. Snow caught in his hair and short beard.

"I'm sorry to displease you, but I've already sent Hermod to Hel to negotiate Balder's return," he said. "She won't deny me if she wants to keep what's hers."

I laughed.

"My, aren't we confident today," I said. "Hel has quite the little crush on him. It's disgusting, really. She will not give him up, especially when she already has victory over you by owning your 'savior'."

His lips flattened. For the first time, a flicker of fear tightened his face. The shudder of uncertainty. Now this is what I waited for. I loved getting beneath his skin.

"You will stop this madness, Loki," he growled.

"You know I cannot control infatuations. I just hope she's gentle with him."

He narrowed his gaze and looked like he wanted to strike me across the face.

"You will stop Ragnarok," he said.

I smiled.

"Oh. *That*." I said. "Afraid that's going to be a no. I'm only doing what's fair."

Pain tightened his face further, but it drowned in the anger that followed.

"Fair..." he spat, as if the word stung. "Like when you broke our oath? When you forced me..."

His skin stretched white over the knuckles of his clenched fists.

"I didn't want this," he said. "Any of it."

"Nor I, yet here we stand."

The wind howled, heaving thickening snow around us. The bite of winter stung our cheeks red. The ramifications of where both our choices brought us. Reminding us what we both lost in the other.

Friendship.

Love.

Everything.

Odin bared his teeth and pushed past my shoulder. He stopped and stared out at the rocks and forest.

I imagined clawing through his back and shredding his guts with my fingernails. It would be easy. Quick.

But where was the satisfaction in swiftness? I couldn't deprive Odin of the death he feared.

"I've thought about you every day," he said.

I chuckled darkly.

"And I thought you said all the sentiment in you was dead?"

He turned and held my gaze. I didn't like the battle of emotions raging behind his eye.

Those memories of him I wanted obliterated rose around me again.

I bent down and picked up another stone and spun it within my hand, stomping each ghost back into the mud where they belonged.

"As it is, I thought about you every day as well," I said, stepping towards him. "How I would kill you. How I would cut out your bowels. How I would watch you burn as I drowned in the venom eating me alive..."

Wet and cold seeped into my palm from the stone. The ocean filled my ears with the crash of venom washing across my chest. The serpent stared down at me. I tasted its venom filling my mouth. I could not move.

I was tied to that rock. Bound.

And it was so dark.

Always dark.

When can I be free?

"Loki?"

Odin gripped my arm, jerking me out of wherever I'd gone. The stone fell from my hand as I surfaced and looked at his confused face.

He stared at the point where he held my wrist. My wrist now riddled with scars and burns and lesions.

I'd fallen out of my illusion.

"Don't touch me." I wrenched myself free, hardening myself, deepening my concentration. My arm returned to its divine form.

"It burns you to have lost," I said. "To know you're finally going to face the fate you keep running from."

His mouth tugged at the corners.

"I haven't lost," he said. "You're going to stop Ragnarok."

I laughed. He was hilarious.

"And why would I do that? I no longer have anything to lose. You saw to that."

His eye glimmered again with that secret that seemed so delicious to him back on the terrace.

"But you do."

Oh, this was going to be good.

"Please, tell me what in all the Nine Worlds would be

worth ending my vengeance for? And don't you dare say forgiveness, because that's such a cliche."

"Sigyn."

My vision went red.

I lunged and curled my fingers into his navy tunic and hurled him against a boulder. My knuckles dug into his chest as I pushed his back harder into the rock. A crack echoed through the pines as stone fractured.

"Don't mock me," I growled.

I crushed my fists deeper into his ribs. His sinew crackled over his bones.

"I don't mock." He winced, struggling for breath. "She's alive."

My grip loosened at the thought. Sigyn...

"No, it's not possible," I breathed. "I saw her die. Frigg stabbed her with a Dwarven steel blade. I couldn't stop it. I couldn't...she was gone."

"Yes, that is what you saw," he said. "But it's not what happened."

"What?"

"She still breathed. She still clung to life as I held her in my arms."

"No one could survive a blow like that. Especially a fledgling goddess."

He gave a rasped chuckle.

"But you know she is different. You know her element is pure hope. And you know no one bests me when it comes to dark charms," he said. "I spoke one over her, preserving what sliver of life her element protected."

That night filled my mind. How he had hovered over her limp body. How he had whispered something...

"The charm would give me enough time until I could

give her a golden apple. I snuck her out of that cave with me. No one ever knew the truth. That she survived."

Idunn's golden apples. They granted immortality to any being that ate of its fruit, or cure a god on the brink of death.

Possibility tugged harder at the roots of my heart.

At what this meant.

"I never intended for them to be slaughtered," he said. "None of it was supposed to have happened—"

"Where is she?"

"Alfheim," he said. "I placed her in a safe house where she has remained during your imprisonment."

And there it was. All I needed to know.

"Bullshit."

His brow arched.

"It's the truth."

"You have no pull with the elves. They'd never do anything for you," I said.

"They didn't do it for me, they did it for you."

I slammed him into the boulder again. His head snapped back and struck the rock.

"You lie," I seethed. "You're telling me anything to stop what's coming for you."

"I'm not lying."

I released his tunic and crushed my hand over his heart. I needed to feel, to see...

Part of my element of chaos gave me the benefit of sensing the chaos in others. I always knew when they lied to me. But with Odin...He was the only one ever able to block my sight.

I dug my fingers into his chest. His element of ambition surged over me and pulled me down at my ankles. Raw. Cruel. Insatiable. I hated how it still enthralled me.

And I went deeper.

I searched for any bit of chaos. Any turmoil to prove his lie.

I found nothing.

As always.

I surfaced from the maelstrom that was Odin and pushed away from him. He drew in large breaths and rubbed where I had touched him, seeming to massage my burn away.

"You have to trust me," he said.

I scoffed and turned my back to him and faced the ocean. I thought only of her.

Sigyn.

My heart thrashed, and I wiped the cold mist from my face. Or was it my own sweat?

"The last time I trusted you it didn't turn out well for me," I said. "And now you ask this of me again?"

Pebbles and sand crunched beneath his boots as he stepped towards me.

"I only ask you to ask yourself if you're willing to take the risk of not believing me?"

I closed my eyes.

All I wanted.

"Take me to her," I said. "I agree to nothing until I see Sigyn with my own eyes."

7

FALAFELS, WITH A SIDE OF SPITE

Alfheim

We rode hard through the rugged kingdom of Fylen and over the soft hills of Ayvadell. Alfheim was a realm alive with woodland creatures and waterfalls tucked among lush forests, mountains, and cities so clean they glistened.

Perfectly beautiful. Perfectly dull. Once you saw one magnificent rainbow, you saw them all.

I noticed none of it. I thought only of her.

Sigyn is alive.

I feared splitting down the middle from the hope swelling inside my chest.

Sigyn is alive.

"She is in good health, if you're wondering," Tyr said, riding next to me. Concern filled his gentle features. "I know your mind must be spinning."

"Oh yes. It's spinning with wonderment at your incompetence at shifting into a hawk or falcon or anything remotely useful. I'd already be to Queen Elénaril's palace by now if it weren't for you and Odin forcing me to journey on horseback."

Tyr sighed and returned his gaze to the forest stretching without end to the horizon.

Good.

I'd grown weary of his false compassion. He'd been a complete thorn in my side the entire journey. Continually asking me if I was alright? If I wanted to talk through my feelings?

Did he think I'd flip over and absolve his sins because of a few charitable words? Fat chance.

I tightened my grip on the reins of my horse, keeping my hands busy. I had to keep them busy, or I'd go back to thinking about *her*.

"If this is all some elaborate trap, I swear I will run you through a sawmill," I said to Odin. "Embroidery and horse don't mix and I already reek of forest."

"You know it's not a trap," he replied. "Otherwise you wouldn't have insisted on this sojourn."

True. He and I were in a stalemate, and it's what kept us safe from the other. I commanding Ragnarok, and he dangling the woman I loved in front of me.

If Sigyn is alive...

If.

Is.

Please.

Shards of light cut through the canopy of maple and oak and darted over an elvish man dressed in green robes and simple leather shoes. He stood in the middle of the road and held a bow, an arrow already nocked between his long fingers.

I recognized his braided black hair that fell past his waist and piercing gray eyes. One of Queen Elénaril's guard.

Cirdan.

Lovely fellow. He'd get pissed after only one pint of mead and try to shoot apples off my head. Which, I would have refused, had I not been far drunker and started collecting bets. Not my finest moment.

Odin clicked his heels into his horse's sides and rode out to him.

"I'm Odin and—"

"I know who you are," Cirdan interrupted, speaking high Elvish.

"Then you'll let us pass," Tyr said, tripping over the Elvish diphthongs. His Elvish always was wretched.

Cirdan snapped his eyes like steel on Tyr.

"I will not. You have no right," Cirdan said. He turned to Odin. "Now take your band of Aesir bullies, turn around, and leave before I shoot this arrow and give you a matching set of eyepatches."

Odin's jaw flexed beneath his beard.

I forgot how much I liked Cirdan. This was the best entertainment after hours of hard riding through stomach churning beauty.

Odin pulled out a thin scroll from his tunic and handed it to Cirdan. Cirdan scowled and yanked it out of Odin's hand and pulled it open and read down the length.

"Actually, Queen Elénaril of the Kingdom of Nilhanor granted me permission to pass into her lands," Odin said. "Or, can't you read?"

Cirdan raised a perfectly arched eyebrow.

"Sorry. No entry."

He handed the scroll back.

"No? You defy your queen?" Odin snapped.

A devious smirk pulled at Cirdan's lips.

"How can I verify this document if, *as you say*, I cannot

read?" he said. "Besides, you've probably stolen it. You'd never achieve such an honor otherwise."

"You're right, he didn't," I said, riding forward. "It was originally bestowed upon me."

Cirdan looked up and met my gaze.

"Loki? Is that really you?"

"Guilty."

A huge smile spread from one of his pointed ears to the other.

The Elves took pride in their lands and in their firm hatred for Asgard. Much deserved.

I was the exception.

I always was.

"You've not been in Alfheim in centuries," he said. "What's kept you away? I hope it's not that pint of mead you still owe me?"

"Not at all," I said. "I've been terribly busy. Imprisoned, planning the end of the worlds, you know how it is."

A crack of laughter exploded out from deep in his gut.

"Always a jokester," he said. "I've missed you, Loki."

I leaned down and motioned Cirdan to come closer. He wiped mirthful tears from his eyes.

"Don't worry about Odin. I know he can be a little..." I scrunched my face and twisted my mouth into an ugly frown. "I'll keep a good watch on him."

Odin glowered.

"I know you will," he said. "Sorry for keeping you. You're free to continue on your journey."

We rode on, Cirdan waving behind us.

"Come back for a pint," he called after me.

Odin grumbled curses beneath his breath.

"What?" I said, switching back to Asgardian. "I can't help I'm popular here. Perhaps had you been more polite and less murder-y, the elves would give you the same courtesy."

He gnashed his teeth harder.

I loved it.

We continued riding along Alfheim's perfectly smooth roads. Queen Elénaril's crests decorated every small village flag. Waterfalls thundered around us, the sunlight sparkling off the crystal water.

The ache clenching my heart only tightened.

This was where I planned to bring Sigyn to escape the gods. Now, here I was surrounded by the lands that were to be our home and without her by my side.

Gods, let this be true.

Let her be alive.

"It will be alright," Tyr said.

Something soft filled his eyes. A caring smile followed. He had to be kidding me.

"Are you reassuring me now?" I said. "We are not friends, so don't flatter yourself."

"I'm also not your enemy."

That was debatable.

I started to give him a nasty retort that would devastate him when gravel crunched beneath the horses' hooves as we rode up to a grand estate.

Arlynn House.

Oak branches twisted overhead as we approached the stately manor of towers and domes and white limestone. Purple aubrietia flowers cascaded over terraces and garden walls overlooking the forests and Lake Eonara.

A waterfall roared, plummeting off a sheer mountain in the distance behind the house.

We dismounted in front of the house's two entry doors covered in carvings of ivy.

"Tyr, inform Lord Falael of our arrival," Odin said. "I suspect that group will help you locate him."

He pointed at a small gathering of men and women gathered reading beneath a willow tree. Some were old, others barely twenty. The hot sun gleamed off their robes of silk and silver thread.

Tyr nodded and walked towards them, narrowly avoiding being trampled by a gang of running children. They laughed, pushing between Odin and me, waving small nets and chasing a dragonfly towards the rose gardens.

What the hell happened to this place? It was all so *pastoral*. I damn near expected a sheep in satin ribbons to walk past me at any moment.

"Not what you anticipated?" Odin asked.

"Last time I was here, I enjoyed a box of toffees with Queen Elénaril that ended up not being only toffee. I woke up a week later, naked, and in a barn with a goat chewing my hair." I sighed, remembering the best party I'd ever attended. "It's just sad to see a good summer home ruined by the sticky fingers of children."

"I'm sure the refugees and orphans who live here now would differ in that opinion."

Oh.

"Come again?"

"Queen Elénaril turned this house over to her nephew, Falael, and dedicated it to the care of any person needing help or safety in the Nine Worlds," Odin said. "But I'm sure it was far better when you could get blitzed out of your mind instead."

I really would enjoy it when he finally quit breathing.

We walked down a gravel path underneath arched trellises dripping with grapes.

To my right, five Jotun men whistled as they repaired a

gate alongside two dwarves from Svartalfheim. And to my left, a woman from Vanaheim recited poetry in her native tongue to a handful of Asgardian youths.

I had to admit, it was quite amazing. Decent. Good. I hated how it inspired a warm and fuzzy feeling in my chest.

"They are educated, fed, given medical care and a bed," Odin continued. "It took serious effort to convince Falael to accept Sigyn here and my terms."

I pushed my hand into his shoulder, stopping him.

"What terms?" I hissed.

He smirked.

"The terms necessary."

I saw now.

"You've condemned her to being a prisoner in this pit." A monarch butterfly landed on my nose. I waved it away.

"Do you really think she could just return to Midgard and her life?" he said. "What possible alternative could there be? You made her a goddess. You tore her out of her world and cast her into ours. You could have walked away..."

I crossed my arms and stared at my feet, not wanting to hear it. Not wanting the bitterness coating my tongue from the truth of his words.

"Just tell me where she is," I said. "Or, is this the point you admit this has all been an elaborate hoax to stall Ragnarok?"

His gaze trailed to the right and settled across the grass.

Blossoming cherry trees crowded a white folly building. Pink petals spun around the children sitting in the grass and floated between the standing adults scratching notes across pads of paper.

They listened to a woman I could not see. But the cadence of her voice...

Blood rushed in my ears.

I walked slowly out to them, trying to peek around the students' shoulders.

I only needed a glimpse.

I only needed...

"I find mixing marshmallow root with a little honey makes an excellent tea for soothing a sore throat," a woman spoke in perfect Elvish.

Gods don't let it only be what my mind wants to hear.

Wants to be true.

I shoved between the students.

Sigyn sat on the steps of the folly building, bundles of herbs in her lap and microscopes, scales, and glass vials covering the table behind her. She rubbed a knotted root between her fingers, looking at it lovingly as she had once looked at me.

My lips parted. My legs turned into jelly, if I still stood at all.

It's true.

Sigyn is alive.

My heart thundered and I knew it could still beat. It could still feel, and there was a future.

And the future was her.

Sigyn put the root aside and picked up a clutch of miniature white flowers. Yarrow. Her pink lips pulled into a soft smile. Cherry blossoms skated down the soft arcs and curves of her face and caught in her honeyed ginger hair I could still feel myself combing my fingers through.

She looked the same. Vibrant. Fierce. Kind.

Although behind the warm brown hues of her eyes, something lingered that was not there before.

I recognized it as loss. I recognized it because my eyes held the same ghosts.

She held up the bundle of yarrow. The students started scribbling and sketching.

"Can anyone tell me one use of yarrow? I realize it's been awhile since we covered it, but it's an exceptionally versatile plant."

My side burned remembering when she had used yarrow in a paste to treat a knife wound I'd gotten thanks to her idiot brother. She had taken me back to her home and when she spread the paste against my bare flesh...

I shivered, recalling the force her element rocked through my veins, shredding them raw. I'd risen into her fidelity. Into the absolute beauty of her hope.

"Anyone?" she asked again.

Fear seared my edges. A million questions and doubts and what ifs.

But my faith was stronger. My need. My love.

"It can stop a wound from bleeding, but damn does it sting," I said in Swiss. My words were only for her.

I stepped forward.

Our eyes met.

The yarrow fell from her hand to her feet. Her eyes rounded and she slowly stood, bracing herself against a column. She rested her other hand against her lips. She trembled.

"Loki?" she breathed through her fingers.

I walked across the blanket of cherry petals towards her. She remained frozen. As frozen as my insides begging me to stay back and forcing me to keep moving forward.

What if?

And forward again.

"I'm back."

Red misted her eyes that kept holding my gaze.

"Class," she choked out the word. "You can leave early."

Students snapped books shut. I pushed between them as I walked up the steps to her.

A tear ran down her cheek. She reached out a timid hand and skated her fingertips down the side of my face, as if uncertain I was real.

"How?" she asked, her voice cracking.

I took her hand. I was real. I was here.

"Does it matter?" I said. "I've found you."

We embraced as if we'd been deprived of air and now we could breathe.

She dug her fingers into my clothes. Into my hair. I closed my eyes and inhaled the rosemary rising from the crook of her neck. I skated my hands that shook across her back.

I pulled her tighter against me, and I was whole again.

I don't know how long we remained lost in the other, seconds or hours, but we slowly pulled apart.

"I never thought," Sigyn whispered, squeezing my shoulders. Tracing my chest. "So often you've come to me as a ghost. I would sleep entire days just for a chance to see you again. To pretend you were here and..."

I looked where she circled one of my buttons, as if expecting me to evaporate.

I caught her face between my hands and stroked her cheeks with my thumbs, gliding over her tears.

"I thought you dead," I said, leaning my forehead against hers. Savoring the touch of her skin against mine.

"For a long time I wished I was. The thought of you being trapped in that darkness," she paused. "I couldn't accept knowing what my life came at the expense of."

She covered my hands with her own and closed her eyes.

I didn't like hearing of the pain I'd left her in. It's not what I wanted.

I smiled through my own tears now.

"I'm not in that place anymore," I said. Reassured. "I'm here now. With you. And we have a future together."

I leaned in to kiss her lips. I had to taste her again.

She stopped me.

"I can't," she said.

She trailed her hands down my arms and held my hands firm at my sides.

"I know it's been a long time since we've done this, but there's no need to be self conscious," I said.

Her palms started to sweat, but she kept her fingers wound tight around mine.

"It's not that," she said. "It's just...Things have changed, Loki."

I raised my eyebrow. What the devil did that mean?

I was about to ask when her gaze fell to someone behind my shoulder. Leather boots snapped against the marble steps and walked towards us.

Perfect.

I turned, ready to rip out the spine of whoever interrupted us.

An Elvish man with a gentle face and thoughtful smile stood with his hands clasped behind his back. His brown hair was pulled half back in a simple braid that matched his simple robes of blue and green linens and cottons. There was an odd comfort about him, like a cup of warm cocoa wrapped in an even warmer hug.

I realized who he was. A page with a message from Odin to hurry up.

Odin could take his message and shove it.

And so could this page.

"If you don't mind, would you bugger off?" I told him. "You are rather ruining our moment."

The page turned from my gaze to Sigyn's.

"Are you alright?" he asked her.

My was he impertinent for a page.

She nodded and released my hands and walked over to him.

She took his arm.

Just who did this page think he was?

"Loki," she said, switching from Swiss back to Elvish. "This is my fiancé."

Everything shifted. Loud carnival music filled my ears. My right eye twitched.

"Sorry, I think I just suffered a minor stroke. Can you tell me that again?"

"We are engaged."

I tilted my head.

"You're with the page?"

"He isn't a page," she said. "I thought you knew. This is his estate."

The man put out his hand to me. I stared down at it and couldn't help my lip from recoiling.

"Please don't worry. I'm often mistaken for a servant." He chuckled softly. "I don't like dressing like your typical Elfish lord. All those layers of fine silks are too formal and distant for my tastes. I'm Falael, by the way."

His hand remained waiting for mine.

"Falafel?" I asked, crossing my arms.

He gave a small grin and let his hand drop back at his side.

"You can call me Fal, if it's easier for you."

Oh, he came to play.

"I prefer Falafel."

He only shrugged, his ever pleasant expression stating *nothing you do can upset me* across his forehead.

I took it as a personal challenge.

"I know this must all be a shock," Falael said.

I snorted.

"A shock? A shock is catching your grandmother naked." I pulled in a calming breath. "So, how did this joyous, *joyous* thing happen?"

Sigyn cleared her throat.

"Well, he was so good with the children..."

"...And she had such passion for care and healing."

Her cheeks flushed.

"Falael spent all his wakeful hours in aiding those who needed help..."

He smiled wider at her.

"...And Sigyn did the same."

They held each other's gaze.

I looked back and forth between them.

"I still don't see the common denominator here."

Sigyn looked at me and pity took root in the arcs of her face.

"Falael started this house in honor of his late wife, Madriel, who passed away in childbirth," she said. "Little baby Lia followed two hours later."

I shrank.

"You see?" she said. "Falael understood my pain in losing you. He understood what it is to lose a child. He taught me how to live again."

Falael took a step closer to me. It made the acid already dancing at the base of my throat pirouette.

"We found comfort in each other's grief," he said.

"And a shared connection in wanting to help others," she finished.

She looked at Falael and he stroked the top of her hand with his slender fingers. The loss he knew was something I didn't wish on any soul.

But it didn't stop me imagining twisting off each of his beautiful fingers one by one.

"That's all very nice and wholesome," I pushed out. "But unlike his wife, I'm not dead."

Pain etched her face that I could not understand what she told me.

"Pretending you dead was better than thinking of you lost in torment," she said, her voice cracking. "Knowing... knowing I couldn't...I..." She paused and pulled in a weak breath. "Did you expect me to remain alone for eternity?"

My mouth dried, and I looked down.

"Of course not," I whispered. The words stung. "I sacrificed myself so you might live and live fully."

"And I owe you everything for saving her," Falael said. "I've met countless who claim bravery. Honor. Truth is, I know none stronger than you. What you did...It's exceptional."

I gave him a smirk.

"Yes, I can be quite noble when the moment strikes me. I'm glad I meet your approval. It will make the blow all the less crushing now your engagement is called off. Since I'm back and all. I'm happy you understand."

I held out my hand to Sigyn.

"I saw a lovely little inn down the road. Then it can be just you, me, and a bottle of expensive champagne."

She shook her head.

"Loki..."

An icy wind rushed through the columns, and a flurry of cherry blossoms twisted around us.

I let my hand fall back at my side.

"You mean you want to stay his prisoner?" I said. "You want to stay *his*?"

Her shoulders stiffened along with the rest of her.

"I've never been a prisoner here," she said.

I laughed.

"Then you suffer delusion. Odin told me of his *terms*."

Falael's jaw tightened. It was the first decent reaction I got out of him.

"As far as Odin was concerned, yes, she was a prisoner," Falael said. "I let him believe I accepted his terms to protect Sigyn. But she had her freedom the moment she stepped foot on my lands."

I looked at Sigyn.

"I don't understand. So you stayed? Willingly?"

The sun disappeared behind thickening gray clouds. A chill bit my cheeks.

"Where else was I to go, Loki?" she said. "We lost our boys to savagery. You were damned to torment because of me. That weighed on my conscience and it nearly destroyed me." She stopped. "I couldn't save our children. I couldn't save you, but I could save others."

"You mean you could forget about me." Bitterness saturated my voice.

Her lips tugged down at the corners.

"Don't twist my words," she said. "I had to make a life to survive. I have a purpose here. I educate. I help those in need. You said you wanted me to live fully, and I'm honoring what you gave me by doing good and making a difference."

The logic of what she said skewered a dagger in my gut.

"And what now?" I asked. "What of me?"

Her mouth parted.

Snow started to fall.

Oops.

Sigyn held out her hand. Fat snowflakes coated her open palm as they coated the lawn and gardens stuffed with rose bushes.

Falael shivered, looking up at a mean sky.

"What's happening?" she asked. "It's summer."

"Oh," I said. "About that. I might have started the end of the worlds."

Sigyn's gaze snapped to mine.

"What?"

I dusted the snow off the railing and leaned against it.

"Ragnarok," I said. "The end of everything. You remember that lovely little prophecy that foretold I was the Destroyer?"

Her eyes narrowed.

"Yes, I very much remember. But you'd never do such a terrible, *terrible* thing."

I scratched behind my ear.

I gave an innocent smile.

"I'm afraid I just couldn't help myself."

Her mouth fell agape.

"I can't believe this."

"I did it for you if that makes you feel better," I said.

She stared knives so hard into me I thought I felt them knick my throat. Her disapproving looks always used to excite me. But this one, not so much.

"Don't worry," I said. "I'm not going through with it now that I know you're still alive. I'm the Destroyer, after all. I started it, and I will just stop it. Easy enough."

The air growled.

The earth heaved and rocked, throwing us off our feet. My knees struck the hard stone. Sigyn's elbow knocked the top of my head and Falael fell flat on his face. I couldn't even properly enjoy it thanks to this earthquake tearing Alfheim apart.

I scrambled towards Sigyn to help her up and out onto the lawn before the entire bleeding folly building collapsed. I clutched her arm, but Falael already pulled her up and out. Damn him.

Fracturing stone and splitting tree branches roared around us as we ran out onto the grass. Cherry petals and snow gusted around our shoulders and chests.

I looked out at an angry world shaking and snarling.

And inside me, without warning, without prompting, my fire erupted and my chaos raced hot and burning white through my seams.

What the?

I looked at my palms. They glowed red and molten, allowing the fan of bones in my hand to be visible through my flesh.

Snow sizzled against my skin. Cherry blossoms shriveled into ash in my palms.

And I couldn't stop it.

So, this was new.

8

WHY ARE THERE NEVER WARNING LABELS?

My hands returned to normal, but I kept staring at them. I didn't like how they had just erupted like that, without my consent. This just didn't happen with me.

It had to have been a fluke. The result of having been dealt a big shock from Sigyn's *news*.

That was a reasonable explanation. A fluke.

It being anything else was too unacceptable for me to consider.

And then there was the whole earthquake thing.

I barely heard a word through my own thoughts and self assurances, but I caught snippets. The earthquake had caused little damage. The foundations remained sound. No injuries. We were lucky. The only casualties were a few tea cups and an ugly vase that deserved what it got.

I rubbed my thumbs across my palms.

It was only a fluke.

"Is something wrong with your hands?" Sigyn asked. She worked on picking up the dozens of books that had been jostled off their shelves and scattered across the patch-work of intricate rugs.

"No, I'm fine."

She dropped a stack of books on the heavy table beside me.

"Really? You keep looking at your hands. I think it's best I inspect them..."

She reached for my hands. I shoved them beneath my armpits.

"I assure you I'm better than anyone has ever been," I said. "You best save your energy for when Falafel falls off that ladder and breaks his neck. What the hell is he doing up there, anyway?"

Falael stood on the last rung of a ladder and leaned far over, running his fingers over the spines of dusty books searching for gods knew what.

I imagined him losing his balance and bashing in his skull against the stone bust of his aunt below him. It would be terribly tragic.

I smiled.

"It's not *Falafel*. It's Falael," she corrected.

"Isn't that what I said?"

She sighed.

The library door swung open with a bang. Odin and Tyr marched in, snow clinging to their hair and furs. Their cheeks were burned red from the wind.

"What have you done now?" Odin snapped at me. "I can't leave you alone for one blasted minute without you bringing down the sky on our heads."

He could come after me all he wanted. But I'd be damned if he stood anywhere near Sigyn. I stood in front of her and moved her behind me.

"Get out," I told Odin.

"Ah, good. You're both here," Falael said. "I think we need to discuss what's going on. I just need a moment to find what I'm looking for."

Was he serious?

"How can you allow these two bastards within the same house as Sigyn?"

Sigyn pushed past me and into the center of the room.

"I don't need protecting," Sigyn said. "Odin and I have come to a certain...civility. Things aren't how they were five hundred years ago."

Sigyn and Odin both shared a glance and a nod, and I noticed a glimmer of something else written in their eyes I could not read. I didn't want to. This was too much for me to accept.

"As I keep noticing," I grumbled beneath my breath.

I went and leaned against a bookcase crowded with minerals and fossils and scowled.

"We have more important things to concern ourselves with," Odin said. He shook snow out of his hair.

"Like why did you cause that earthquake?" Tyr asked.

I scoffed.

"Of course. Always throw the blame at me. You see, Sigyn? They've not changed."

Falael cleared his throat.

"The earthquake is the second sign of Ragnarok," Falael said. "This is really quite invigorating."

I narrowed my eyes.

"Second sign? How do you know that?"

He smiled, and I hated how sickeningly genuine it was. How much stronger it made his jaw look. It could cut marble.

"Researching Ragnarok is a hobby of mine," he said. "I

find all its peculiarities fascinating. Its nature, its overall role in the cosmos. I devour all I can on the subject."

Sigyn gripped her Elven gown into fists.

"If Ragnarok caused the earthquake..." Sigyn looked at me. "I thought you said you weren't going through with this insanity. Why did you do this?"

Her blame hurt the most.

I threw up my hands.

"I didn't make that earthquake happen," I said. "I meant what I told you."

"He's right. It's just the nature of Ragnarok. Ah. Here we are." Falael's face brightened, pulling out a heavy volume from the shelf. "There are five signs in total. First Fimbulwinter, then earthquakes, as we've experienced. Next comes the sun darkening, oceans boiling, and finally the sound of a divine horn called Gjallarhorn. It's your typical end of the world scenario. The earthquake was not Loki's fault. He may be the catalyst to start it, but Ragnarok has a life of its own, I'm afraid."

Odin's brow twisted.

"What do you mean, *not Loki's fault*?" he asked. "He's the Destroyer. The Breaker of Worlds. Ragnarok is in his control."

Falael shrugged.

"Yes. And no."

Falael slid down the ladder from the top shelf, holding a book fraying from age. He walked to a table covered in green felt and opened the book to a page in the middle. Flecks of dried leather and mildewed paper covered his fingers.

Odin's eye widened. His mouth parted.

He padded slowly towards the ancient volume as if in the presence of a relic. He always got weird around books. Poetry and literature were like a drug to him.

"You have a copy of *The Foretelling of the Nine Worlds*?" He skated his index finger across the fading ink. "You mean to tell me it's been here all this time?"

"Only one in existence," Falael said proudly.

"I've searched eons for this book," Odin breathed. "Since I first learned of Ragnarok and devoted my life to stopping it. It contains the missing pieces I needed."

Falael smirked and brushed Odin's hand away from the manuscript.

"Maybe had you been more genteel in your approach in finding knowledge, people would have willingly shared with you instead of hiding it away," Falael said.

"See?" I said to Odin. "I told you a little politeness goes a long way."

Odin shot me a nasty look as if imagining me being punted across Alfheim by a rather aggressive elephant. It made me chuckle, seeing his face all contorted like a scarecrow.

"Anyway," I said, forcing my laughter away. "You were explaining how the earthquake wasn't my fault. This is a novelty for me to not be blamed, so please, do go on."

Falael scanned the page, his hazel eyes running left to right. Odin peeked over his shoulder.

He tapped his finger on a paragraph.

"Here we go," he said. "Ragnarok is a cycle. It hungers to destroy in order to create. Once Surtr is woken, the cycle is complete, and it begins again."

"Meaning?" Odin said.

"As long as Loki didn't accept his role as the Destroyer, Ragnarok remained dormant. Like a sleeping dragon beneath the earth. But when he accepted his destiny, when he broke out of his bonds and started fulfilling his role..."

"The dragon woke," Tyr finished. He kept twisting his beard between his large fingers.

Falael nodded.

I crossed my arms and leaned back against the bookcase again.

"Well, I'm not going back into that cave if that's what you're all thinking," I said.

"It wouldn't matter anyway," Falael replied. "Ragnarok is a chain reaction. A series of falling dominos, and you tipped the first over. It's too late."

And there it was. Putting the blame back on me.

"This is all fine and good, but what I still don't understand is why Ragnarok is continuing despite Loki's wishes to end it." Odin pointed at me, the silver rings on his fingers catching the cold, winter light. "He's the Destroyer. It's under his command. He should be able to stop it."

Falael shook his head.

"And that's the nugget of knowledge you missed, Odin," Falael said. "How Ragnarok truly works. You think it's something to be controlled. It's not. It can't. Once the Destroyer began Ragnarok, it became its own force. Its own life. No one controls Ragnarok, it controls us."

A chill flooded the room as wind and snow rattled the window panes.

I rubbed my thumbs against my palms again, removing any residual heat from where they had exploded during the earthquake. Had it truly been out of my control?

I didn't like that thought.

Apparently, neither did Odin.

Emotions tightened the muscles of his face, a storm of anger and worry and fear.

"This is ridiculous," he said. "I thought I had this all taken care of. Sigyn is the only person Loki would stop this madness for, and now you're saying he's not even in control of it? Her being alive was supposed to stop him."

The thin thread holding me together snapped. And something deeper cracked. Splintered.

I shoved off the bookcase and marched towards him.

I saw it now.

The truth of his *noble* act of saving her.

I lunged at him and shoved him against the wall. He grunted and books fell down around us, their spines cracking open as they struck the floor.

"You son of a bitch!" I shouted. "You never saved her life out of pure decency, did you? It's all been another con. Another hustle to manipulate me into stopping what you fear. Me."

"What did you expect?" he said. "That I'd take no precautions after you promised to bring Ragnarok?"

I threw him to the carpet and stood over him. He glowered, looking up at me.

"My motive might have been double edged, but the fact remains I saved her life. You should be grateful you've even gotten these moments I've given you. Not that you deserve them after what you did."

"What *I* did?"

He rubbed my wounds raw with salt.

I dropped my hand to my dagger at my hip. I'd show him just how grateful I was to him.

Someone grabbed my wrist and stopped me.

"You will not do this," Sigyn said. She squeezed into my bones.

"How can you ask me that? Have you forgotten what he did? To you? To us? He doesn't deserve to live. He doesn't deserve to win."

Confusion washed over her face.

"Win? What are you talking about?"

My mind reeled. I was gone. Lost somewhere in a fog of red. Lost to a hunger for blood I had to slake because anything less would kill me.

I pulled out of her grip and clasped her hands in mine.

"We could do it together," I said, holding her tighter. "Make their knees crack. Watch as Ragnarok burns their worlds and their stars. Their lives would be ours."

"No, Loki," she said. Definite. Firm.

"No?" I spat. "How can you be so complicit? And you stayed. You actually stayed their prisoner…"

I looked into her eyes, searching for an explanation.

It hit me. Hard.

"I see how it is," I said. "You've all moved on, haven't you? It's why you can even stay in the same room as Odin and Tyr. Why you've found someone else and forgotten about me. Well, I've not had the luxury of being able to move on and forgive and forget."

Her eyes moved down to my hands that were rigid around hers. I looked. Scars and gnarled flesh bled through my illusion. I couldn't even control my bloody emotions anymore.

I wouldn't have her see.

I let her go and walked to the window and looked out at the snow. It fell heavier now. I breathed in the cold, wanting it to calm the rage burning inside me.

"I realize I must be a disappointment." Pure scorn fell from my mouth. "I'm sorry I'm no longer the man you remember. Or want."

I felt her near me.

Worse, I felt her shatter.

"You gave everything to save me. Don't throw it all away by wanting to continue down this path," she said. "Promise me you will put your vengeance aside. Not just for me, but for you. Promise me, Loki."

She touched my shoulder, and I was undone. A shock of her fidelity tore through me, flooding my veins and chambers. Her hope swelled in my chest and I was found.

The red cleared.

I surfaced.

I turned and faced her. Shame pierced me at seeing her heart breaking in her gaze. And it was because of me. I never wanted to cause her to look at me like that again.

"I...I promise," I rasped, holding her gaze. Meaning it. I always would.

She grasped my upper arms and squeezed.

"We will get through this."

I pulled in a breath and nodded.

She continued to hold on to me. She even stroked her thumbs against the silk of my jacket. She stopped, as if catching herself, and returned her hands to her sides.

I wish she hadn't.

I cleared my throat and faced the others.

"So," I said, my voice still husky. "If I'm not in control of Ragnarok, which is very disappointing, how do you recommend we stop this thing?"

"Balder." Odin whispered the word, staring at nothing. "He's our only hope now. Our salvation against Surtr."

I frowned. Now that was depressing. In fact, I wasn't sure what upset me more. The prospect of dying a fiery death, or Balder being my saving grace.

"He's right," Falael said. "Balder is the only way. Where is he? He must be made ready."

"Why don't you ask Loki where he is?" Tyr nodded my direction.

All eyes fell on me.

I rubbed the back of my neck. Today was just not my day.

"I'm afraid he's rather dead. After I stabbed him in the neck," I said. "That one is totally on me."

Falael grimaced.

"Ah. Well, that is a problem," Falael said.

Odin cleared his throat and squared his shoulders.

"It would be if I hadn't sent Hermod down to Hel to negotiate Balder's return," he said. "We should have him back soon."

Did he really still believe it would be so easy? That she would bend from a few words from his little toady?

I walked to the book and looked at the handwritten script. I hoped it contained some other secret to get us out of this particularly sour pickle.

"Do you have a plan if she refuses?" I asked. "I don't think you realize how deep her infatuation with him goes. She made him an altar. She will not return him easily."

Sigyn tapped her fingers against her arm.

"Can someone explain Balder's significance in all this?" she asked.

Falael flipped through the pages of the book, stopping on one with an illustration of a great beast with a volcano for a mouth gnawing on a few screaming skeletons before dropping them into ladles of fire. Not very reassuring.

"Surtr is a darkness that consumes all and ends all," he read. "Only one who contains a pure element of a contrasting force can conquer Surtr and save us."

"Which leaves Balder," Tyr said. "The god of goodness and light. Everything Surtr is not."

"And Surtr is?" Sigyn tapped her fingers faster now.

"Just a thousand foot fire giant I'm supposed to wake," I said casually. "I was really looking forward to seeing that."

"My father told me Surtr was a weapon," Odin said.

"Actually," Falael pushed in. "No one truly knows what Surtr is, other than lethal. It could be all or none of those things. I theorize Surtr is really an element like a god, but far more powerful. Pure dark matter. Straight darkness."

My stomach churned looking at the screaming skeletons. I really could do without that experience.

"If this Surtr character is the main issue here, and I'm the one supposed to wake it, I just won't. If we can't control Ragnarok, we can at least control that. Maybe we won't need Balder after all."

That was a happy thought indeed.

Falael grimaced, pouring a nice bucket of ice water over all my hopes and dreams.

"Prophecies don't work that way," he said. "You can actively try to work against something and really be working towards it. Prophecies are ambiguous things until they become wretchedly plain."

He didn't have to tell me that twice.

Two ravens tapped at the window. Hugin and Munin. Did his bloody birds never die? Nothing would make me happier than seeing those two impaled on stakes and roasted over an open fire.

Odin opened the window and they flew in with a burst of snow that blew across the rugs. He closed it behind them.

They hopped on the table. Odin leaned down to them and stroked their beaks. They clicked and purred with their news.

News that sank Odin's face and shoulders.

"It's a message from Hermod," he said. "Hel refuses to return Balder. She said she's displeased I sent a lackey in my stead. If I want to negotiate his release, and stop the march of her army, she will only speak to me."

I wondered if now was an appropriate time for an *I told you so*.

Yes. Yes, it was.

"I warned you she wouldn't give him up lightly."

Odin rubbed his mouth.

"This is bad," he said. "We can only be grateful at least her brothers are not an active threat like her. Fenrir and Jormungand remain banished where they cannot escape. For now, we are safe from them."

I was grateful for another reason. They remained safe from Odin. I'd see to resolving their banishment in due course, but for now, it was better they remain where they were until this all blew over. Fenrir could stay busy on his island, and Jormungand in the Midgardian oceans.

"But..." Tyr said, his voice oddly shaken. "What if they happened to get out...to escape?"

"Then it would be another fallen domino closer to the end," Falael said.

Tyr looked awfully pale, almost as if he was going to be sick. But why would he care?

"I have to go to Hel," Odin said. "Getting Balder back is our only priority now. He's our only chance at stopping Surtr and winning this thing. She wouldn't dare refuse me in person."

I noticed a slight tremble in his voice, as if he wasn't so convinced by his own words.

I know I wasn't. Hel liked to play with her prey before she pounced. This was a game. A deadly one.

Odin waved at Tyr to follow him as he walked towards the library doors.

I followed. He turned and stopped me.

"Where do you think you're going?"

"I thought it might be good I come with you as a mediator. She is my daughter, after all. I might get her to see reas—"

"I wouldn't trust you two in the same chamber for all of King Midas' gold!" he said. "No. I do this alone. In fact, you are to stay right here in Alfheim. Go nowhere."

"You can't be serious."

"We can't afford any more risks. Besides, I thought you'd like to catch up with the woman you've caused all this for." Bitterness stiffened every word.

He made to leave. I grabbed his forearm and leaned into his ear. I hated the memories of him gnawing at my insides as his heat sank into my fingers.

"You might have swindled me into your camp to stop Ragnarok," I whispered. "But when this is over, I'm still going to kill you. I may have promised Sigyn to help stop Ragnarok, but I didn't promise to spare your life. You might escape Ragnarok, but you can't escape me."

He bared his teeth, but pain etched every line of his face.

"You seem to think you haven't already killed me when you broke our oath and made me do what I did. You might as well finish the job."

9

IF AWKWARDNESS BE THE FOOD
OF LOVE

I was back on Vigridr. Dried grass crinkled beneath my boots as I walked through smoke and ash and cinders.

The spirit stood waiting, its white shroud billowing around its thin frame in the hot wind.

"Back so soon?" it asked.

"I'm afraid I need some clarification."

"What's there to clarify? Nothing could be more straightforward. Burn them. Kill them. Destroy them."

Its mantra echoed through the field of stone and parched turf. Brimstone filled my lungs.

"The earthquake," I said. "I didn't invoke it. Nor did I invoke my chaos that sent fire into my palms."

"Of course you didn't," it said. "Ragnarok is unraveling as it should. Beyond you. Beyond all."

Damn. Falael was right. I wasn't sure which news upset me more.

I took two steps closer. Sparks snapped between my fingers and through my hair.

"Stop this," I said. "Call it off."

It chuckled, the sound like rattling dried bones.

"Call it off?" it said. "This is Ragnarok. It cannot be called off. It cannot be stopped now you've started it."

"The hell it can't," I spat. "I'm the Destroyer. You said Ragnarok was mine to command. End this."

It held out a finger to me.

"*You* said," it replied. "Your self assuredness always blinds you to the facts. Ragnarok has begun and you will wake Surtr and raze the worlds together at the final battle. There is no choice. There is no hope. There is only inevitability. Fate. And this is yours."

My blood turned to ice despite the burning embers crackling around me. Despite my fire twisting and popping in my depths lashing to get out.

"I refuse to believe this. I am not controlled by fate."

The spirit laughed, and this time, I knew it laughed at me.

"Really? Are you sure?"

My chaos thrashed against my ribs. It wanted out. I grit my teeth tighter, refusing it. I wouldn't succumb.

"I won't summon Surtr."

"You will." Its breath blistered. "One way or another. It is your destiny, and destiny is inescapable."

I grunted as my chaos burst out of me, engulfing my hands in flames.

I felt a kick to the chest. I was sucked out of Vigridr and back into Sigyn's private study surrounded by books, minerals, and pots of dried herbs. I sat on a leather sofa. I looked at my hands.

My palms burned and the heat from them broiled my cheeks. They glowed red and yellow just as before.

Except this time they were hotter.

A ringing filled my ears along with a chorus of voices. I

winced as the sound hammered against my skull. Within my skull.

Burn them. Kill them. Destroy them.

I focused on sucking my fire back into myself as I'd done countless times before.

My hands continued to smolder.

Come on...Stop.

Burn them. Kill them. Destroy them.

They wouldn't extinguish.

For the first time, I couldn't control my fire. My chaos. My own element. It ran wild through me and a spark of fear exploded deep in my bowels as to what this meant.

A door creaked open. The laughter and talk from children and adults rushed in, chasing away the chattering voices in my head.

I glanced over my shoulder. Sigyn.

I stood, hiding my hands behind my back so she couldn't see. This fire thing was turning into a real nuisance.

"It's complete mayhem out there," she said, walking in. "Nothing but questions from the older ones as to what's happening, and questions from the younger if they can play in the snow."

"You can't say I don't keep things lively when I pop in."

She smiled and closed the door behind her, throwing us into silence again. Sigyn walked around tables cluttered with microscopes and glass vials. Her study reminded me very much of her home back in Basel, packed with heavy furniture and medical equipment.

Sigyn went to a desk shoved in front of a window and set down a green bottle and two clean glasses.

"I thought you could use some of this." She popped open the bottle and poured them full with fareth, clear Elven brandy made from pears. "I know I could after today."

I stepped towards her, relief relaxing my muscles as my hands finally cooled and returned to normal.

Bookcases with science and anatomy books lined the wall to my left, and to my right the shelves were stuffed with jars, canisters, and urns all filled with salves and ointments. It was everything I'd ever wished for her.

She poured my glass to the rim and my mouth watered. I was about to take it when a stack of notes written in her hand took my attention.

"What's this?" I asked.

She brightened, handing them to me.

"I'm revising a book I wrote on women's health. Every year I go through it and update with new information or advancements made in the field."

I flipped through dozens of pages. Diagrams, equations, cross sections of women mid-childbirth.

"This is marvelous."

"I'm always trying to find ways to make the information more accessible and easy to understand. Especially for our new arrivals."

I smiled, loving how very different she was. How beautiful her soul.

"You never were one to stand aside."

She leaned against the desk and it was like falling back in time. When we spoke for hours about medicine in her house on Heuberg after a good dinner of potage and bread bursting with grains.

"The lack of education in some realms is shocking. I had to do something. I've been adding to this little work since shortly after I arrived here. It's become my passion project."

I handed her back her manuscript. Her fingers skated against mine as she took it from me.

Stillness settled between us.

She looked up into my eyes. I neared her, removing the remaining distance.

Her breaths deepened along with my own.

My lips burned hungering for her kiss.

She pulled back.

"Do you find it drafty in here?" she asked. "That wind is really howling through these shoddy windows."

She turned away and walked to the leather sofa. She sat on the far end in front of the fireplace and fiddled with the lace of her gown.

I sat on the opposite end, forcing my racing blood to calm.

I suppose it was only natural things should be awkward between us. We had both risen from the grave to the other.

Plus, she with a fiancé and me with the whole ending the worlds thing didn't help. It was quite the large elephant in the room.

"About Ragnarok. Earlier. If I knew..." I said. "I'd never put you in danger."

"I know. But you shouldn't have put anyone in danger."

Her disappointment in me was crushing.

But what more could be said?

Everything.

Nothing.

And we both knew it.

I traced the patterned stitching on my sleeve, wishing the silence would end. Wishing to move on to other subjects. To better ones.

She cleared her throat.

"What's this whole thing you have going on?" She pointed at my jacquard blazer.

"What do you mean?"

"Your jacket nearly matches Auntie Elénaril's embroidered pillows."

"It's Gucci," I said, horrified.

A hint of teasing lifted the corners of her mouth. Her eyes sparked with that playful spirit that always captivated me.

"And should I be impressed?"

"I'm told it's only worn by the most discerning Midgardians. You don't find embroidery like this just anywhere these days."

She laughed gently. I loved making her laugh.

"I guess I wouldn't know what's popular in Midgard anymore. I keep myself busy here with Fal—with the students."

And the moment died.

I stared at the fire, scratching my nails against the leather armrest.

"Yes. I'm sure it's difficult to pull yourselves out of each other's embrace to find the time for travel."

I didn't intend the sentence to be that harsh. To drip that much scorn. But the idea of them together...

Her shoulders tightened.

She rose and stood before a painting of two small children on the wall. Fresh and rosy cheeked. Their red hair reminded me of our boys.

Is this what Narfi and Nari would have looked like, had they not...

A burning flush seared my lungs.

"Don't make the mistake thinking you're the only one still haunted by ghosts."

I hated myself in that second. I always seemed to say the wrong thing to her.

"I never even got the chance to tell them goodbye," she whispered.

Pain bit the back of my throat.

"I will never forgive myself I wasn't fast enough," I said.

I got up off the sofa and stood behind her. I could feel the heat of her body. I could smell the rosemary from her hair that cascaded down her back. For a split second, we were hurtled again into another time. Into the time before all the horror.

I reached out and touched the side of her hand, not daring more. Not wanting more.

"I can sometimes still hear them in echoes or in the breeze," she said. She turned and faced me, letting her hand remain in mine. She held my gaze. "As I heard yours call to me."

A need took me over to hold her and never let her go.

The door squeaked open and the din from outside flooded in along with footsteps.

Sigyn stepped back and smiled as Falael walked in.

Gods. Would I ever be rid of this man? If Sigyn wasn't so violently opposed to murder...

"I've brought you both some blankets," he said. "This house was made for a hot climate, not the blizzard raging outside."

Sigyn walked to him and took the bundle of thick, wool blankets in her arms.

"Thank you, that's very kind. Isn't it kind, Loki?"

I rolled my eyes.

"Oh yes. So very, *very* kind. Whatever would we do without your generosity?"

He raised an eyebrow.

"Have I come at a bad time?"

Sigyn plopped the blankets on the sofa.

"Actually—"

"No," Sigyn interrupted. "Not at all. We were just catching up."

Falael took a flannel blanket off the top and wrapped it around her shoulders. He kissed her cheek.

Gods.

I walked to the desk and shot back the drink Sigyn had made me. Sweet. Fruity. Brimming with alcohol. I poured myself a second. A bigger one.

"I'm glad you can enjoy that stuff, I've never been a fan of fareth myself," he said. "But then, I prefer tea."

"How incredibly predictable," I grumbled.

He stepped closer to me. I shot down the second glass, savoring the sting.

"We've actually met before, you know," he said.

"Did we?"

"While you were waiting on Auntie Elénaril, we spoke right here in this room for an hour about the overpopulation of Solean Goats in Vanaheim."

"That sounds more like it was a hostage situation."

His dark eyebrows twisted.

"Don't you remember?" he pressed. "Your solution to the problem was throwing an enormous barbecue?"

His face came into my mind at that. Younger. Beaming.

Perfectly irritating.

"Oh, that's right. I do remember you and your glittering conversation," I said. "I see you've not changed a bit since then."

He gave that amused grin again. The kind that told me I was as bothersome as a snug kitten in a shoe.

"And it seems, neither have you," he said.

Bastard.

I turned to Sigyn.

"You've found quite the shining star in him," I told Sigyn, switching to speaking Swiss, wanting to keep him out of our conversation. "Is there a place we can go without his glaring brightness?"

"I can leave, if you'd prefer, Sigyn," he told her. Also in Swiss.

"No, you can stay," she replied.

My neck grew hot.

"Oh, you also speak Swiss?" I asked him. "How *perfectly* delightful."

He chuckled.

"Sigyn taught me," he said.

"Of course she did." My neck grew hotter. I didn't like the flashes I kept seeing of them alone.

"I was such a bad student at first," he said.

He smiled at Sigyn, holding her gaze. I wanted to claw out his eyes.

"It wasn't any worse than you teaching me Elvish," she said. "I think I insulted the entire household at some point, telling them they should shower instead of wash their hands."

He shifted and looked at me again.

"I'm utterly fascinated by Midgard," he said. "Their topography, the art, the clothes."

I poured a third drink as he kept chattering away, intent to flush out the mental images of them together.

"I visit Midgard often, actually," he continued. "Sigyn has taught me a lot about life there. Not just of the languages, but of the cultures, the climates, and the food. Is there anything those Midgardians won't put cheese on? It's truly fantastic!"

And there it was. A way to wound him.

"Let me get this straight," I said "You visit Midgard often, yet, she has never returned with you? Odd. I'd think you'd take her with you on one of these ventures, being she isn't your prisoner?"

Falael's mouth flattened.

I sneered, enjoying my victory.

"It's not a question of being free to go back," she said. "I won't. Can't."

"Why?"

Falael squeezed her shoulder, and I hated the deep sincerity bleeding through his eyes looking at her.

"We all deal with grief differently," he said. "When I lost my Madriel, instead of dying from my sorrow, I channeled my grief into creating this house. Grief fuels Sigyn's mission to do good. And you've used your grief to..."

"Burn this all to the ground? Don't think I'm the best example."

He sighed.

"I was going to say it's given you a fierce determination, misguided as it may be," he said. "The point is, it's difficult to face the memories head on. I think you more than anyone can understand that."

I shrank.

"Midgard has become a place only of loss to me," she said. "I lost the life I loved. I lost our children to insanity, my father to illness, and my brother to war."

Guilt washed cold down my back at that last one. Simon dying in war was the lie I fed her. It was far better than the truth. That I had killed him to save her. If she ever found out...

I pushed that unhappy thought away.

"I've tried so hard to move on," she said. "But the thought of even going back there..."

"I wish you would have shared this with me," I told her.

Pain stitched the lines of her face.

"You don't deserve to be burdened by my demons. You have enough of your own."

I took in a breath, preparing to tell her to hang my demons. That she could tell me anything that bothered her. That she could rely on me.

The door shot open again.

Tyr stood in the doorway. Snow fell off his broad shoulders and boots in sheets.

Dammit! Was everyone in Alfheim walking through that bloody door today?

10

SEND IN THE WOLVES

I ce crystals clung to Tyr's beard and hair. He almost looked like the fabled frost giants of Northern Jotunheim. Except ten times smaller, and without that hungry look for wanting to crush your bones into their lentil soup.

Falael pushed passed me and waved Tyr over to sit on the sofa.

"Come closer to the fire," he said. "You're nearly frozen solid. Sigyn, get him a shot of fareth to warm his blood."

I stepped in front of him, blocking his path to the fire.

"Why the blazes are you back?" I said. "I thought myself finally rid of you."

Tyr threw me a nasty look, another slough of snow falling onto the inlaid wooden floor.

"Then it will please you to know I cannot stay. Odin doesn't know I'm here. If he found out..." he swallowed. "There's something urgent I need to tell you."

Sigyn rushed to Tyr holding a full glass of fareth. It dribbled over the rim and splattered the floor in a trail behind her.

I couldn't believe the generosity I was seeing. The concern. Every kind word to him, every kind action, tore out my insides piece by piece.

"First drink this." She handed him the glass.

Tyr's chapped lips pulled into a grin behind his dark blonde beard as he lifted the glass to his mouth.

I couldn't do this.

I ripped the glass out of his hand and threw it into the fireplace. A million clear pebbles exploded against the stone.

"Say what you've come to say and leave."

Sigyn glared at me, pointing at a chair in the corner. A very dark corner.

"Go and sit."

I scoffed and crossed my arms.

"Am I a child now?"

"Do you really want me to answer that?"

I did not.

I marched to the chair and plopped on the worn cushion and rubbed the side of my face, allowing Tyr to see a very particular finger glare back at him.

He sighed.

"I know you see me as an enemy, Loki. I deserve it. But you must understand, I come on your behalf."

I shot my gaze to his.

"Is that supposed to make everything better?" I asked. "Am I supposed to thank you now?"

"It's about your son, Fenrir."

I lowered my hands to my lap.

"What of him?"

He shifted in his boots. He scratched his nose.

"I never gave it a second thought until this afternoon

with all the Ragnarok talk. If I had known...what with dominoes and all...well...Fenrir...he's...uh..."

"Dammit, spit it out."

"He's free, Loki."

My breath hitched. I slowly leaned forward in the chair, the leather groaning beneath me.

"Free? How are you certain?" I asked.

He tugged his ear and bit his bottom lip.

"I...I'm the one that freed him. Centuries ago."

A million cold worms wriggled in my stomach. I stood and braced myself against the mantel and stared into the fire.

If this was true, Fenrir was no longer safe. *We* were no longer safe.

"Why did you free him?" Falael asked.

"Just because I am in the inner circle of Aesir gods doesn't mean I always agree with their decisions," he said. "Hel at least gained an entire kingdom, and Jormungand had the seas to rule. Fenrir..."

My heart stung. Bitterness filled my mouth. What had happened to my boy?

"He was never going to be banished to an island where he could run free, was he?" I said. "Where then?"

I turned and looked at him. His shoulders fell.

He pulled in a heavy breath.

"It was wrong." He looked me in the eye. "And conning you and his mother into thinking you were sending him away to a good place, a safe place...I couldn't bear it."

I walked to him and stared up at his wind beaten face.

"Where?" I snapped.

His cheeks hollowed.

"They actually did plan to send him to an island. But it was Lynsvi Island, in the middle of Lake Amsvartnir."

I clenched my teeth and pain radiated down the length of my jaw.

Lynsvi Island was a slab of black rock in the center of a black lake. Nothing but mist and stone and darkness.

And once more, Odin had betrayed me.

"We trusted them," I growled. "Angrboda and I believed we were giving our children their best chance, but it was only ever for Odin's own good."

He nodded.

"They wouldn't dare tell you the truth," he said. "The gods charged me with taking him there and chaining him to a boulder. Then, I was told to drive a sword through his bottom jaw, pinning him to the earth so he could no longer bite. He could no longer eat. He could no longer be a threat."

My skin iced. I'd agreed to give my son the same fate the gods gave me. To suffer eternity alone and cold and starving.

I tasted venom in my mouth.

And the melting snow trickling off Tyr's cloak to the floor in rhythmic drips only made me taste it more.

"If you knew Odin's true motive, why didn't you tell me?" I said. "I would have done something. I would have prevented it."

His mouth twisted into a crooked line.

"Because I knew how you get when you find out you've been crossed. It was not the time for one of your scenes."

"I don't make scenes."

He gave me a look.

"Maybe sometimes," I said.

"I loved Fenrir," he said. "He was my friend, and to punish him for simply existing...He never broke a single rule. He never spoke a rude word out of turn. He didn't deserve that fate."

The smallest grain of gratitude for Tyr grew in my chest. But the cruel reality swept it away, knowing what the ramifications of this merciful act meant.

He made Fenrir a wild card. There was no telling what Ragnarok whispered to him. And I knew it whispered to him, pushed him, as it did to his sister and to me.

And what of my other son, Jormungand? What did Ragnarok whisper to him?

I pushed that thought away, but the hair on my arms remained raised.

"The fact remains, Fenrir is free, and that's a problem. For him, and for us," I said.

Falael wiped his mouth. Shadows played across the soft arcs and dips of his face that sharpened with thought. With concern.

Grave concern.

"And we are all another domino closer to Ragnarok," he said.

He put his hands behind his back and walked to the window and stared out.

"I don't understand," Sigyn said. "Why is Fenrir so significant to Ragnarok? Why was he singled out to be damned and not the others?"

Tyr sighed.

"Odin believes Fenrir his undoing once the final battle begins," Tyr said. "He thought if he could trap Fenrir..."

"He could escape that part of his fate," I finished. "He does enjoy caging what he thinks will kill him. He needs a better hobby."

Tyr walked to the fire, his bulky shoulders and layers of

fur blocking most of the firelight throwing us into a gloom that matched our thoughts.

He spread out his large hands, warming them.

"As for Fenrir, the great wolf, he will crush Odin between his jowls," he whispered, echoing the prophecy Golda had told me when I found out I was the Destroyer.

Golda was a formidable witch. The best. It still annoyed me she took my mother's dagger, *Truth,* in exchange for the knowledge I sought. I could barely stomach the thought of her gutting fish with such a beautiful weapon.

"Where is Fenrir now?" I asked.

Wood popped in the fireplace. Cinders crackled and burst.

"On Midgard," he said. "In Vienna, Austria. I don't know where, only that he's confined to the city. It was better than being strapped down on that godsforsaken island."

"And if Odin finds this out?" Falael asked, still staring out the window. Somberness imbued his translucent reflection in the glass.

Tyr didn't answer this time. He just stared into the flames that coated him in gold. But I knew.

"He will kill him," I said.

Tyr swallowed. "And I don't need to tell you why that can't happen."

The fire snapped and logs collapsed further into embers.

"How can I trust you?" I said. "How can I be sure this isn't another ruse?"

He straightened and rolled up his sleeve and thrust out his right arm to me. The hook he used in place of his missing hand reflected the flickering fire.

"Did you ever wonder how I lost my hand?" he asked. "Of course not. You were always too busy with some orgy or pissed on claret to bother asking."

"There are a frightful many severed appendages in Asgard. I'm sorry if I can't keep up with them all."

He flattened his lips.

"The gods feared Fenrir would suspect trickery unless one of us laid a hand in his jaws as a sign of good faith," he said. "Of course, this meant one of us would inevitably lose a hand. But they viewed it as a necessary sacrifice for protecting the Nine Worlds."

"I don't understand."

"Only one way would prove to the gods I'd done what they wanted. Only one way would keep them from discovering the truth. That I never chained Fenrir at all." He paused. "I made Fenrir bite off my hand."

I stilled. Even my breaths stopped.

"You did that for my son?"

"It's not the only thing he did," Sigyn said.

I turned to her.

"When Frigg ripped Narfi and Nari out of my arms and pulled out her knife…" She paused. She swallowed. "Tyr let me slip from his grasp."

I looked at him, puzzled.

"I told you I'm not your enemy," he said. "You were a son of a bitch to break your oath to Odin, but you didn't deserve that. I did the only thing I could without revealing myself, just as I had done with letting Fenrir bite off my hand. I let her go so she could defend your children. As I let Fenrir go to live in peace."

That little grain of gratitude swelled. Dammit. Why couldn't I just remain in hatred for him forever?

"We have to find Fenrir," I said. "We have to prevent Odin from discovering him. We have to protect him."

Falael made a worried noise.

He turned away from the window and stepped next to us.

"It might seem counterintuitive, but I feel it far safer to leave him where he is," Falael said. "Now is not the time to meddle."

I tilted my head so far I thought it would snap off.

"How can you suggest such a thing?" I asked.

He sighed and pinched the bridge of his slender nose.

"Again, you don't know the consequences our actions will have. Whatever we do could very well work against Ragnarok, but it could also push us closer towards it. Please be reasonable."

He obviously didn't know me well.

"You expect me to just leave Fenrir a sitting duck?" My voice grew louder.

His pointed ears flushed red.

"No. Of course not. It's not what I mean. Just, we have to practice caution. We are in a very rocky boat."

"If you haven't noticed, the boat has a massive hole drilled in the middle and is already sinking," I said.

I marched towards the doors.

"What are you doing?" Sigyn said.

"I'm going after him. I won't have another son slain. And if he kills Odin...we lose our only chance at retrieving Balder and stopping Surtr, at stopping Ragnarok. This is the only course of action we can take."

Tyr stepped in front of me, looking more grim than a skeleton in a dusty tomb.

"Get out of my way."

"You can't be the one to find him. Same as me," he said. "If Odin catches you outside Alfheim..."

I chuckled. Was that all?

"Please, if I worried about Odin and his wishes, I'd get nothing done," I said.

"He has eyes everywhere."

"Ah yes, his flying rats," I said. "I'm well acquainted."

I tried to step around him. He blocked me again. I calculated how much force it would take me to push him over. Probably whatever would be equivalent to pushing over a boulder. Or exceedingly large mammoth.

"He will find out."

"Not if I find Fenrir before he does," I snapped. "Fenrir is my son. I must do this."

Sigyn walked over and stood next to me.

"I will go with you," she said.

Falael's mouth parted and his brow pressed together.

"Go to Midgard?" he said. "Are you sure that's wise? I don't know if that's the best option considering...well, remember? You pulled out last minute accompanying me to the premiere of Don Giovanni in Prague. You said playing cards with Mozart and Casanova after the opera would be too taxing. Now we are talking brink of war, end of worlds scenarios. I know you're strong, but...please consider the issues."

"As much as I hate admitting, I agree with Falafel." Those words hurt me to say. "It's better you remain here where it's safe."

Falael laid a supporting hand on Sigyn's shoulder.

"I just don't want you hurt," he said. "But I support your decision, whatever you choose."

She nodded.

"Nowhere is safe as long as Ragnarok looms over our heads," she said. "Don't fight me. My mind is made up and I must do my part. I won't see another child harmed by the gods. Not if I can prevent it."

Gods I loved her strength, even so, I wasn't particularly thrilled with her being put in harm's way. I hadn't sacrificed myself for her just to put her at risk a second time.

Tyr shook his shoulders and fastened his cloak tight beneath his chin.

Falael and Sigyn spoke together in terse whispers.

"I must go before I'm missed," Tyr said.

He opened the doors. I tugged his cloak, stopping him before he walked through.

"I'm not accustomed to saying such things." I itched the top of my nose. "In fact, it makes my stomach churn already, but..."

He gave a faint smile.

"You're welcome," he said.

* * *

"I can't believe I'm doing this. I swore I'd never go back to Midgard," Sigyn pushed through a mouthful of chocolate.

Falael slumped a pile of Midgardian clothing on her bed. Her eyes widened, taking in the mountain of shirts, dresses, and wool coats.

She rustled out another square of chocolate from the box she held in an iron grip. She popped it in her mouth. It was her twelfth piece.

"Again, it would be much better if you stay here," I said.

She rummaged through a heap of silk scarves. I didn't like how her hands shook.

"And here I was thinking you'd be happy to see me outside Alfheim...since you consider me a prisoner and all."

She got me there.

"I'm going," she said. "I must. I will. I am. What is this?"

She pulled out a mini skirt and knee high patent leather

heeled boots. Her eyes widened, and I wasn't sure if her expression leaned more towards confusion or horror.

"How...How do you even wear such garments?" She held the mini skirt against her waist.

I smiled.

"Actually, I think that would look quite fetching on you," I said. "Especially if you paired it with this halter top."

She grabbed another handful of chocolate and chewed forcefully.

"Back in the sixteenth century one had to wear at least five layers of wool and linen and be neatly stitched in," she said. "These new fashions are overwhelming."

I waded through the blouses and slacks, wanting to help. I found a lovely black blouse that would set off her hair quite nicely.

"Try these." Falael held out a stack of folded clothes. "You might find them more familiar."

Did he never cease in one upping me?

Skepticism tightened the angles of her face, but she took the stack and walked behind a changing screen.

Laces raced through eyelets.

Stitches snapped.

Silk rushed down skin.

"If this wasn't already stressful enough..." she grumbled.

She tossed her gown onto a small side table, almost knocking over a porcelain washbasin.

Falael moved next to me. He was a beige nightmare in his own Midgardian clothing. Beige trousers, beige chunky sweater, beige loafers...and somehow it only made him more attractive. More huggable. I wanted to die.

Trying to escape him, I stepped away and went to the full-length mirror next to Sigyn's vanity. Where a variety of remedies and herbs cluttered her study, for herself she kept it simple. A pot of rouge. A comb.

"How long do you think we have before Odin's ravens spot us?" Falael asked me.

Could he not take the hint I didn't want to talk to him?

I combed my fingers through my hair, admiring how it waved wildly around my sharp face.

"Odin being away in Hel has bought us some time, but not much. This needs to be quick. In and out before they can report back to him."

"That will be difficult."

I chuckled.

I straightened my lapels and pushed the sleeves of my exquisite jacket up to my elbows. Damn, I looked good.

"Maybe for you," I said. "I find a ticking clock and death on the line invigorating. Perhaps it would be better you sit this one out. You'll only slow Sigyn and I down."

Sigyn groaned behind the screen.

"Not this again. It's been settled."

I had looked forward to Sigyn and I finally getting some much needed alone time. And if I knew anything, it was that nothing heated the blood faster than a rich and exciting danger like we were about to dive into.

It promised to be quite the scintillating trip.

Until Sigyn informed me that Falael would join us, and just like that they made me the third wheel.

Now all that thrilling danger was wasted.

"Again, I really must protest," I said.

"Have you ever been to Vienna, Loki?" she asked.

I went and sat on the bed, sinking into layers of cotton and feathers.

"Yes, actually. During the Black Death of 1349 I made a grand tour of Europe."

Falael perked and leaned against the bedpost, crossing his arms.

"Really?" Falael said. "Wouldn't a less diseased time have been better?"

"On the contrary, it kept tourist crowds low during the summer holidays. Plus, the plague pits were marvelously grim."

"You really have unique tastes," he said. "Some might even say deeply disturbing, but, I admire that you are true to yourself. More should follow your example."

I smiled.

"Thank you. People would find life vastly more fun if they did."

Wait. Why was I even talking to him? I hated him. He always kept finding ways of pulling me into pleasant conversation. This man infuriated me to no end.

"As I'm sure you realized," Sigyn continued. "Times have changed since the fourteenth century. Gods! These stockings are worse than any pair of stays or corsets I've worn. I feel like a sausage wrapped around the middle."

"What are you saying?"

She sighed.

"Falael has more experience than both of us with modern Midgard. He knows all the new technologies and can find Fenrir faster than both of us together."

I scoffed, straightening my silver rings.

"Please. I'm sure I can find my son. I've tracked down more people than I can count," I said. "I am quite as adept as Falafel. No. *Better*."

She sighed again.

"Do you even know what a mobile is?"

"A what?"

"He's coming."

Damn.

"I'm coming out now," she said. "Don't laugh. I've not worn Midgardian clothing in five hundred years and I feel a fool."

She stepped out from behind the screen. My heart hammered against my chest so hard I thought it would pop out between my ribs.

She wore black tights, a houndstooth skirt, gray sweater, and, oh, I was proud. A leather jacket to match her leather ankle boots.

Falael laid his hand on her shoulder.

"You look perfect," he said.

I couldn't find my voice.

That same awe that hit me when I accidentally caught her bathing in the Rhine struck me.

Gathering her hair up into a high ponytail, she passed me and walked to the full-length mirror. She made a sour face looking at herself.

Her eyes found mine in the mirror's reflection.

"Yes...perfect," I whispered.

She wound her honeyed hair faster into a bun and looked away.

And I had lost her.

Lost her?

No. That wasn't possible. I didn't lose to men who wore beige and sensible shoes.

I smiled.

It was clear.

Falael was just a temporary infatuation. Yes. That was all. It had been a long time since she and I were together. It was understandable she would find comfort with another while I was away.

I turned to him. He shoved his solid arms into a camel

coat and pulled it up over his shoulders. He was like a tall glass of whole milk. Rich and nourishing.

And utterly boring.

I smiled wider.

Maybe I had been looking at him joining us on this little adventure all wrong. This was an opportunity.

I'd save my son, I'd save the worlds, and I'd prove to Sigyn the truth. I was the better man.

She just needed a reminder, and the infatuation would end.

"I've booked us rooms at the Sacher Hotel," Falael said, his voice breaking my thoughts that brimmed with a thousand schemes and plots. "We will need a place we can meet away from any eyes. Especially with Hugin and Munin flying about."

This wasn't even fair.

"What a brilliant idea." I stood next to him and draped my arm over his shoulder and tugged him against me. Even his biceps were perfect and firm.

Facing me, his brow knit with confusion. I smiled wider.

"Why are you looking at me like that?"

"Oh, I'm just thinking I maybe underestimated your usefulness on this trip."

"I just booked two hotel rooms, it's really not that big a deal."

"So humble! You are more helpful than you realize, Falafel."

"*Falael*," he said.

"Whatever."

11

KNÖDELS ON PARADE

Midgard

Vienna, Austria

Sigyn was right.

Vienna had changed a lot since 1349.

The uneven timber framed homes were replaced by grand and opulent buildings of limestone and marble. There was also the lack of pestilent corpses rotting in heaps on every corner.

Vienna was now a city of statues, filigrees, and capstones covered in varying layers of gilding instead of mud and shit.

A welcome change.

Wind tore through my hair and flapped my clothes around my legs as I stood in the center of Stephansplatz and stared at the only thing I recognized. The two front towers of St. Stephen's Cathedral remained just as tall and solid as when I saw them seven hundred years before.

People bustled in every direction, leaning into another

cold gust that snapped around the sharp corners of the cathedral and howled across the square.

I pulled my coat higher over my chin. Sweat clung to my back despite the frigid gales and snow. Winters in Vienna were always somehow simultaneously freezing and humid. But that's what you got for thinking it a good idea to plop a city in a basin between the Alps and Carpathian mountains.

Falael, Sigyn, and I took off down Kärntner Strasse, a wide shopping street that cut through the center of the city. Baroque buildings were sandwiched between modern ones of smooth glass and flashing, neon signs. Horse hooves clapped against the cobblestone streets and classical music mingled with the growl of cars and busses. Vienna was a city stuck somewhere in between the old and the new.

Like me.

We sifted through Vienna's numerous districts looking for Fenrir. Down quiet alleys. Up noisy boulevards of trams and taxis. We trudged as far as the Prater with its red ferris wheel that moved almost imperceptibly, and came back towards the city center along the graffiti lined walls of the Danube river.

And every chance I got, I slowly and meticulously chipped away at Sigyn and Falael's relationship. I beat Falael to every door and opened it for her first. I insisted on carrying her purse when it started to strain her shoulder. I even popped into a store called Cartier's and bought her a fantastic bracelet. Simple. Elegant. Sigyn.

When she opened the box, she thanked me and put it in her pocket instead of on her wrist.

No matter. She only needed more time.

Falael was just a passing fancy.

He had to be.

Exhausted, we dragged ourselves to the Hotel Sacher, a

building of marble, mahogany, and thick, red velvet. I spoke to the concierge and sent a dozen red roses up to her room. The fact she shared it with Falael made the burn to him even more delicious.

We woke before the sun even broke the horizon and met in the quiet elegance of the lobby.

I heard nothing about the flowers.

And worse, Falael didn't even seem the slightest bit annoyed. He didn't even seem to see me as a threat at all. In fact, he wished me a good morning and handed me a freshly baked semmel roll.

I threw it in the nearest bin out of spite, even though it smelled delicious.

We left the Sacher and went out into the snow and diesel and cigarettes. We pushed harder. Looked farther. Turned the entire city upside down, shaking it at its scruff for any hint of Fenrir. It gave us nothing.

The wind wailed. It grew colder.

And something worse followed...

The sky turned a slight shade of red. Like a bead of blood dropped into a tub of water.

At first I thought my eyes played tricks on me, but Sigyn and Falael noticed it too.

The sun was darkening.

The third sign of Ragnarok.

Burn them. Kill them. Destroy them...

I dove my hands into my pockets so they could not see how they glowed like hot irons.

But the call remained.

Burn them. Kill them. Destroy them...

Time was running out.

We had to find Fenrir. Now.

"Can we hurry this up? You've been pounding at that

blasted glowy rectangle in your hand for hours," I said to Falael.

His thumbs flew over a screen of illuminated glass making a storm of clicks and clacks. Each keystroke pulverized my last nerve further into pulp. I learned this was the elusive "mobile."

"I'm searching for leads," he said. "It takes time to comb through social media. If we are lucky..."

Another storm of chinks and snaps followed.

I massaged my temples.

"I swear Falafel, if you make one more *pop* on that infernal machine—"

"My gods..."

Falael's eyes widened.

"What is it?" Sigyn turned from the white stallions she'd been watching. The horses chewed hay in their stables on the other side of large panes of glass. We'd been waiting inside a covered passage of the Hofburg Palace that connected to Michaelerplatz and the Spanish Riding School.

Falael smiled and held out his phone to us. He scrolled down a collage of square photos of food. Green smoothies, slices of Linzertortes, and salads piled with cranberries and sunflower seeds.

It was official. Falael was losing it.

"That's a very nice menu, but I don't see how this is helpful," I said.

He chuckled.

"This isn't a menu," he said. "It's an app where people post their photos, and this particular account specializes in highlighting all the best vegan food of Vienna."

"What does this have to do with my son?"

He smiled.

"Everything," he said. "This account is Fenrir's."

My heart stopped.

Sigyn clapped her hand over her mouth.

"How can you be sure?" I asked.

Falael tapped and swiped. He clicked one of the photos. A picture of a young man with long, brown hair and bright, emerald eyes filled the screen. Fenrir. He had an immense grin plastered across his angled face as he held up an ice cream cone in one hand and gave a thumbs up with the other. Apparently, it was made entirely out of coconut milk and totally worth eight euros a scoop.

I cocked my head.

I snatched the phone and looked at it closer.

"My son takes photos of his food instead of eating it?"

"You're missing the point," Sigyn said.

"You're right. Thank gods we found him before this gets anymore out of hand. This requires an intervention."

She rubbed her brow.

"These pictures can help us locate him. If we can find any pattern of places he visits, we can get to Fenrir before Odin. Before this madness continues any further." Sigyn touched my arm and gave me a reassuring squeeze. "Loki, we found your son. It's all going to be ok."

I gave a small smile and tried not to think of the voices in my head chanting otherwise.

Falael pulled the phone out of my grasp and sped through more photos of soups, breads, strudels, and "I Can't Believe it's Not Meat" schnitzels. A parade of knödels, Austrian dumplings, followed: Spinach knödels, semmel knödels, apricot knödels, potato knödels...If you could think it, you could knödel it.

I was about to rip it back away to end the knödel nightmare but his smile stopped me.

"Look!" Falael said.

Sigyn and I leaned in to see.

Fenrir stood outside of a cafe called *L. Heiner* eating a cookie filled with nuts and dried fruit. Another photo sped by. This of a coffee and a fancy puff pastry drizzled with chocolate. Photo after excruciating photo of soups, desserts, and—I sighed—knödels.

I guess there could be worse hobbies, although none came to mind.

"He goes there every day," Falael said. "And always in the morning around nine."

Church bells clanged through the city. Deep and rhythmic and settled in my bones.

It was nine.

* * *

WE ENTERED cafe *L. Heiner* just off of Wollzeile, a narrow street packed with cars, pedestrians, and bikes.

Coffee, butter, and sugar filled my nose. Radiators rattled pumping out waves of heat that made me question if we'd mistakenly entered a sauna. It was like this with every building in the city. The Viennese seemed terrified of catching a chill, and so preferred to lightly boil.

"Grüss Gott," a gray haired woman said to us from behind an immense glass counter filled with tortes and pastries.

We turned right and walked into a smallish room paneled in mahogany (it was always mahogany in Vienna) and lined with round, marble tables. Sigyn pulled out a red velvet chair (it was also always red velvet) and sat at a table next to a large window.

Falael slid his camel coat off his shoulders and hung it on the coat rack in the corner.

"I'm going to speak with the manager to see if they know of any regulars. If we've ended up missing him, we might at least get an address. It's likely he's had deliveries."

"What would you have us do?" Sigyn asked.

"Wait and keep watch," he said. "He could walk through the entrance any minute."

Falael took off back towards the stairs that led to another level of tables and chairs and pastry.

"I'm going to go after him. If he mucks this up..."

She grasped my wrist and stopped me.

"Stay," she said. "Please. I need to talk to you."

My skin seared beneath her touch, awakening every nerve of my body.

Sigyn's cheeks flushed.

She released me as if I had burned her.

I ran my hot fingers through my hair and sat opposite her. She wiped her palm against her skirt.

I tried to focus on anything else but my racing blood. The soft conversation surrounding us pertaining to the odd weather. The scraping of forks across plates as old men wearing tweed shoveled piles of whipped cream and apfelstrudel into their mouths.

Sigyn cleared her throat.

"I know this trip has not been easy for you, but the snide remarks need to stop. Falael is trying to help you. He's trying his best given the...*difficult*...situation we've all been thrown in. You need to cut him some slack. You don't have to like him, but you can be nicer."

"Nicer? I had ample chances to shove him into the Danube, and I didn't. How much nicer could I be?"

She rolled her eyes.

"He has a kind heart."

The muscles in my shoulders tightened.

"As you've said multiple times already. I get it. He's *wonderful*."

I pulled out the menu and flung through each page.

"I'm sorry, I don't mean to cause you pain."

I snorted.

"Why ever would you think me seeing you with another man would cause me pain?"

I peered over the menu at her and immediately hated myself.

I parted my mouth to apologize when a server stepped next to us, pen in hand ready for our orders.

They always had excellent timing.

"A melange. Thank you," Sigyn said.

"Double whiskey for me." I tossed the menu on the table.

Sigyn's eyebrows shot up to her hairline.

"It's nine in the morning."

I nodded.

"You're right. Make it a single."

The server scribbled across her pad and left us alone again.

"You also need to stop giving me gifts," Sigyn said.

I smiled and leaned forward, laying my arms on the table.

"Ah! So you received the roses. Good," I said. "I almost threw in a string quartet, but decided that would be a tad excessive."

"Loki, I know what you're doing."

"Treating you as you deserve? Yes. I take it seriously," I said. "Unlike Falafel. I've not seen him buy you anything from Tiffany's or Chanel."

"You have to accept…"

The server returned with two silver trays, one for Sigyn and one for me. I frowned as she scooted a fiaker in front of me. Strong coffee mixed with rum and topped with whipped cream. I guess it was a no on the whiskey.

"Accept what?" I asked.

Sigyn took the little napkin from beneath her melange and twisted the corners.

"You have to accept he and I are together now."

I leaned back in the chair and the wood creaked. So, she still thought them well matched? She just needed more time.

I just hoped she'd hurry before we all blew up in the fires of Ragnarok if this didn't go well.

"Whatever you say," I said. I sipped my drink, loving the burn of the hot coffee and bite of the rum on my tongue.

She crossed her arms.

"I am not a prize to be won."

"You aren't, I agree," I said. "This isn't a contest. I understand what's going on and I'm just waiting it out. Falael is just a passing fancy."

"Passing fancy? Is that really what you think?"

"What else should I think? After all we've been through. After all we shared…You just need time."

"Loki…I've had time. Five hundred years of it. And…"

Something restrained welled in her eyes. Something she fought against. As if reason and heart were at war in her.

I put down my coffee.

"What are you saying?"

Sigyn stiffened.

"I…"

"You loved me beyond anything."

"I did."

"And you love me still."

She didn't answer. She twisted and tore at her napkin faster. White bits of paper fell into her lap.

I didn't like how long this pause stretched.

My chest constricted.

"Sigyn...do you still love me?"

Her eyes misted.

My breaths thinned.

"Please...don't do this," she said.

I hung on her every word. In all my millennia of life, in all my close calls and desperate acts, this was the most scared I'd ever been.

"Sigyn, what's wrong?" Falael asked behind me.

"Nothing," she said. "I'm fine. I'm...I'm fine."

He shook his head.

"I was afraid it would be too much for you coming back here," he said. "How can I help?"

I scratched my nails into the wood of the table. I was done with his constant interruptions.

With his existence.

"You can help by going away," I said. "This is nothing that concerns you."

I stood and faced him.

His eyes narrowed and he stepped closer. I could feel his breath. I could smell his overly spiced cologne.

"If she's upset, it most decidedly concerns me," he said. "What did you say to her?"

I scoffed.

"You dare blame me for her tears?"

"She didn't cry until you came back."

He drove a spear into my bowels with that.

"You overstep, Elf." I pressed my finger into his chest.

"Can't you see what this is all doing to her?"

"Both of you, stop," Sigyn snapped, her words echoing somewhere in the background.

There was only Falael and the anger lighting behind his eyes. He looked at me as if I were a beast.

"I kept excusing your behavior as it being just a healthy sense of self-esteem," he said. "But now I see. You're just inconsiderate and care about no one's needs besides your own."

"Are you saying I'm self-centered?"

"The sun is smaller than your ego."

I started to push him and his cable knit sweater into all the whipped cream delights on the table behind us—*it would make a glorious mess*—when a man walked in the door.

I stopped.

The man peered through the counter at the pastries. His brown hair was tied back, and dark stubble covered his chin and jaw. He pulled out his phone, lifted his perfectly groomed thick eyebrows, and snapped a photo of a strawberry tart.

Fenrir.

12

SALT AND BLOOD

Everything I wanted to forget from the last time I ever saw Fenrir cut through my veins like a stinging knife.

The smile on his face when he believed my lie.

How soundly he slept that night, not realizing it would be his last in his own bed in Ironwood.

And I didn't tell him goodbye in the morning.

I couldn't survive seeing his face once he knew the truth.

It is for his own protection.

None of that mattered now.

I pushed Falael out of the way and walked to Fenrir. He bent forward, looking at rows of lemon tarts and custards. A string of red mala beads tied around his wrist clicked with his movement.

"What vegan options do you have today, Anna?" he asked the young server standing behind the counter. Her blonde hair was pulled into a French braid that showed off her round face.

I heard an echo of my voice in his, but his timbre was far darker and deeper. You could almost swim in it.

I stood behind him and opened my mouth to speak. Nothing came out.

I never had a problem with finding words. In fact, my problem was quite the opposite, but now, I couldn't find a single one.

Fenrir's shoulders tensed.

The skin around his navy scarf rose with gooseflesh. He straightened and lengthened his posture.

"You could have come before now," he said in Jotun, his voice almost a growl that made the language sound more threatening than it already did.

He was a shifter. A wolf. It didn't surprise me he sensed me before I made myself known to him. It made it awfully hard to play hide and seek with him as a child.

"You know I couldn't. There were rules."

He kept staring forward at the wall cluttered with wrapped packages of chocolates.

I could see his lips pull into a wry smile in the display case's reflection.

"I didn't think *rules* were a sentiment you prescribed to," he said.

"There were terms."

He scoffed.

He turned and faced me. His face was angular like my own, though not so sharp. We shared the same green eyes, though his were more gentle. Fenrir looked pulled from the pages of a brochure on camping. Rugged, yet soft around his sturdy edges.

"You haven't changed. It's always excuses with you."

"What are you talking about?"

His hands clenched into fists at his sides.

"I saw you break plenty a rule with glee. You viewed

them as dares. So don't lie to me. You've only come because you want something."

I stepped closer to him. His shoulders tightened further.

"You're right," I said. "I have come here because I want something. To save your life. You're in danger."

His eyes changed from green to gold. To the piercing eyes of the wolf that lurked deep within him.

He rushed me and shoved me back. Anna shrieked, her voice rattling between my ears as I struck the floor. My breath knocked out of my lungs.

He curled his fingers into my coat, pinning me beneath him. I struggled to pull in air. He was far heavier than I remembered.

"Don't pretend you actually care," he snarled. "That you came here purely out of fatherly concern. You aren't a father. You are just an opportunist."

He bared his teeth. They flashed white against his dark stubble.

"I'm not," I said.

"Chain my son to save my own skin," he mocked, feigning my voice. "Accommodating Fenrir won't mind, because he has no mind at all."

"Stop this! I've never once said or thought such a thing."

He lowered his face to mine.

"You don't have to," he spat. "Your actions that day spoke loud enough. You never thought me your equal with all your cleverness and mind games. I was a liability."

He dug his nails into my throat. I pushed my palms into his chest stiff with muscle, trying to shove him off me.

I needed air.

"You chose your place with the Aesir over your own son!"

"No," I rasped. "I never did that. Tyr told you the truth. I was lied to."

He chuckled darkly.

A black halo expanded around his head as my vision wavered.

"Then tell me, *Father*, how did I end up here if not for you? You didn't even tell me goodbye. You are a coward."

That curdled my insides. Because that much was the truth.

His face was red with rage. A large vein bulged down his forehead.

I clawed at his iron fingers, trying to unhook them from my neck.

"Fenrir..." I wheezed.

His hold didn't loosen.

For a second, I thought he might kill me.

His eyes cleared.

He looked around the room and locked eyes with Anna, who cowered against the back wall.

Shame softened his features. Horror turned them rigid.

"No..." he said, releasing my throat.

I sucked in a breath, filling my prickling lungs. My vision cleared.

Fenrir scrambled off me and backed away until his back struck the counter. Leaning against the glass, he drew up his knees to his chest and looked at his hands that trembled.

"I'm sorry," he said. "I...I don't know what came over me. It's the energy of this room. It's not right. I..." He scrubbed his face. "I must get out of here. I need a cup of chamomile tea. Yes, that will help. Always does the trick."

I forced myself up, rubbing the burn from my neck, coughing between gulps of air. Damn it stung.

Patrons rose from their tables and shuffled around us. Curious whispers followed. Someone mentioned the police. That was the last thing we needed.

I held out my hand to him. He took it and I tugged him to his feet.

"To help what's happening to you is going to take a lot more than a cup of tea," I said.

* * *

AFTER INTRODUCTIONS WERE MADE and it was decided that we would conduct all further correspondence in Asgardian, we set off for Fenrir's flat. Anywhere we could avoid Hugin and Munin and their gaze.

We walked down Wollzeile and cut through the busy square of Hoher Markt with its astronomical clock, and took a right on Marc-Aurel Strasse. His raw denim jeans stretched with his long strides, and his laced boots sank into the snow. He tugged his green quilted jacket tighter together, bracing against a gust of wind bursting with sleet.

Shoving a key into a brass keyhole, he pushed the door open with his shoulder. We walked into an arched foyer of white plaster and proceeded to the worn, stone steps lined with an iron railing.

We jostled up five painful flights and marched through a final set of thickly painted, double doors nearly double my height.

Heavy incense, banana, and granola hit me in the face, entering his flat. Herringbone wood floors spread throughout the room, their warmth contrasting the cold white walls. A small altar stood to my right, stuffed with figures and depictions of all manner of gods and saints.

Fenrir maneuvered around a jungle of fiddle leaf fig trees and yucca and walked into the cramped kitchen in the back. Cabinets opened. The clink of porcelain followed. A kettle hissed.

"Can I get you all a cup of tea?" he asked. "Or, perhaps a shot of wheatgrass? It tastes dreadful, but it's rich in antioxidants."

"A cup of black tea would be lovely," Falael replied quickly, leaning down and inspecting a brass statue of Ganesh sitting beside a hefty chunk of rose quartz.

Sigyn stared at a genuine Albrecht Dürer depicting St. Francis receiving the stigmata above the altar. Good ol' Francis. Now there was a man who knew how to throw a decent masquerade orgy. Until he decided he cared more for his soul than having a spot of innocent fun.

Fenrir came out of the kitchen carrying a tray filled with floral, demitasse cups and a silver teapot.

Bending beneath a rather aggressive palm, he placed the tray on a dark and thick oak table—12th century, at least—shoved against the wall. We joined him, squeezing around the table as best we could. Although, I probably didn't need to kick Falael's leg out of my way as hard as I did.

The seat cushion relaxed beneath me, and I thought I'd damn near fall through the gilded frame. Balancing myself as best I could, I shoved bottles of herbal supplements to the back of the table, clearing more space. Sigyn's brow knit together and she picked up a white bottle.

"Holy Basil?" she said. "I take it you've been feeling anxious?"

Fenrir poured orange pekoe tea into the cups and scooted one to each of us. I grimaced as steam rose out of the little floral painted horrors. I was not accustomed to drinking poached plant water.

Falael squeezed a wedge of lemon into his tea and stirred, smiling as if looking at a prized cut of beef.

I was as disappointed in him as I had been with Francis when he told me the news. Brown wool just wasn't a good look on anyone.

"My stress has never been so hard to control," Fenrir said. "I cannot become stressed. Stress attacks every system of the body. It leads to anxiety, which leads to irritability and...gods, it's happening already, isn't it?"

He opened a nearly empty bottle of St. John's Wart and coaxed out a capsule into his palm.

"No, I wouldn't say that," I said. "Calm people crush the windpipes of others all the time."

Sigyn scowled at me.

"I don't think now is the time..." she pressed through her teeth.

"Please don't let what I did back at the cafe paint a terrible picture of me," he said. "I abhor violence in any form." He swallowed the capsule with a swig of tea. "That...*episode*...is what's been stressing me."

I leaned forward, pushing my teacup out of the way. *Far* away.

"It wasn't the first time?" Falael asked.

Fenrir squashed his lip between his teeth and opened another plastic bottle. He spilled out an unreasonable amount of vitamin D.

"I've tried so hard to fight my anger." He shot back the golden capsules. "As you can see, practicing mindfulness and achieving inner peace is important to me. But..." He opened a third bottle, this one vitamin B12. "A pressure has started building in me. Like a thunderstorm raging in my head. It's been lashing out, and when I saw you, Father..."

He paused. He met my gaze.

"All I've fought for, all I've tried to be, disappeared in the hatred of a second, and what I've battled to keep tamed forced itself free of my control."

I knew to what he referred.

"The wolf?" I asked.

He shifted in his seat.

"The wolf. It's as if it's being called out of me, despite my will to keep it in."

This news wasn't great.

"I had found happiness," he said. "I even forgave you and Mother. But lately, there's a growing hatred in my soul. A hunger for blood that rubs salt in wounds I believed healed. I feel I'm losing control and...and that *it* will win."

I bit the inside of my mouth at that word. At the thought that Ragnarok really was all beyond us. Controlling us.

I tasted iron.

"I'm sure that's not the case," I said. I hoped, though a deeper part of me knew I only lied to myself.

Fenrir's face twisted. He circled a knot in the wood with his finger. His cuticles were torn and ragged.

"How would you know?" he asked. "Everything annoys me." His tone shifted. He rubbed the table harder. "Grates me. I used to be free in nature, in the Ironwood, and now I'm stuck in a city of stone and cement. Fresh air is clogged with diesel and cigarettes. All because of you...because of Odin..."

His eyes flashed gold. He scratched his nails across the table, drawing his hand closed into a fist.

He caught himself and relaxed his hand and filled himself with breath.

"You see what I mean?" he said. "It gets away from me so easily. And I hate it. After what happened to Tyr, I swore I'd never spill a drop of blood again from any living creature. I don't want to hurt anyone. But the wolf..." He stared out. "It's why I'm in danger, isn't it? It's almost like..."

A ringing filled my ears.

Burn them. Kill them. Destroy them.

"Almost like what?" I asked, pushing the voice away. "Almost like Ragnarok?"

He chewed his thumbnail, making it even more jagged.

"It really is happening, isn't it? I hoped I was wrong. I shrugged off the first pulses, but as they grew..."

"Is Ragnarok speaking to you?" I said, trying to ignore its echo in my head. "It does to your sister."

Sweat beaded at his temples.

"I just want the call to stop. I want it all to stop."

He gripped his head, sinking his fingers into his long hair, as if trying to smother the words I knew were being whispered to him.

My heart tore.

I hated this. Hated seeing him suffer. What I hated more was not knowing the breaking point. When this would all cave in around us. Ragnarok drew closer, and the signs kept coming and the voices grew louder.

Burn them. Kill them. Destroy them...

I shut my eyes, forcing the voices to silence.

All that mattered now was getting Fenrir out of Vienna.

"Odin will soon know you aren't where he put you," I said. "He will come for you."

He looked at me, and he knew the reason.

"He's going to kill me, isn't he?" He leaned back in his chair. "Tyr told me about the prophecy. About my role in Ragnarok. Odin sees me as his biggest threat. I never asked for any of this. I don't want it. Or to be a part of it."

"Nor do I," I said.

His brow furrowed.

"You? What part in Ragnarok do you have besides seeing your fun times end?"

I guess no one bothered to tell him I was the Destroyer. It was probably for the best it stay that way.

"Oh, he didn't tell you that bit. Never mind. Forget I mentioned it. It was just a funny joke."

I forced a laugh.

Sigyn crossed her arms.

"Loki, he needs to know the truth," she said.

"The truth?" Fenrir asked. "What truth?"

This was going to be delightful.

I scratched the back of my ear.

"Did Tyr ever talk about the *Destroyer*?"

He nodded.

"Of course! They are the asshole that started this whole mess."

"Well, that's a bit harsh," I said. "I'm sure they had a perfectly good reason..."

He cocked his head.

"Good reason? What possible reason could—" Knowing filled his gaze. "Oh my gods. It was you, wasn't it?"

My lips pulled into a sheepish grin.

"Sorry..."

"Typical you," he spat. "You get slighted and suddenly all the worlds need to burn to satisfy your petty squabble."

I stood, letting the chair fall back and crack against the floor.

"Petty?" I said. "I'm sorry if being tortured for five hundred years kinda puts you in a bad mood."

He scoffed.

"Torture? What madness are you spouting now? You know what. I don't care. I can't afford to be in a negative space. Not now."

He got up and walked to a purple yoga mat in the living room and sank into the lotus position. I wanted to grab the Athenian vase sitting beside a carved oak hutch and hit him over the head with it.

"Are you serious right now? We are literally on the brink of an apocalyptic war and you want to meditate?"

He kept his eyes closed, and forefingers pressed against his thumbs.

"Do you know how to stop it?" he asked.

"I'm working on it."

He chuckled.

"While you're *working* on it, I need to work on making sure the wolf doesn't escape and eat you all. If it gets out...I wouldn't survive myself if I hurt anyone."

"You're more of a threat if you stay. If Ragnarok makes you lose control of the wolf...if you kill Odin, or he kills you..." I paused. "Either way, Ragnarok would win, and everyone would be hurt."

He opened his eyes and stared at me. I saw fear behind them.

"I get you're trying to help me. But..."

"You don't trust me?"

"You are the god of lies," he said. "Besides, the last time you tried to help me...well..."

That day in the Ironwood suffocated my mind with more memories. I forced them out. Away. Back into my depths.

"I thought you said you forgave me?"

"Forgiveness doesn't mean I will willingly be fooled again."

"Listen to your father," Sigyn said.

She marched towards Fenrir and stared up at him.

"Whatever issues you have with your father need to be set aside," she said. "He is here in earnest to protect you. We all are. And that should count for something to prove good intentions."

Fenrir shrugged.

"Sorry if I'm going to need a little more than 'good intentions'," he said. "I appreciate you trying to help me, and I'm sure you mean well, but I've never known him to put anyone before his own skin."

Her eyes flashed blue for two seconds. A pulse of her fidelity washed over me.

I shuddered from its peace.

"Never known?" she said. "Your father sacrificed himself for me and our children. He endured utter hell...and..."

She stopped.

Her shoulders slumped.

A hush weighed down the room.

"Sigyn..." Falael said. "Please. You swore to yourself..."

She waved him away.

"No," she said. "He must know. This lack of faith and trust must end. I will not let the gods kill again."

Confusion deepened the creases of Fenrir's forehead.

"Again?"

Her breaths deepened. Her hope radiated off of her.

"The gods hunted us because of what we were to the prophecy," she said. "Like you."

"But why? What were you to them?"

"Everything," she said. "I bore the sign that instigated Ragnarok. I bore sons." She glanced at me. "Narfi and Nari, our twin boys..." Her voice cracked, but her eyes blazed blue. "The gods believed them their undoing."

"I don't understand," he said.

She returned her gaze to Fenrir's.

"Loki made a bargain with Odin. His life for ours. The gods took the deal and bound him in a cave. They tortured him with venom pouring over his body," she choked. "You think you know the man, but he's so much more than you realize. And he's willing to go farther for you than you can even conceive."

She stopped, and her eyes returned to normal.

Fenrir looked at me. I could tell he wanted to believe, but skepticism still lingered within his eyes.

"Is that the torture you referred to?" he asked.

"Yes," I pushed past the growing lump in my throat.

He shook his head.

"Wait. The venom of the Vanir Viper scalds any flesh, even that of a god."

He was rich. But what more could I expect from him, when I had never given him reason to trust me.

When I'd only ever hurt him.

"Are you inferring I look too good?" I asked. "I guess you've forgotten my skill with illusions."

I suppose it was now or never.

My bowels turned to water.

I let my magic fade.

My illusions dissolved.

All of them.

Horror filled Fenrir's eyes.

Sigyn covered her mouth and Falael turned rigid.

It was a reasonable reaction, really.

My natural state was a lot to take in.

Wet scars laced between my fingers covered in blisters that bubbled up my arms. Tight ribbons of skin twisted down my neck.

And my face...

I chuckled darkly to myself at that.

What face?

A gaping hole was all that remained of my nose. The rest was flesh and bits of exposed bone.

"Five hundred years of straight up venom is not great for the skin," I said. "No one can even recognize me anymore. No one can..." My words died as I held out my hand, inspecting my cracked knuckles. I no longer had fingernails.

Sigyn took slow steps towards me, her eyes searching mine. I wanted to step back, away, but she reached out her hand and skated her fingertips across my cheek before I could.

"I recognize you." She traced my jaw. Delicate. Gentle. "I can still see you. And I...I..."

Her hand fell away, and I exhaled.

"And I shouldn't have come," she whispered. "I shouldn't..."

She ran to the door and left down the stairs. Everything in me screamed to follow her...

Falael stepped next to me.

"I've only heard her tell that story once before," he said. "She promised herself she'd never let it fall from her lips a second time."

I called back my illusion, drowning myself in false divine beauty.

"What happened to the children?" Fenrir asked, his voice soft.

I stared at the floor.

"They died." That word still stung. "The gods broke their word to me. They murdered them. Their betrayal is the *petty* reason I started Ragnarok." I met his gaze. "And now you know the complete truth. And the stakes. Don't make me suffer seeing another son die at their hands."

I looked at the door where Sigyn had left through.

I felt a hand on my shoulder. Falael's hand.

"Go after her," Falael told me. "You need to grieve together."

13

INTO THE FIRE

I walked down the stairs and the air grew colder.

Sigyn leaned against the white arched walls of the foyer, her arms crossed tight against her chest. She stared at the marble floor.

I cursed myself. She shouldn't have had to relive that night. She shouldn't have had to see the truth of how I looked.

I could barely stand the truth myself.

Plaster angels and gilded filigrees blossomed above our heads on the ceiling as I walked into the foyer. Car engines roared on the other side of the door outside. Shoes struck pavement.

Sigyn kept her eyes firmly on the stone floor. She dug her fingers harder into her sweater.

I stood next to her, trying not to think how warm she felt in the cold.

"I lived with the terror of knowing where you were. Strapped down. Alone. Suffering." She gripped her arms tighter. "It's different to actually see it."

"I never intended for you to know the...*effects*," I pushed out. "I didn't want to burden you with that truth."

Silence fell between us, broken only by the muffled conversation of a passerby. The spinning spokes of a bicycle.

"The truth." She spat out the word as if it were bitter. "The truth is...The truth is I hated the world for forgetting you, but I hated myself more because I envied them. Because everywhere I looked was a ghost waiting to rip out my guts."

Without thought I pushed back a stray lock of her hair and tucked it behind her ear. As I had done in the past so many times when we were together.

"Sigyn, don't—"

Her eyes rose to mine and they knit with a million emotions that fought together.

"I wanted to forget you like they could," she continued. "To consider you a legend, a distant memory long buried. Anything to stop the pain of losing you. Of knowing what was happening to you and that I was helpless to stop it."

My throat dried.

She twisted her sweater between her fingers.

"I reinvented myself to survive. With work. With a new life. With a new—" she paused. "But no matter how much I tried, how much I wanted..." She reached out and cupped my cheek. "I never stopped loving you, Loki."

Where she touched my illusion melted, but she didn't retract her hand from the decay. She didn't flinch feeling the marred flesh beneath her palm.

"Everything in me wants you," she said. "Needs you. Your heart, your touch...I want to be yours, Loki, fully and utterly—but we can't be together."

I rested my hand over hers, wanting to still her trembling even though mine trembled more.

"Why?"

A sad smile cracked her face. Pity infected its edges, as if I couldn't see something she knew to be painfully clear.

"When you returned...when I first saw you, I was happy," she said. "I had you back. I found you again. Then came the rush of hurt. Fear. Everything I tried to push down and lock away. It all bubbled to the surface. What loving you means. What being with you means."

A chilled gust of wind forced its way beneath the heavy door, making it chatter.

"And what does it mean?"

"Pain."

"That's ridiculous."

"Our love brings pain, Loki," she said. "To you. To me. And now, to all the worlds as Ragnarok breathes down our necks. Don't you see? Being together isn't fair."

I didn't see.

"This isn't rational."

"Our love lost us our children. Our love damned you to a fate worse than death. And now, our love might lose us everything."

I felt her slipping from me with every passing word.

"What are you saying?" I said. "That we shouldn't have loved each other at all?"

"It would have spared us all this heartache. We would have spared everyone and...and..."

"And what?"

Her eyes rimmed in red.

She looked weathered. Beaten. Grief deepened the lines around her eyes, dimmed with a fatigue that matched my own.

I took her hand and pressed her fingers over my thrashing heart.

I had to reach her. To make her understand.

"This darkness won't last forever. We will find a way."

I opened my element to her. She gasped as my chaos seared into her fingertips, through her veins, and crashed against her insides.

Reminding her.

"I am yours, Sigyn. Now. Forever. To my last breath."

She clasped my face between her hands, pulling me closer.

"How can you still want me?" Her eyes searched mine. "After all you suffered because of me. For me."

She rubbed her thumbs across my cheeks and through my tears.

"And I'd do it all again."

Our mouths locked in a kiss. Torrential. Tender.

Starving.

I could have died in that kiss.

She sank her fingers into my hair and I stroked the curves of her breasts and hips.

Her tongue entered me.

The shock of her element followed.

Fidelity struck my chaos in an explosive vortex. She stormed through my body like a cooling balm and I gasped as her energy scalded the roots of my heart with hope. With the promise of salvation.

The discord in my soul calmed, and I rose into a plane of peace.

I slowed our kiss to savor her. I trailed my mouth down the gentle arc of her neck, wanting to venerate her. To stretch out this moment and live in it as long as we could.

Time ceased in this slice of tranquility.

The past dissolved. The future didn't exist.

There was only us suspended in being.

We hovered on that cusp, and then we fell.

Her breaths deepened. Want tightened between my legs.

She slipped her hands beneath my shirt and clawed her nails across my naked back, wanting more. Needing more.

She grew impatient. I understood.

My chaos scorched her chambers, flooding her to the brim with my recklessness. She deepened our kiss, needing even more of it. Sucking me into her. Drinking me down.

I was happy to oblige.

Hoisting her up, I pressed her back against the plaster wall. Holding open her legs, I ground against her hungry body, nestling my hips between her thighs.

Our lips crushed together and our tongues tangled. Her pulse thundered. She moaned into my mouth and pulled me closer, collapsing us further into fire.

Her fidelity penetrated into my bones and deeper into my marrow. Every inch of my skin she touched obliterated me further.

Electric. Dizzying.

She ripped at my hair and tore at my belt, drunk on my chaos. Drunk on the same need that wound that aching coil tighter in my core.

All thought left me.

There was only rushing blood and pounding hearts and the need to bury myself in her heat.

I had to feel her surround me again. To devour her fidelity. To have it quench my fire raging in my depths and then to fall into that shiver of release lost in her hope.

I unzipped my trousers and lifted her skirts over her hips and moved her underwear aside.

She kissed me harder and rocked against me.

I nudged her.

Her body tensed.

She broke the kiss and gripped my wrist, stopping me from pushing in.

"I want to," she rasped. "But I can't...I can't do this. And I won't do this to him."

We shared each others breaths. Felt our bodies cradled against the other.

"Even still?" Our lips grazed, making the ache in me for her more painful.

"He's a good man, and I've made a promise to him."

Every word she spoke splintered me deeper to the bone.

"Don't marry him," I whispered. Begged. "I love you."

She pushed me back.

Cold air swept between us.

Sigyn straightened her skirt and sweater. She wiped the wet from her eyes.

"I think it's time we returned upstairs."

14

WHY IS IT ALWAYS THE UNEXPECTED?

I didn't return with Sigyn upstairs. I couldn't.
I needed to be alone.
I left.
And I walked.

I walked without caring where I ended up.

Snow melted against my hot cheeks. I rubbed my mouth, trying to erase her taste from my lips. Did she truly believe our love caused pain?

Or worse, was she right?

No. Such a thought was abhorrent to me.

A squall of snow swept across the sculpted gardens of the Schönbrunn Palace, forcing me to tug my coat tighter over my chest.

Ice and gravel crunched beneath my boots as I kept to the path between squares of withered summer flowers and frost crusted bushes. I walked further down the length of the Great Parterre, leaving the yellow palace to loom behind me like a stretched out giant.

The entire grounds were empty except for me.

I tried not to notice the sky and how it swirled an even

deeper shade of red now.

A grating screech detonated within my ears, drowning out everything else in its squeal. A stampede of voices, some yelling, some whispering, charged through my eardrums.

Burn them. Kill them. Destroy them.

I rolled my eyes. Here we went again.

Dead grass spread out beneath my feet, gobbling up the paths, topiaries, and palace. A storm of hot wind and ash replaced the howl of winter. The wasteland of Vigridr surrounded me and the spirit stood waiting.

This was getting terribly exhausting.

"Do we really have to do this now? I'm not in the mood for all your doom and gloom today."

I tried to breathe out the sulfur stinging my nostrils. But that's all this place was. Sulfur, smoke, and burnt flesh. And it seemed stronger than before...

"Surtr grows restless for your call," it said.

"Surtr can stuff it."

Even though I couldn't see its stupid face behind its stupid shroud, I could sense it smile.

"Still fighting your fate, are we? When will you learn?"

I crossed my arms.

"That this is Ragnarok? That this is all inevitable? Yes, I got that the first thousand times you've told me."

I gave it several rude signs, turned on my heel, and walked away through smoke and sparks.

"And still you refuse to accept it." Its voice crackled like a hearth.

I faced it again. I marched towards the spirit, and every step closer I took my chaos rattled stronger against my ribs. Hungry and seething to be set loose.

"Do you really think I'm just going to wake Surtr because some spirit says so? Please. I will not be commanded by a piece of muslin with a chip on their shoulder."

My fire churned in my veins. My element thrashed, and I stiffened my muscles, ignoring how viciously it gnawed and scratched at my core.

I could sense the spirit smile again.

"You still hunger for their lives," it said. "You still want to burn their worlds."

My chaos boiled my insides, loving their words.

"That's not true," I said.

My blood heated even more. My fire swelled. I clenched my teeth fighting against it.

"It doesn't look that way to me." It pointed at the cinders cracking between my knuckles. "Every time you see them you want them dead. You want what I promised you. Vengeance. Justice. Their suffering."

Slices of my fire escaped and raged down my arms and doused my hands in flames. My mind broiled with the thoughts of their screams spilling out of charring throats as their flesh blistered.

At the absolute thrill of it all.

At the absolute relief of having completed my destiny.

I grunted, forcing myself to lengthen and stand taller. My body jerked and sparks popped.

"I won't do it," I said.

The spirit leaned into me. I stood my ground, though I wanted to crack from the pressure of keeping an absolute hailstorm tight inside of me.

"Hope doesn't suit you. Especially when you have none left." It pressed a finger into my chest. I thought it tore me in two as it turned my chaos loose.

My element stormed out of me, wild and burning. A blaze exploded and spiraled us in a vortex of flames that consumed the earth beneath our feet, scorching grass and splitting stone.

I was fire and I was death.

I was judgement.

"Understand now? There is no choice. Fighting is useless," it said. "Surtr will be woken, and it will be by your hand."

A white flash. Gravel prickled my scalp.

I stared up at the red sky laying on my back in the Schönbrunn gardens. A frigid gust nipped at my cheeks. I pressed my palms against the frozen gravel and sat up. Steam hissed beneath my hands and curled into the air between my fingers.

I looked at them. Wet and soot stained.

I hated the cold dread in me. I detested the sensation and how fully I felt it. And worse? I wasn't sure if I had a choice anymore.

The shrill croak of a raven broke the still air.

Shit.

I wiped my hands clean on my trousers and stood.

In the branches of a larch, two ravens stared at me. Hugin and Munin. They flapped their wings and clicked and purred. They pointed their black beaks at the Gloriette standing on top of a hill behind an excessively large fountain of Neptune consorting with sea nymphs.

A man dressed in a Midgardian gray trench coat and common wingtip shoes leaned against one of the building's stone pillars. He stared back at me, a black eyepatch covering his right eye.

Odin.

He found me.

This day just kept getting better and better. What other delightful surprises awaited me?

I walked up the steps to the landing. Odin braced himself against the railing, the striking contours of his face hard and pensive. He stared out at the palace and over the entire city of Vienna. Orange roofs spread along the base of the low hills, punctuated by rising monoliths of green domes and white stone.

He scratched his short beard, and I couldn't help noticing the shine of sweat at his temples. His flushed cheeks and heavy breathing made him look as if he had just endured running a marathon across the Alps.

"Given the circumstances, I thought maybe, just once, you would listen to me and remain where I told you to stay," he said.

Thank gods. It was just a lecture. I never thought I'd be so happy for one of his sprawling speeches on the importance of responsibility.

I relaxed and leaned against a stone pillar and inspected my nails.

"You know I just can't help myself." I ran my thumb over the smooth tips. "Midgard is at its most beautiful before the apocalypse. How could I stay away from a once in a lifetime experience?"

His only eye twitched and his anger brightened the blue of his iris.

"Damn you!" he spat. "We are on the brink of war, and still you rock the boat. Do you really never have a care for the gravity of anything?"

A wry smile tugged at the corners of my mouth.

As much as I enjoyed his rage, I needed him to leave. I couldn't risk him poking his nose where it didn't belong. I'd hate to have to lop it off.

"You know thinking sensibly gives me a headache," I said. "As it were, I think you'd be much more comfortable back in Asgard. You really look like you could use a bath. Or two."

He crushed his fingers into the stone and split the railing. I grimaced.

"You really must try to do better about controlling your temper," I said.

He took one step back and faced me.

"Hel refuses to return Balder," he said.

Everything tilted. Ice trickled down my back.

He wiped the sweat from his brow.

"I've never seen her so crazed," he said. "She brought Balder out to me. My own son. Dangled him in front of my face and said if..."

"If what?"

He dug his fingers into his dark hair and combed them through.

"If I kneeled before her, she would return him," he said. "What choice did I have? I lowered myself before her and asked for the return of my son. She smiled, and then told me no. *Me*. The bitch made me beg just for the satisfaction of refusing me."

Had this not been so bad, I would have been awfully proud of her for getting Odin to grovel. No easy feat, that. She truly was my daughter, but right now she was making me incredibly depressed.

"Well, I did tell you so."

The corners of his mouth twitched.

"Don't even start. I don't need to tell you how bad this is. Without Balder..."

I scrubbed my face, trying not to think of the voices still murmuring in the recesses of my mind.

If I would somehow wake Surtr...

"What if I went?" I said. "Surely with me—"

He shook his head.

"There's no use," he interrupted. "She's mad with Ragnarok. There's no negotiating anymore. It's over. The look in her eyes...It was the coldest, most unslakable hunger for death I'd ever seen in another being." He paused. "I imagine it's similar to the look in Fenrir's eyes?"

My stomach clenched.

"I wouldn't have the foggiest idea," I lied.

He chuckled beneath his breath.

"Do you really think me a fool?"

"I'm not sure how to answer that."

He stared out over the city again, and the fine lines crinkled around his eyes.

"I've known Fenrir has been free since the beginning."

I sat on the railing, ignoring the cold from the rock seeping through my clothes.

"I don't understand."

He locked his gaze on mine and pain swam behind his eye.

"I learned of Tyr's plan to rescue him," he said. "In fact, I'm the one that gave him the idea."

"You? Tyr told me you didn't even know."

He chuckled.

"That's what I needed Tyr to think. I allowed him to steal Fenrir away in the night and banish him to Vienna. Confined to the city he would be safe from the gods, and we safe from him."

I pushed off the railing and stepped towards him. A blast of snow surged between the pillars of the building.

It made me sick how he spoke like he did me a favor.

"I don't believe you," I said. "You wanted him chained. You wanted him abandoned on that shit hole Lynsvi Island, like you left me in that cave..."

Darkness ate at my edges as the coldness of the stone sank further into me. My skin burned as if the pain of the venom had been branded into my cells. I shook it away.

"So it appeared," he said. "It was safer that way, so Frigg could think she'd won. It was the only way to ensure she didn't chase him anymore."

My guts twisted just hearing her name.

"Frigg? What does that woman have to do with this?"

He sighed.

"She's the one that came up with the plot to chain him in Lynsvi. What Yggdrassil revealed to me to do with you inspired her. What was good enough for the father would surely be good enough for the son."

That woman. My business with her was hardly through.

"It was foolproof," he said. "It would have protected us."

"If it was so *foolproof,* then what stopped you?"

His face softened, looking like I asked him the most obvious question in all the worlds.

"Surely you know?"

"I don't."

A bitter gale stung my cheeks.

"I did it for you," he said. "I know you want to hate me, but I've always tried to find alternatives. Even for you, the man destined to destroy me. And now, everything I tried to stop is crumbling around me. Had you just listened. Had you not forced my hand..."

I rolled my eyes.

"Forced? Here it comes. The blame. The pointing finger," I said. "You drove me to Ragnarok with all your deceptions."

He stood so close to me his nose nearly touched my own. I felt his hot breath.

"Me?" he said. "I begged you to leave that girl alone. I

begged you to stay in Asgard all those centuries ago. This could have all been avoided had you just listened to me." He broke. Cracked. "But you never listen. Same as now. Same as always."

My vision turned red and I saw only blood and steel.

Burn them. Kill them. Destroy them.

I grabbed him and twisted my fingers into the lapels of his trench coat and launched him into a pillar. He grunted as the building shook and bits of stone and dust rained on our heads.

"My boys died because you broke your word to me." I crushed him harder into the limestone.

"I didn't break it."

Every tendon in me tightened. Snow gusted around us, whipping our hair around our faces.

"Then tell me, how did they die? Because I seem to recall you promising their lives for mine?"

His teeth flashed white beneath his beard. He gripped my wrists, flexing my bones, and threw me into a set of French doors. Glass shattered and wood splintered behind my back. Beads of broken glass spilled off my shoulders.

Odin marched up to me and grabbed my shirt and pulled me up to his face.

"I tried to stop Frigg!" He shook me. "I tried to stop it all."

I sneered.

"Excuses."

I drew back my arm and punched him across his jaw. A clap echoed through the stone and cold as I struck bone and cartilage, channeling all my strength into my fist.

He stumbled back and wiped his nose with his finger. Blood flowed out of his nostrils and splattered the snow with bright red circles. I smiled, my lips barbed with the delight of having drawn first blood.

Odin looked at me, a delicious mix of shock and rage. I gorged on its beauty.

He screamed and lunged at me and shoved me to the floor. My head cracked against the stone, sending a jolt down my legs. My eyes swam with stars. I chuckled.

He always did like it rough.

There was a time this kind of foreplay would have excited me. But now, nothing would give me greater pleasure than burying my dagger into his bowels.

"You keep saying you tried," I said. "But you could have done more."

I wrapped my arms around his torso and pulled him down. Catching his left foot with my right leg I hooked his shoulder with my arm. Forcing all my power into my legs, I thrust up and flung him on his back.

He grunted.

"What more could I have done?" he rasped, staring up at me. "You put me in an impossible situation."

Mounting him, I took out my dagger and pressed the edge of my blade against his pulsing artery in his throat. He hissed, stirring my blood further.

"As was I."

A clattering noise filled my ears along with the snap of twigs and crunch of snow. The rumble shook the stone beneath my kneecaps.

Odin's anger melted into dread.

"They're coming," he whispered, the words tight with fear.

I looked out at the tree line. Snow fell off the branches and leaves as the thunder neared.

"Who?"

"A gift from Hel," he said. "They chased me the entire way here. I used every charm in the book to hold them back as long as I could..."

At least a hundred of Hel's warriors dressed in black armor tore out from behind the trees and charged us. Thirty more ruptured out of the ground, clawing their way through the earth. An absolute hurricane of shriveled corpses, skeletons, and rotting hunks of flesh.

Well, this certainly wasn't something you saw every day.

"This is only a handful of the legions she commands," he said. "And they collected a few friends along the way. She's commanded the dead of the entire the Nine Worlds to rise and join her to fight against us."

I got off of Odin and stood, grounding my feet. I unsheathed my second dagger and reversed my grip on the second.

Odin removed a pen from his inner coat pocket and transformed it into his spear, Gungnir. He took a fighting stance next to me, his weapon catching the pale light.

"You could have mentioned this earlier," I said. "Might have been nice to have a little heads up."

The warriors raced up the stairs towards us, growling and snarling and eyes clouded. Our blades struck their sickles and swords. I found it slightly unsettling how their receded lips made them all look like they were grinning.

"You didn't even give me a chance before you started tearing into me."

"Yes, it's always my fault. How could I forget."

I buried my blade into the head of the closest warrior. My steel scraped along the bone of its skull as I pulled it out and slit through the stomach of a second, emptying their festering guts at their feet.

I smiled as the thrill of battle lit my veins. I smiled wider, noticing some carried swords of Dwarven steel. The risk of death made this entirely more electric.

This day was finally turning around!

I swung my daggers at the onslaught, stabbing eye sockets and cracking open sternums dropping four in a row. I breathed in the rush of each I slaughtered.

Odin impaled three warriors through the chest with his spear. A tug and a spin and he forced his spear up, masterfully cutting them in half. He butted it into the jaw of a warrior armed with a long sword. A lovely crunch rang out. He thrusted the spear forward, twirling it around him, flaying open warriors left and right.

Six surrounded me. They attacked. I blocked one swinging a sickle, disarming him and kicking him back, and lodged my blade firmly between the ribs of a woman. Waving my blades, I stuck one behind the leg and then the back.

I jumped.

I latched onto the skull of a skeleton and twisted. Snap. Pop.

I ripped off the head and hurled it at a bloated and unfortunately gooey soldier square in the chest.

He flailed and pirouetted in a kind of gruesome ballet in an effort to keep his balance.

Odin took advantage and planted his boot hard into the warrior's side and sent him flying into a group of twenty. They all crashed to the floor, a flurry of armor and weapons and growls.

I guess we had not changed in this way. We could always anticipate the move of the other without a word spoken or plan given. Like finishing the other's sentences, but with death. It's what made us exceptionally lethal on the battlefield.

We had been well matched back then. Unstoppable. Friends. Brothers. More.

I hated the rush of memories fighting by his side awoke in me of the old days.

How they made me mourn them.

It must have lit the same disgusting sentiments in Odin.

"I gave my life for you at Yggdrasil so you wouldn't know that fate it wanted for you." He skewered the liver of a shriveled corpse. "And how was I repaid with my sacrifice? With a broken oath and your hatred."

More warriors rushed me. I ducked, barely missing a scythe slicing off the top of my head.

"Is this really the time?" I asked.

I crossed my forearms and pushed against the soldier. I hooked behind his withered neck with my dagger, and slashed across his chest with my other, dropping him.

"I lost the only one who ever knew me that day."

Apparently it was. He always had to spoil the fun.

I disarmed the sickle of a woman and threw it, nestling it nicely between the eyes of a beefy warrior more bone than flesh.

"You lost me long before that."

"Did what we share mean so little to you?"

I met his gaze, wiping gore off my face. Nasty bits were splattered across his chest. Nothing beat this. Although, I was going to need a master dry cleaner if there was any hope for my Gucci jacket.

"And what did we share, Odin?" I asked. "Lies? Spite?"

"Love."

I constricted.

Pulling my eyes off his, I locked blades with a warrior as a second onslaught barreled down on us. Odin and I pressed our backs together as we fought hard.

I tried not to think how his heat sank into me.

How fiercely I had loved him.

"At one time that was true," I said. "But any love I have for you is now dead."

We both jumped onto the railing of the Glorietta, breaking the contact. We had to make it down the Grand Parterre towards the palace and then out if we wanted to survive this. A little ingenuity would be required.

Men and women warriors flooded behind us. They tried to tear at our clothes and pull us down.

Odin and I looked at each other and nodded. It was now or never.

We leapt off the railing and down onto the lawn. They scrambled over the railing after us as we ran down the hill towards the Neptune Fountain.

Odin and I slid across the ice, angling for the center of the fountain. We clambered up the statues of horses and sea nymphs. The frigid stone burned my fingertips. That was nothing to the warriors that followed us.

I crunched the heel of my boot into the nose of one and severed the fingers off a second. Odin slashed at least a dozen with a powerful swing and thrust of his spear.

This was seriously the best day I'd had in centuries.

"I don't know why you're so upset," I said. "You've spent the last five hundred years trying to forget me. Like everyone else."

We sheathed our weapons, and both grabbed an arm of Neptune who was twice our size. A shove and a push and we broke him out of his shell.

We flipped the statue on its side, I taking Neptune's head, and Odin grasping his massive ankles. We jumped down and charged towards the fresh wave of warriors that ran towards us. They all screamed and held out their swords and axes.

We didn't stop.

Their eyes widened. Well, those that had eyes.

We plowed through them, running down the Grand Parterre. Tibias and femurs flew in an explosion of bone and slippery globs as we slammed the statue into them.

"Forget you? What the devil are you talking about?"

"I saw my old rooms in Asgard." A head rolled between us. "It was shut up. You wanted to pretend like I never existed. Don't worry, it seems a very popular way to get over me."

We were feet away from the front of the palace.

"I ordered them locked because it hurt too much to remember," he said. "I never wanted us to die, Loki."

My edges softened.

I hadn't either.

But here we were.

We threw the Neptune statue into the arms of the warriors making them collapse beneath it, and ran through the front courtyard of the palace and out into the busy street.

We raced across the street, dodging traffic. The corpses followed, far angrier than earlier. Cars skidded to a stop, their breaks screeching louder than the pedestrians. A Mercedes struck a skeleton, scattering its bones across the pavement.

Odin and I rushed down the tiled stairs of a subway station. The rumble of armor and boots followed.

A train waited. We ran into the orange cabin filled with business men wearing slim suits and women wrapped in thick scarves.

They all looked up at us. And then they all screamed, looking behind us at what followed.

The doors shuffled closed.

Could the bloody things move any slower?

Corpses and skeletons shoved their arms through the tightening gap, trying to wedge themselves in.

Odin and I forced the doors shut the final three inches.

Squish.

Thud.

An unlucky warrior's arm twitched and squirmed on the train floor. The train sped off, swaying back and forth, its wheels screeching and the whoosh of tunnels sucking the pressure from my ears.

Odin and I turned.

Men and women's mouths hung open.

Humans.

They never could handle a little dose of the supernatural.

The arm still twitched at our feet. I kicked it beneath a seat away into the shadows.

"There, all gone!" I tried to assure. "Nothing to worry about."

Their shrieks melted into the squeal of the track and they clamored over each other and huddled at the far end of the train. No one ever appreciated my helpfulness.

I shrugged and plopped into an exceptionally ugly tan seat. Odin sat opposite me.

"We can point fingers for an eternity about what happened, but in the end, it was a horror beyond us all," Odin said. "And now we face the end because of it."

I wiped the sweat and grisly globs from my brow, not wanting to acknowledge his point. Not able to.

"The dead are rising and will wreak havoc across the

Nine Worlds as they all march towards Vigridr to join Hel's armies," he continued. "I need to prepare my troops in Valhalla. Without Balder, we do this the old fashioned way."

"War," I breathed.

"War," he echoed. "The final battle."

There is only inevitability now. Fate. And yours is to wake Surtr and raze the worlds together at the final battle. The spirit's voice filled my mind.

I would not succumb to fate. That just wasn't my style.

I snapped my gaze to his.

"I will do all I can to stop Ragnarok. I will fight this war alongside you," I said. "But don't think this changes anything between us. When we win this thing, I'm still going to kill you."

He gave me a crooked smile.

"Unless a miracle happens, there is no winning this."

15

INCONVENIENT FAIRY TALES

Mayhem engulfed Vienna.

People raced up the cramped streets and spilled out into open squares in a panic. They broke store windows and carried out packages of toilet paper twice as wide as they were. Burning rubber and smoke seared my nostrils from cars drenched in flames left wrecked on sidewalks or crashed into light poles.

Everyone either screamed, ran, or prayed for mercy from higher powers they'd forgotten about until now.

Your typical human reaction to when things didn't go so well.

And then there were the corpses.

All manner of mummies and skeletons burst out of manholes and broke through church crypts.

Of course, we had to be in a city built entirely on top of bloody graveyards. Vienna would soon crawl with the dead. And as much as I'd like to have seen such a spectacle, I had to get back to Sigyn, Fenrir...and I suppose even Falael.

Although, I couldn't help from smiling imagining a peckish cadaver eating his brain as an omega-3 rich snack.

I really made harrowing sacrifices trying to do the right thing.

I kicked a growling corpse out of my way into the gutter, dug my blade between the eye sockets of a second and slipped inside Fenrir's building. Grabbing an abandoned umbrella from a corner, I braced the door shut and bounded up the stairs and into Fenrir's apartment.

Sigyn and Falael stood in the middle of the living room armed with various cutlery. Fenrir stared out the window, mouth agape and holding a frying pan.

"Loki!"

Sigyn brushed the branch of a palm out of her way and raced towards me, clasping kitchen shears in a white knuckled grip. She spread out her arms as if to embrace me, but stopped, lowering them back to her sides.

It was for the best. Had she touched me, I would have broken into pieces.

"Where have you been?" she said. "I've been worried sick."

"Whatever for?" I pulled a severed finger out of my hair. "It's just the dead rising from their graves. Trust me, it could be worse."

Fenrir turned and cocked his head.

"How could it possibly be worse?" he asked.

I shrugged.

"They could be the cannibalistic kind. Or draugr. Nothing stops those bloated menaces from drinking your blood but a good stake of iron into the brain," I said. "Seriously, you must learn to count your blessings when you have them."

Sirens blared somewhere in the distance. The rhythmic thunder of helicopter blades followed.

"But why are they rising from their graves at all?" Falael said.

Falael patted his coat pockets. He shoved his hand into the right one and took out a small, black notebook stuffed with index cards and bits of paper and unwrapped the cord keeping it tied all together.

"This isn't one of the signs." He flipped through notes and diagrams. "Trust me, I know them all well."

"Yes. You hardly let me forget that fact," I said. "As it so happens, this is an early Ragnarok gift from Hel. The dead of all the worlds are joining her ranks."

Glass splintered outside, along with cries and the rumble of tanks.

Fenrir's posture slumped.

"My sister is responsible for this?" he asked.

He turned his gaze back to the window and peered through the clouded pane coated with dust. A pair of skeletons danced on top of a smoking Mercedes Benz.

Disappointment tugged the corners of his mouth lower into a frown.

"I never believed her capable of such evil," he said.

I laid my hand on his shoulder, his muscle solid beneath his flannel shirt.

"Ragnarok has taken over her mind," I said. "She's drunk on it and wants to ensure Balder remains hers forever."

Sigyn's shoulders drew up.

"You mean?"

They all looked at me now.

I guess there wasn't a good way to tell them the truth.

"She's not letting him go." I said. "Balder is to remain with her, and our fates are sealed."

Sigyn sank onto a lumpy sofa upholstered in fraying satin and crumpled in on herself.

"Balder?" Fenrir asked. "Golden boy Balder? What does he have to do with this whole mess?"

Falael set next to Sigyn and rested his elbows on his knees and planted his face in his hands. Red tipped his pointed ears.

"He's the only one who can defeat Surtr," he pushed between his fingers. "He's the only one with a pure element of a contrasting force. He's the only one that can save us all from death."

I'd never seen Falael so glum and without an answer before. Had it not been for the impending doom on my own life, I would have found it absolutely delightful.

Sigyn shot up and paced, the herringbone wood floor squeaking beneath her every step.

"How did you find this all out?" she asked.

"Er..."

I walked to the table and scanned for something, anything, with an alcohol content. I found only cups of cold tea. My lips recoiled.

"Odin—oh, you will laugh—*well*—Odin paid me a visit," I said.

Sigyn snapped her gaze to Fenrir.

Fenrir stepped back and into a small forest ficuses in wicker baskets.

"He's here?" The leaves rustled around his shoulders and waist. One of the trees teetered and fell, striking the wall.

I put out my hands to calm him.

"You're safe," I said. "Turns out, Odin has known you've been in Vienna since the beginning."

I bent down and picked up the tree, propping it back upright.

"Then why am I still alive?" he asked.

"I will explain that all later," I said. "But right now, all that matters is what he told me. Ragnarok is coming, fast, and without Balder we've no choice but to finish this the old fashioned way."

Falael tapped his knuckles against the back of his notebook.

"What's the old fashioned way?" he asked.

"Dying honorably in battle," I said. "Which isn't as glamorous as it sounds. Especially the dying bit."

An explosion went off in the next building, shaking the small crystals of the chandelier above our heads.

Sigyn pressed her lips thin.

"This can't be it," she said. "There has to be something else we can do. Some clue we might have missed that could stop Surtr...Balder can't be the only way."

"Trust me, I'm all ears," I said. "But unless you can pull a miraculous plan out of the air, we've reached the end."

Sigyn ran her fingers over her bottom lip as she often did, lost in thought. Falael returned to paging through his scribbles.

Fenrir cleared his throat.

"*He* might be aware of another weakness of Surtr's..."

"Who?" Sigyn asked.

Please don't say his name.

"Jormungand."

Blasted bloody demons and damnation.

I pulled my hands down my face.

"Out of the question," I said. "Do you forget how *intense* he can be?"

Fenrir bobbled his head, looking like he knew he practically just suggested we take a swim in a pool with irritated piranha.

"Do you have a better suggestion?" he said.

I sighed, not having one.

Jormungand was like a morose poem wound with barbed wire and dipped in black nail polish. And I suspected being banished into an ocean with whispers of Ragnarok hadn't much improved his mood.

Falael stood and that ever present sparkle of hope returned to his eyes I wanted to gouge out.

"What does Jormungand know about Surtr?" he said. "Anything might give us an edge."

Fenrir scratched the dense stubble covering his chin. He looked at me.

"You know how Mummy loves inviting the most eccentric people she can to her parties," he said.

"Of course," I said. "Her leather themed soirées were not to be topped. I'd never seen so many spread eagles, which isn't easy when you're wearing—"

Sigyn shot me a look, telling me that my leather themed soirée tales were not currently welcome.

"Not important, please continue..." I said to Fenrir.

"When we were children, this old man came to stay," he said. "I think his name was Bjarke. No. Halvor. Yes. Halvor had fought alongside Odin's father, Bor, during the Aesir-Vanir wars. Could barely remember what he had for lunch, of course, but the stories he told...They were chilling. And bat shit crazy, but the point is, they enthralled Jorg."

I took two steps towards him.

"Enthralled how?" I asked.

"He believed them."

"Of course he did."

"What kind of stories did this *Halvor* tell?" Falael asked, also taking a step closer to Fenrir.

"The story of Gullveig."

"Never heard of her," I said.

"No one had. Not even Mummy, and she knows everyone's secrets. She called it 'hogwash.'" Fenrir said. "Anyway, he told us Gullveig was a völva. A seeress. The most powerful that ever lived. Bor started to fear her and ordered her killed, but every time he killed her, she was just reborn. Three times he tried, and three times he failed."

I shook my head.

"Leave it to the Aesir to get in your business," I said.

He sighed.

"As I was saying," he continued. "Of course, Gullveig didn't take kindly to this continual murder and vowed to bring Ragnarok and end the gods. Obviously, she didn't succeed as life continued on. Well, until now."

"Life continued on because this is all fiction," I said.

"You were just a fiction to me," Sigyn said. "And we see how that turned out."

True.

"What does this Gullveig have to do with Surtr?" Sigyn asked.

"Halvor said she entwined herself with this dark force," he said. "She walked into the fires of Muspelheim and drank it down, taking its power into her veins. That's when she became darkness. That's when she became Surtr."

"Now this is just sounding silly," I said.

Fenrir shook his head.

"Silly it may sound, but Jorg was convinced of the truth of the tale, and set out to find proof that Gullveig existed."

"And did he?" I asked.

"He said what he found changed everything."

"And what did he find?"

Fenrir shrugged.

"To be honest, I didn't bother asking," he said. "Once he

started yammering on about Gullveig, you couldn't get him to stop."

Jorg always liked dark and wounded things and saw the beauty in their scars and pain. He felt layers of nuance others missed, which made him incredibly perceptive, but also lethally idealistic.

"What he found isn't important," Fenrir said. "What is important is that if anyone would know another weakness of Surtr, it would be Jorg. We must ask him."

I stiffened.

"That would mean releasing him," I said. "What if he's as mad with Ragnarok as your sister? It's best to leave him right where he is. We can't afford any more mistakes."

"What more mistakes could be made?" Fenrir said. "If you haven't noticed, it doesn't much matter anymore. We need to take what chances we have."

I ran both my hands through my hair, trying to take all the madness in. This was daring, even for me.

"I don't have a clue where he is," I said. "Not to mention, oceans are rather large and spread out, and we haven't even gotten to the question of how to break the spell keeping him in the sea."

Fenrir walked up to me.

"You are the cleverest of the gods," he said. "You always have some trick up your sleeve. Surely you know something that can help us? This is our only shot."

I smiled.

I didn't know something, but I did know some*one*.

"I might know who can help us find and release Jorg," I said. "She's a bit off her rocker, but in a time like this, that's exactly what you need."

"Who?" Falael asked.

16

IN A NUTSHELL

"Golda," I said. "She's a witch. The best I've ever met. I went to her for help before...she's who told me the secret Odin kept from me, that I was the Destroyer."

I fell back into that day. How the rot of her abode had filled my sinuses. How I unraveled when the truth fell from her lips. How that was my last day above the earth until...

"Where is she?" Fenrir asked.

I sucked in a breath, extinguishing the damp and cold rock from my nostrils.

"A particularly nasty little corner of Midgard," I said. "It's called Florida."

"Then we better get going," Sigyn said.

She secured her kitchen shears between her waist and belt and walked into the kitchen. Cabinets creaked and a chorus of clanging metal and plastic utensils ensued.

"There's a minor problem with that," Falael said over the smack of drawers.

Sigyn walked back out and handed him a serrated knife.

Fenrir took the overly large and overly pointy serving fork she held out to him.

"Which is?" I asked, refusing a spatula crusted in layers of dinners past. I'd really have to get them some proper weapons...

He pointed out the window.

"How are we supposed to get through that?" Corpses chased a man holding two bottles of vodka. A car sped by and crashed into the grocery store across the street. "I'd say normal modes of transportation are out."

Fair point.

My eye caught a Da Vinci in the back corner depicting Leda and the swan.

Of course.

"Air travel is our only option," I said. "I can do a nice little trick and shift into a falcon. Anyone else able to shift into something with wings?"

They just blinked.

I sighed.

"Really?" I said. "You have centuries at your disposal and no one else has bothered to learn something actually useful?"

I tapped my chin.

An idea popped into my head.

Risky.

Foolish.

I loved it.

"I could transfigure you three into something I could carry in my falcon aspect," I said. "It would have to be small. Like a nut." I snapped my fingers. "Like a hazelnut."

Sigyn's mouth opened, and she cocked her head.

"Are you being serious right now?" she asked.

I shrugged.

"I've done it before when I had to rescue Idunn from Thiazi," I said. "I'll give you it has been a long while since I wielded such magic, but..."

I laced my fingers together and stretched them, enjoying how my joints cracked down my knuckles.

This would be such fun.

"You fill me with the greatest of confidence." Fenrir cradled his forehead in his right hand.

"Loki's right," Falael said. "Flight is the only way we will make it to Golda. I see no other recourse."

I jerked up my sleeves to my elbows and shook out my hands.

"Then it's settled," I said. "Now, I'll need you all to stand right over there. In a row, please. Yes, like that."

Fenrir stiffened and tiptoed back.

"I'm afraid I won't be coming with you," he said. "You must do this journey alone."

"No, we do this together," I said.

His mouth twisted into a defeated smile.

"I'm trapped here. Remember?"

Dammit. I forgot that delightful little wrench.

I chewed the edge of my nail.

I thought harder.

I smiled again.

"This is a non-issue," I said.

"How do you figure that?" he asked.

"Magic," I said. "Transfiguration breaks you down and rebuilds you into something else. It rearranges molecules. Re-stacks atoms. It makes a new mosaic of all your bits and pieces and essences."

"It *what*?" Sigyn said.

Oh dear. I forgot how that sometimes made people a bit skittish.

"It rarely ever causes any long term side effects if that's what concerns you," I said.

"*Rarely*?"

"Point is," I continued. "You aren't, well, you and that means--"

"The spell can't deflect Fenrir," Falael finished.

"Exactly," I said. "You still look unsure. The chance of your eyes switching to where your ears are is only five percent..."

"It's not that," Fenrir said.

"What then?"

He slouched into a velvet chair stuffed with springs and stared out.

"Odin might not want my life anymore, but the wolf wants his. It keeps fighting to get out of me. To tear the worlds apart. I will not become a killer."

He shut his eyes hard and rubbed his temples as if trying to stifle the voices raging in his head.

It tore my heart to shreds.

I stepped beside him and laid my hand on his shoulder and squeezed.

"You won't," I said. "Because I won't let you."

He looked up at me, and a desire to believe me swam behind his emerald eyes.

"You see how my sister has succumbed to Ragnarok. I can't take the risk. If I see Odin..."

He scrunched his face.

I understood his fear of losing control. But fear was such a useless thing. It was far better to close your eyes and jump and enjoy the thrill.

That's what I kept telling myself as the voices in my own head grew louder.

"We are all taking risks," I said, trying not to think how

my fire had ignited back at Schönbrunn. "But taking risk is our only chance. I will not abandon you again."

Sigyn stepped forward.

"Nor I," she said.

"Or me," Falael added.

I looked into Fenrir's eyes.

"Can you trust me?" I asked him.

He stood and wiped his nose on his sleeve and pulled in a forceful sniff.

"Yes," he said. "I think so."

"Good," I said. "Shall we try again, then?"

They reformed their row, and I faced them.

"Now, this will take extreme concentration, especially with there being three of you. But, nothing easy is ever worth doing."

I stepped before Falael first. Because, if I did muck this up...Well, it wouldn't be that much of a loss.

My natural inclination for magic meant I never had to rely on runes or spells, although they were fine in a pinch, but to transfigure three beings in a row...this promised to be a prickly challenge, even for me.

And I couldn't wait. Otherwise, what fun would it be?

I hovered my hands over Falael's chest and imagined him smaller.

Much, much smaller.

Rounder.

And stuck in a shell.

Magic sparked against my ribs and through my veins. Absolute potential vibrated through my core. Gods I missed this feeling.

I concentrated harder.

Pop!

Plink!

A perfect hazelnut spun on the wooden floorboards.

I still had it.

Wrestling away the temptation of accidentally stepping on him, I bent down and picked him up off the floor and dropped him safely into my pocket.

"Who's next?" I asked.

"I suppose me," Fenrir said.

He stood still and I held my hands over him, focusing on transfiguring him into the same form as Falael.

It was harder this time. Spells always sliced off little slivers of your energy, but this was like whacking a hatchet into an éclair.

I closed my eyes, centering myself and my magic on bending his every cell to my will. I imagined him smaller. Rounder. Stuck in a shell...

My fingers shook as I pushed more of myself out.

"I haven't all day," Fenrir said.

I grumbled a few choice words as I forced out another blast, trying to reserve enough for Sigyn.

A suction pulled in the surrounding air.

Pop!

Plink!

I smiled and picked Fenrir up off the floorboards and slipped him in my pocket along with Falael.

Sigyn remained, and I cursed the fatigue eating at my body. I massaged the spot above the bridge of my nose, trying to slacken the tension coiling and coiling.

Sigyn stepped before me and looked into my eyes. She pressed her lips together, making mine heat with the memory of our kiss.

She fiddled with her fingers.

"Loki. About earlier...I didn't mean to hurt you, and—"

"Please," I said. "Don't worry about me. I'm okay. Really."

I was not.

"Now, let's start this party. The worlds won't save themselves."

I summoned my magic up again, demanding all I had, and pushed it through my deepening exhaustion. But that once delicious spark now sputtered.

Nothing more came.

Ridiculous.

There was always more.

I called it up again, reaching deep into the well of my core. Deeper.

My muscles twisted and strained.

I pushed back my hair sticking to the sweat beading across my brow.

"Apologies," I said. "This is quite embarrassing. I swear this is the first time something like this has ever happened."

"You look so tired," she said.

I forced a smile.

"On the contrary, it's exhilarating," I lied.

"Let me help you."

"I'm afraid there's nothing much you can do," I said. "But don't worry, I will manage. I won't let anything happen to you."

"I know." Her words were soft and warm. Sincere.

Sigyn reached out and touched my arm.

A new energy not my own swept through me where her fingertips brushed. It surged through my insides and filled me. Recharged me.

Gave me hope.

Somehow, inexplicably, my magic reignited and reared to go again, just as fresh and powerful as before.

But how?

Never mind.

I didn't have time to consider what this meant. If she simply had the gift, or if she possessed something more. Something greater.

"What?" she asked.

I grinned.

"Hold tight."

The air stilled, collapsing in on itself and...

Pop!

Plink!

Sigyn dropped to the floor. I picked her up and tucked her gently away with the others.

I walked to the tall windows and opened them. A cacophony of chaos filled my ears from the streets below and destruction spread out before me.

All the chaos I swore I would bring.

All I wanted.

And now I went to stop it.

Irony really was a bitch.

I stretched my neck and rolled my shoulders.

Shifting into my falcon aspect, I flew out of the window and over the city that now burned. Over a world that split at the seams.

And I wasn't sure we could put it back together.

17

LIFE'S A WITCH

Miami Beach, Florida

The clock struck noon.

But Miami Beach drowned in twilight.

Street lights flickered.

Pressure built and pushed down on my neck. My shoulders.

The rhythmic thunder of waves crashing against the beach cut through the eerie still, along with the soft rustle of palm trees.

The entire stretch of A1A stood still with abandoned cars. People had apparently realized it was faster to flee on foot rather than remain stuck on the bridge over Biscayne Bay.

The first snowflake was probably enough to scare them away long before the sky darkened and the dead Hel rose from their graves marched through on their way to Vigridr.

We walked down Ocean Drive, a tight street lined with palms and squat buildings of stucco and glass. Fenrir called their uniquely sleek style "Art Deco." Apparently it was all the rage in the 1920s and 30s, along with jazz, cocaine, and cold gin. I was sad to have missed that.

We stopped and faced a vivid white building with six stories of sharp edges, windows, and chrome detailing. White umbrellas lined its front, and palm trees tall enough to reach the fourth floor stood on either end.

A blue neon sign flashed: The Hotel Pompano.

"Are you sure this is the right place?" Sigyn pressed her face against a frosted window etched with flamingoes. "You said it was a hut in the middle of a mangrove swamp."

I shrugged.

"Apparently things have changed since 1526. It's probably for the best. I don't think I ever got all the muck out of my hair," I said. "But this is the spot."

"It might be the spot, but Golda surely is long gone," Fenrir said. "When the developers moved in—"

"—She sold her land and negotiated lodging," Falael interrupted. "Völvas don't leave a spot once they set down roots."

Well, he was right.

"Furthermore," I added. Louder than Falael. And with more authority. "She spoke as if she had no choice but to remain where she was. No, she's here. It's just a question of where."

The Atlantic roared behind us and salt saturated the air. A chilled gust beat our backs and flapped our clothes around our legs as we headed inside.

The rotating glass doors skidded open, and we walked across polished terrazzo floors and into a chic lobby. Coral vases and paintings of teal oceans, yellow umbrellas, and gray seagulls added pops of color to the white walls.

Something rattled in the gift shop next to the elegant front desk.

I pulled out my daggers and snuck closer. Sigyn and Falael both clutched their kitchen knives and shears. Fenrir gripped his paring knife.

An alligator sauntered out beneath a collection of orange t-shirts with hideous logos of daiquiris and parrots. The beast drifted across the lobby, whacking over wicker chairs and side tables in its wake.

I guess some things still hadn't changed.

We walked down a marble tiled hallway and opened door after door and found everything we didn't need.

A pool.

A gym.

A ballroom.

No witch.

"How many rooms does this bloody place have?" I kicked down a door, sending splinters of wood everywhere and...it was a utility closet. "Dammit!"

"I'd make a guess at there being at least seventy-five," Falael said.

Sigyn groaned.

"This is going to take forever," she said. "We need to break up and cover more ground. Golda could be anywhere."

Falael looked out a large window at the end of the hall facing the roiling ocean across the street. The water seemed meaner. Hotter. Froth and foam slipped and thickened on the black, churning surface.

He tapped his fingers against his trousers and bit the soft flesh of his bottom lip.

"We are running out of time," he said. "The third sign approaches. Soon the oceans will boil, and then it's only the blow of the Gjallarhorn that remains. We can't let it get to that."

"Why?" Fenrir asked.

Falael kept staring at the waves. Still. Contemplative. That ever present glow of hope and possibility flickered. His soft cheeks hollowed. His skin turned ashen, and I could see the faint lines around his eyes deepen. He looked as ancient and weathered as an oak.

"Once the horn sounds, it's over," he said.

Fenrir shrank.

Of course. Why couldn't we add just a little more pressure? Although, I loved the buzz of facing the insurmountable. Nothing was more delicious, but I didn't like how it filled Fenrir with worry.

Sigyn rested her hand on Fenrir's shoulder and squeezed into his army jacket.

"It will be alright," she said.

As if woken from his reverie, Falael turned and forced a smile at both of them.

"Yes," he pushed out. "It will all be fine."

His words were comforting, but his hazel eyes told the truth. As did the flame of chaos I saw burst in his chest from his lie.

He wasn't sure.

And neither was I.

"Let's meet back in the lobby in an hour." I swiped my thumbs against my hot palms. I tried not to think how they felt hotter.

Sigyn nodded and let her hand fall away.

"An hour," she repeated.

We didn't say more. We broke off in different directions of the hotel.

Sigyn took a sharp right and raced down a hall plastered in paintings of seashells and starfish. Falael swerved left.

Fenrir pushed open the door to the stairwell and bounded up the stairs.

I kept forward, venturing deeper into the guts of the building.

We had to find Golda.

I split open doors and broke locks. Every room was the same. Mirrors, chrome, teal and more teal. Annoyingly empty.

Frustration lit my blood.

I half destroyed the penthouse rummaging through closets and flipping over the bed in case she was playing a game of hide and seek.

The hour was nearly up.

I grumbled my entire way back to the lobby.

If I saw one more bedspread decorated with tropical fish...

I stopped.

A curious room of purple ambient lighting and terrazzo floors with intricate geometric patterns spread out before me.

And then my breath left my body.

Standing in the center, shining like a beacon, was a full bar with white glowing shelves lined with bottles and bottles of alcohol.

Thank gods.

This new age truly had it all.

I walked towards the absolute beauty, weaving between dark wood tables and chairs of taupe velvet and black leather.

A television hanging on the wall at the far end of the room remained switched on. The mouth of a man holding a microphone moved rapidly, though I couldn't hear a word. His forehead glistened with sweat.

He disappeared. Scenes of destruction replaced him.

Mudslides, fires, earthquakes swallowing buildings... disaster after disaster flickered past the screen. The entire world was in chaos.

And the chaos was mine.

My palms heated more...

I had brought the worlds to their knees as I swore I would do. I made them crumble. And while I hated I was responsible for the wreckage speeding before my eyes, another part of me loved it.

That terrified me the most.

I turned away, needing to remove the bitterness from my mouth. Leaping over the bar, I swiped a bottle of dark Cuban rum off a shelf loaded with whiskeys, tequilas, and vodkas. I twisted off the lid and knocked back a big slug.

Toasted sugar cane burned down my throat.

My eyes settled on the mirror behind a row of vermouth and bourbon. A woman stared back at me.

My heart leapt and I spun around.

Golda stood in front of me, a smile cracking her square face and solid jaw. Her eyes beamed, lined in a perfect cat-eye. A clean, white linen shirt covered her sturdy arms, and gold earrings hung from her ears. Last I saw her, she was sweat and grime and leathered skin. But now...

She tapped her gold watch wrapped around her strong wrist.

"Right on time this visit!" she exclaimed. "My, you've certainly updated yourself since I saw you last. You really can pull off those tight-fitting trousers."

I cocked my head, trying to take it all in.

"And you...you look more...hygienic."

She chuckled and ran her manicured fingers through

her now platinum blonde, curled hair. Her red nail polish matched her red lipstick.

"The benefit of living in a place with a spa and good housekeeping," she said. "You try doing your laundry in a swamp full of alligator piss. Your flawless complexion would have fared no better."

Her gaze fell to the bottle of rum I still clutched. She tsk'd and joined me on the other side of the bar and snatched the bottle out of my grip.

"Excuse me, I wasn't finished with that." I swiped at the bottle, but she tossed it behind her shoulder. The stone floor annihilated the bottle in a torrent of cracked glass and rum.

That hurt me deeply.

"Rum isn't a very celebratory drink for the end of the worlds. This calls for something special."

Golda bent over and it took everything in me not to wrap my fingers around her neck and squeeze.

She grabbed two champagne flutes out of a low cabinet and placed them on the smooth, dark wood of the bar. She took a bottle of good champagne and unwrapped the gold foil from around the neck and popped out the cork with a squeal.

"The last thing you told me was you were going to decide your own fate." Froth slid down the bottle and over her fingers. "How did that work out for you?"

My insides tensed and my eyes burned as needles wiggled in my corneas.

"A little heads up about the five hundred years of torture would have been nice," I said, blinking the pain away.

Laughter lit behind her eyes.

She tipped over the bottle, letting an arc of champagne fill each glass. Delicate bubbles swam to the surface.

"I did warn you to tread carefully." She spun and picked

up a bottle of absinth. "But no matter. You finally accepted your destiny, and Ragnarok has been beautiful to watch unfold."

A tornado tore through a small town somewhere in Indiana on the television. My jaw tightened.

"You're right," I said. "I did accept my destiny. I did start Ragnarok. And now, I want to stop it."

She burst out laughing as she cracked open the absinth and poured a shot into the champagne, turning everything a milky green.

"Still on this, are we?" she said. "There is no greater honor than being the Destroyer. The Breaker of Worlds. Why do you keep wanting to throw all that away?"

"Things are different."

She studied me. She knew.

"The woman," she said. "You really will do anything for her."

"Mercilessly."

She smiled, but something beneath the surface frosted my nerves, and not only because she was a creepy old bat.

"That's good. I'm glad. We all need something to fight for, and what is more noble than fighting for *love*?"

A spiteful ghost seemed to haunt that last word...

She gave me the glass. She smelled like earth and pungent French perfume.

My lips recoiled, remembering the last time she handed me a drink. Roaches had scuttled all over the glass thick with filth. And that was before she filled it with straight, putrid rotgut.

"It's called *Death in the Afternoon*," she said. "A much more fitting drink for these final hours. The absinth gives the champagne a nice kick."

This did look far more appealing.

I took the flute glass.

"All that awaits is for you to wake Surtr, and then your destiny as the Destroyer will be complete," she said. "So, let's cheers to the end."

She clinked my glass with hers.

I lost my desire. I set my drink back on the bar.

Her lips pulled into a frown and pity knit the fine, weathered creases of her forehead.

"I know, my child," she said. "You think there is a way to stop all this. It's why you want to find your son, Jormungand."

Still the best, after all these centuries.

I lengthened and leaned forward, eager for any information she might have.

"And do you know where he is?"

Her eyes twinkled, as if I asked her exactly what she wanted most to tell me.

"Of course, but it will do you no good. Ragnarok is here and there's no stopping it."

She always was unyielding in her belief of fate to the point of being exceedingly annoying.

"But there is," I said. "Surtr has a weakness."

She stiffened.

"Balder the Savior, you mean?" Scorn doused each word. "Yes, his element of goodness was formidable...But now his light is snuffed out, leaving room for the coming seething darkness that is Surtr. With Balder's death, there is no more weakness."

I ran my thumb across my silver rings on my fingers.

"Balder can't be the only weakness. There must be some other hope..."

She raised her perfectly shaped right eyebrow.

"Without light, what hope is there against the black?"

She said it with an element of glee that unnerved me. She picked out a maraschino cherry from a silver bowl and tore it off the stem and gobbled it down.

My nerves frayed as another way lanced my gut.

Could I even...

I could.

Because I would do anything for Sigyn.

Even if that meant...

I shot back my drink and drained the glass dry. A punch of black licorice. A bite of champagne.

I needed something to dull the venom searing my skin.

And the sting of my last resort if Jormungand truly did fail us.

"What if..."

"What if *what*, dear?"

I could barely say it.

"What if I returned to the cave?" I forced the words past the lump swelling in my throat. Past the taste of venom filling my mouth. "What if I went back into torment? I couldn't wake Surtr locked away and out of my mind in pain. It would stop Ragnarok. It would save everybody."

She laughed again. Louder than the first time.

"My poor boy. What delusion," she said. "I told you Odin only delayed the inevitable with all that rubbish, and the inevitable is now here."

She plucked out another cherry, snapped it from the stem, and plopped it in her mouth.

"I refuse to believe that," I said. "Surtr must have another weakness."

She chewed slower. Harder. I think she imagined the cherry my head.

"Surtr has only one weakness," she spat. Bits of cherry

flew out of her mouth. "And he's trapped with your daughter in Hel. You best start accepting things as they are."

Holding her gaze, I bared my teeth and closed the space between us.

"Never."

She swallowed and then smiled.

"Stubborn, as always. It's what makes you so perfect."

"Do you know where Jorg is or not?" I snapped. "I'm rather in a hurry to prove you wrong."

"All you had to do is look out the window."

She pointed out at the thrashing waves.

I buried my face in my hands.

"Do you ever give straight answers? No. Why would you?"

"I thought it clear," she said. "He's in the Bermuda Triangle. And the tip of the triangle starts right here...in Miami."

I raised my head.

"Why would he stay in such a small area when he has the entire seas to roam free?"

She blinked.

And I knew.

My shoulders slumped, and I grew angry.

Heat radiated off my neck. Off of my chest, my arms.

"He never was just banished to the seas," I said. "He was imprisoned in them. In the triangle."

"They are the walls of his prison," she said. "What do you think makes the waters there so dangerous? Mysterious? Chaotic? All those ships and planes didn't go missing by themselves. No. I suspect being crossed didn't put Jormungand in the best of moods."

My fingers curled into fists, thinking how time after time the gods had tricked me.

How nothing ever worked out, no matter how much I

sacrificed. I lost Sigyn. I lost my chance for vengeance. I lost Ragnarok...

Ragnarok.

The word echoed in my head. Beautiful. Poetic.

My insides blazed, and I took in a sharp breath, feeding on the prickle of heat.

The television flashed again with more scenes of collapse. Lava flooded out of a volcanoes in Iceland and Hawaii, the later flowing beautifully into the ocean where steam rose into the red sky.

And I couldn't peel my eyes away.

"You still want it, don't you?" she asked.

"What?"

She stepped closer to me. I felt her breath skate hotter than my own across the fine hairs on the back of my neck.

"To make them suffer. To make the worlds burn at your feet. To make the gods pay for what they did to you. You want Ragnarok."

Burn them. Kill them. Destroy them.

I didn't.

And yet, I didn't tell her no.

"Loki?" Sigyn's voice cut through my thoughts. "Is this her?"

I turned and faced Sigyn standing in the doorway. Her presence soothed the voices in my head like a cooling balm.

I nodded.

Golda beamed and walked to Sigyn. She took Sigyn's hands in hers and squeezed, messaging her thumbs over her fan of bones.

Sigyn's muscles tightened, drawing up her shoulders.

"So, this is who captured the lie-smith's heart?" Golda said. "The one who bore the sign that instigated Ragnarok.

It is a pleasure to meet the woman who started the Destroyer on his path. Who gave him purpose."

Sigyn narrowed her eyes and pulled her hands out of Golda's and stepped back. She wiped her palms against her skirts. I couldn't blame her. Golda was a lot to take in.

"Pleasure," she pressed out. She looked at me. "Does she know where Jorg is?"

"Apparently we are going on a lovely sojourn into the Bermuda Triangle."

"Then let's go."

Golda made a funny noise.

"Aren't you going to ask me if I know how to break Odin's spell and free Jorg from his watery prison?" she asked.

Völvas never missed a chance to show off.

"I take it you do, because of course you do."

She smiled and nodded.

"Excellent," I said. "Are we talking blood magic, cut your palm with a knife type deal? Or, an incantation only able to be spoken on a full moon during the summer equinox thing?"

She smiled wider.

"You know this isn't how this works," she said. "There's a price."

I sighed.

"There always is with you."

"How else do you think I can keep this platinum hair flawless? It's murder on the bank account."

Sigyn stepped in front of me and crossed her arms.

"What do you want?" Sigyn asked.

Devious glee tugged at Golda's lips and eyes.

"I like this one," Golda said, looking at me. "Last time I asked for your mother's dagger. I think this time it won't be anything quite so sentimental."

I hoped not. I never was one for sentiment, and so such items were hard to come by.

"Spit it out."

"Take me with you."

I narrowed my eyes.

"Why in all the Nine Worlds would you ever want that? Even I don't want to go. Jormungand has always been a little high strung..."

She shrugged.

"Well, seeing the legendary Midgard serpent happens to be on my bucket list. And since we are all about to die fiery deaths, this might be my only chance."

Sigyn tugged my arm and pulled me down closer to her.

"I don't know about this," she whispered in my ear. "There's something about her that makes my skin crawl. Like a dark void is in her sucking me dry."

I chuckled and patted her hand. I tried not to let my fingers linger.

"Trust me, she makes everyone feel that way," I said. "Probably why her only friends were toads, snakes, and alligators."

Sigyn squished her bottom lip between her teeth.

"She looks at us like we are pawns."

I knew what Sigyn meant, but witches rarely looked at you any other way. If they didn't look at you as their drones, they looked at you as their supper. Especially if you were a child.

"The only way we can break the spell and get to Jorg is with her help. This is our last chance at stopping Surtr and all this mess."

Sigyn looked out at Golda who gave us a cheery wave.

"Fine, but I don't like this."

Neither did I, but what was one to do?

I turned back to Golda.

"It seems we have a deal," I told her.

Golda clapped her hands and rubbed them together, her gold rings clacking like ricocheting marbles.

"Wonderful! Now, let's release us a serpent."

However could this go badly?

18

VOYAGE OF THE DAMNED

We raced to the Miami Beach Marina near the tip of South Beach. Seagulls swarmed over our heads, their squawks and croons cutting through the pounding of ocean waves. Brown pelicans sat on buoys and edged the dock.

We walked along the floating pier, passing rows of sailboats, fishing boats, and luxury yachts all bobbing in their slips.

But which to take?

A sleek, white speedboat named *The Last Nail* seemed the best option. Not a foreboding name for a vessel at all. Nails and death were definitely what I wanted to think about heading into the Bermuda Triangle.

Climbing aboard the boat we fiddled with batteries, breakers, valves, and wires trying to get the bloody thing to run. Tempers flared. Groans pressed between tight teeth that clenched tighter. "No, do it this ways" were hurled like a tennis ball in a volatile match.

The starter activated before it came to death threats. The boat rumbled beneath our feet. We revved the diesel engines and sped out of the marina and towards the triangle.

The bow cut through the surf and darts of water sprayed our faces with each hit of fiberglass against water. Warm ocean met cold air. Froth and steam churned and swelled around us as we sped deeper into a black and very angry sea that seemed to simmer.

I stood next to Golda, her eyes firm on the dwindling white Miami coastline. Her platinum hair tangled in the wind, lashing her round cheeks and square chin.

"I never thought I'd get off that rotting piece of land," she said.

"I would imagine scraping the mold off your heels would get vexing," I said.

She braced herself against the smooth fiberglass.

"But I endured," she said.

A rush of primordial power radiated off her every movement.

The oddity of it all pricked my curiosity.

Usually such ancient beings weren't hidden away in swamps of no consequence without a reason.

I moved in closer.

"You once said you didn't choose to live here," I said. "That it was chosen for you."

She smirked.

"Chosen." She spat out the word. "'Chosen' is like covering dog shit in vanilla frosting and calling it a cupcake."

My curiosity turned into a blaze.

"You must have been very naughty to end up here," I said. "What did you do?"

She huffed.

"I only wanted peace," she said. "Promises were made, and promises were broken. But not by me."

Her gaze hardened, looking somewhere in the past. Somewhere teeming with pain.

"They should have known better thinking they could...could..."

She gripped the boat harder, pulling the skin tight over her knuckles. This seemed like an awfully sore subject. I wanted to know *everything*.

"Could what?"

Her hands relaxed.

She smiled and patted my cheek as if I were her dearest son. As if I held some key. She never stopped making my skin crawl.

"All water under the bridge," she assured. "I really can be awfully dramatic sometimes. Is my lipstick smudged? Red is such a fussy color!"

She took out a black tube of lipstick from her pocket and spread a fresh coat of red over thin lips. It didn't hide the little blossom of chaos igniting in her chest. Apparently, it wasn't all water under the bridge as she let on.

"Now," she said. "If we want to find your son, I must help Falael navigate, otherwise we might end up in Nassau!"

Before I could press any further, Golda turned and walked to the helm in the middle of the boat. She sat in the seat beside Falael, who held the chrome wheel and kept it steady, ensuring everything remained safe and tidy and frightfully dull.

What was the point of all this speed if you wouldn't even take advantage of seeing how long you could remain airborne after catching a six foot wave?

I honestly didn't see what all the fuss was about.

And that's probably why the mutiny happened.

My stint as captain of *The Last Nail* had lasted only five minutes before Falael replaced me. It was decided he was far more responsible.

I never saw the allure of responsibility. Responsibility was so limiting.

I looked through the helm to the front cockpit of the boat. Sigyn planted her knees in the leather cushion and gripped the railing, facing the ocean spreading out endlessly before her. Sigyn's hair spiraled and twisted across the tops of her shoulders and down her back, as wild and untamed as the surf and mist exploding on either side of her.

She looked behind her shoulder at Falael and held his gaze. She smiled. Joyful. Bright.

Alive.

And it tore me apart.

I looked away and slumped on one of the long benches and folded my arms on the table. I continued to shrink in my despair until I planted my forehead in the crooks of my elbows, shutting out the world.

Shutting out it all.

Leather squealed. Someone joined me.

I sprouted thorns.

I looked up, ready to tell them off. I would not have my private session of self-loathing interrupted.

My thorns immediately retracted.

Fenrir scooted down the smooth, beige leather and settled next to me. His small smile teemed with concern as he handed me an ice cream cone wrapped in blue paper.

He was already halfway through a strawberry popsicle.

"Found these in the freezer below deck. Thought we might as well enjoy a last meal if this doesn't go our way."

Well, if I wasn't allowed to wallow in my wretchedness...

I took the cone and tore off the paper and my heart

somersaulted. Vanilla ice cream dipped in chocolate and covered in peanuts. I took a big bite, loving the silk of cream and zing of chocolate rolling over my tongue.

"I will miss these frozen delights," I pushed through a full mouth. "Wondrous things."

Fenrir pulled out the popsicle from his mouth.

"I think there's something you're already missing..."

I annihilated my way down the cone.

"What do you mean?"

Pity thickened his features.

"Sigyn."

My breaths shallowed.

"Are you trying to give me advice about women? *Me*? I think I'm quite fine in that department."

"I just thought—"

"You just thought you'd give me a few encouraging words and make it all better? Thanks, but I've never been one to talk about *emotions*. Useless, irritating, gnawing things. I find it best to lock them in a box, throw away the key, and shove that racket deep, *deep* down."

He rolled his eyes and leaned back in his seat.

"Yes, I recall all your sage council. Suppressing your emotions can't always be a solution."

My lips curled into a wry smile.

"You're right. Steel and mead also work wonders."

He and I both chuckled.

His gentleness astounded me. His integrity. It filled me with pride. For all my faults, I felt blessed knowing that at least in him, I had created something good.

I held his gaze.

He pushed himself further into his seat.

"Why are you looking at me like that?"

"Like what?"

"*Lovingly.*"

"What's wrong with me looking at you lovingly? You are my son."

He rubbed the stubble shading his angled jaw.

"It's a little disconcerting coming from you is all," he said.

I took in a breath.

"I know," I said. "And I'm...I'm sorry. I'm sorry I wasn't a better father," I said. "I should have been there..."

The words turned to cotton in my mouth.

I should have been there when they took you.

He reached out and laid his hand on my shoulder.

"It's alright," he said. "I told you I forgave you. I meant it."

I nodded.

The roar of the engines filled the silence that settled between us.

I looked at Sigyn again.

"It hurts to be in love when the other doesn't feel the same," Fenrir said.

Pins and needles grated my throat.

"That's not the problem." I picked up the paper wrapping. "The problem is, she *does* love me."

He cocked his head.

"Then why is she with Falael?"

I snorted and ripped the paper, shredding it slowly into ribbons.

"Because she finds us *ill suited*."

"And are you?" he asked.

I stopped.

Falael caught a small wave, giving the boat a nice bounce. Sigyn laughed and her eyes blazed with adventure.

She motioned for him to do it again. He chuckled,

hitting another gentle swell. She bounced and glee lit her face, and that fearless spirit I so loved about her radiated even through her pores.

Her lips stretched into a smile of purest happiness.

I wanted her to always be this happy.

"I used to make her smile like that," I said. "But I also made her cry. I promised myself I'd never hurt her, and that's exactly what I've done."

I tore off another jagged sliver of paper. Each represented a lie I'd told her. An arrow of pain I shot into her heart.

Fenrir shook his head.

"Love is complicated, isn't it?" he said. "It can cut us deeply, but it's also what heals us."

"When did you get so philosophical?"

He grinned.

"Well, it's simple really," he said. "Loving someone is putting their needs before your own."

Falael blew Sigyn a kiss, and she looked even happier.

And I knew what I had to do.

I gathered the ribbons of paper off my lap and opened my hand to the wind, letting them fly away into the sea.

I needed to speak to her.

I got up and started walking to the front of the boat through the helm where Falael had his nose against the navigational screens with Golda.

Sigyn caught my gaze and pushed off the railing and stood. A wave struck the boat, pitching her forward. She flung out both arms, trying to keep her balance.

Falael didn't see.

She tumbled to the left.

I raced to her as she swayed to the right...

I caught her. She laughed in my arms as if she had the time of her life. Gods she was perfect.

"Thank you," she said. "The cold made me stiffer than I realized."

Her face beamed, but her teeth chattered. I sat us on a bench and pressed her hands between mine, trying to warm them. Even though the sea was hot, the wind was frigid with the bite of winter.

"Your fingers are ice."

"It was worth it," she said. "I've never experienced such speed before! The sensation of wind in my hair and surf on my skin. It's exhilarating."

I chuckled.

"I can't fault you there," I said.

I slid my leather coat off my arms and handed it to her.

"At least wear this if you want to stay up here."

"Really, I'm fine," she said. Her teeth still chattered.

"Yes, I can see that," I said. "Are you ever not stubborn?"

Mischief sparkled in her eyes. It weakened my knees.

"Would you have me any other way?"

I smiled.

I would not.

And I would not lose this game of wills.

I held my coat out closer to her. She sighed and grabbed it, and struggled to shove her frozen arms inside.

"Let me." I slipped it over her shoulders and tugged it closed over her chest.

My fingers accidentally grazed the nape of her neck.

Her cheeks flushed.

"Apologies."

The mirth drained from her face and an emotion I couldn't place took over.

"Don't apologize," she said. "Not to me."

My throat dried.

A yellow glow sheathed her face in warm light.

She looked down and her eyes widened.

I followed her gaze with my own.

Fire coated my hands and fingers in thin flame.

No. Not now.

I turned and ran to the helm, Sigyn's voice trailing behind me.

Flinging open the cabin door, I headed down and away, ignoring Falael's concerned questions.

If they knew...

My heels slipped off the edges of the stupidly small wooden steps that led below deck into a stupidly tight cabin of leather, cedar, and fiberglass. Actually, tight was too generous a word.

After almost bashing my head against a cabinet, I steadied myself and leaned against a small wall. I stared at my hands. They continued to blaze.

The door clicked open.

I hid my hands behind my back, careful not to have them touch anything. This would be a really inconvenient time to start burning holes through the boat.

Sigyn descended the steps and squeezed between me and the narrow sofa behind her.

"What's wrong with your hands?" she asked. "Ever since Alfheim you keep getting preoccupied with them."

She looked up at me. The ship tossed us back and forth. I worshipped the seconds of contact each wave caused.

"Everything is perfectly alright," I lied. "I just thought I'd pop down here for more ice cream," I said. "Nothing like ice cream on a blustery ocean cruise."

I tried to shove past her to get to the freezer. She blocked my way.

"Loki…"

"What? I thought you liked ice cream?"

She crossed her arms. I held my breath as her elbows brushed against my chest.

"Tell me."

Her expression was an exquisite portrait of a woman done.

Well, I guess the cat was out of the bag.

"Fine," I said. "I'm having an itty, bitty, seriously small problem."

"Which is?"

I opened my mouth to speak. Nothing came out.

"I…I can't seem to control my fire anymore. My chaos. My element."

"How can you not control your own element?"

I tightened, not wanting to say the truth I'd been denying.

"Because Ragnarok is taking me over."

She furrowed her brow.

"Taking you over?"

My lips tugged into a grim smile.

"The prophecy foretold I'm to raze the worlds in fire beside Surtr," I said. "Can't you see? I'm succumbing to Ragnarok's control. Every day I fight against the battle raging in my insides, and every day I lose just a little more ground." I swallowed. My throat was raw. "I don't know how much longer I can keep my chaos chained."

She shook her head.

"You won't succumb." She said it with such confidence. I almost believed her.

But the reality remained a twisted, barbed wire.

"Ragnarok calls to me," I said. "Voices continually

whisper in my mind to burn. To kill. To destroy. And they grow louder."

"Loki..."

My jaw flexed. Why wasn't she understanding?

"Do you know how I survived five hundred years in that cave?" My words cut like razors. "Burn them. Kill them. Destroy them." Black darkened my vision. "That mantra raced in a loop in my head as venom seared my skin and into my bones. Burn them. Kill them. Destroy them."

I pressed my eyes closed, trying to stop the pain of a thousand needles boring into them again and again and...

"The words gave me a purpose," I said. "And purpose gave me a will. A promise to have my need for blood sated."

I couldn't move.

I couldn't...

And the darkness.

Always darkness...

When can I be free?

"But you don't want Ragnarok anymore," she said.

I forced my eyes open, forcing myself out of the horror the gods had cast me into.

I shook away the smell of my own children's flesh from my nostrils.

I shook away the agony of drowning in venom, choking on bile...five hundred years of it...

Five hundred years endured to come through on a single promise.

All I wanted.

I chuckled darkly.

"That's the worst thing," I said. "I do want Ragnarok. Still."

My palms grew hotter behind my back. I was grateful

the rumble of the engines hid the crackle of cinders snapping between my fingers.

"What do you mean?" Her words remained calm. That would soon change.

"When I first learned you were alive, I was overjoyed. And then..." I revolted myself even admitting such a thought. "I was angry. Angry because I knew I'd have to give up my vengeance. Everything. I want them to pay with their lives for what they did to us. I still want Ragnarok to end them."

I braced myself for the coming hatred. For the resentment and disgust.

But none came.

There was only compassion.

Of all the things I deserved, that was not it.

"Why aren't you livid?" I growled. "You should hate me for saying such a vile thing."

"Why would I hate you?" she said. "You have a right to feel as you do. You have a right to be angry. It's what we do with our anger that matters."

Now it was I who didn't understand.

"You might still want Ragnarok, but you've made a choice to not bring it," she said. "You've chosen to not act on your anger. You've chosen to forego your vengeance. Making a choice is half the battle."

Choice.

Bitterness coated my mouth as the spirit's voice echoed in my ears.

There is no choice. There is no hope. There is only inevitability. Fate. And this is yours.

"And what if I don't have a choice anymore?" I said.

My chaos snarled and bit at my ribs and my guts. I held out my hands that blazed and crackled for her to see.

"Look at me," I said. "I can't stop it. I can't call it back into myself. What if the voices are right? There is only inevitability. Fate. And mine is to end everything."

Sigyn grasped my hands and held them tight. I tried to tear out of her hold. I would not scald her. She gripped them tighter. Cinders popped beneath her palms and my fire licked between her fingers. But I did not burn her.

No one had ever been able to touch my exposed element but her.

And I was not prepared for the strike of her fidelity tearing through me. Raising me out of my depths and into the sky.

"There is always a choice," she said. "That can never be taken from us. Are you Loki the Destroyer, the Breaker of Worlds? Or Loki, the man who gave everything to spare the lives of those he loved?"

She held me tighter. My flames flickered over her skin. Up her wrists. Her fidelity caressed my chaos, healing it. Quieting it.

I dared to meet her gaze.

"I don't even know anymore."

"I do."

And tighter again, forcing my fire to dance over her knuckles and down her fingernails.

I searched her eyes.

"After everything, how can you still believe in me?"

She clasped me against her and wouldn't let me go.

"I always will."

She squeezed harder. Another deluge of her hope washed through me. Coated me. My chaos collapsed into stillness as her fidelity embraced me.

Fed me.

Quenched every cell of my body as if I'd been thirsty my whole life and only now been able to drink.

My blaze extinguished.

There was only hope, and she filled me to the brim with it.

She slowly pulled back, but kept latched onto my fingers, rubbing and rubbing her thumbs over the tops of my hands.

Her touch softened.

Became tender.

I smelled the rosemary in her hair.

She continued to hold my gaze.

And still she didn't let me go.

"I'm sorry for what I said to you in Vienna," she whispered. "I was wrong. I shouldn't have ever said any of it."

I swallowed, fighting the urge to take her into my arms again.

Because she didn't belong in my arms anymore.

I wanted her happy, and that meant not being with me.

"But you were right," I said.

She opened her mouth as if to counter me.

"We are here," someone called from above deck.

19

A PIECE OF SNAKE

We went above deck and walked out to the back of *The Last Nail*. The frigid wind battered my cheeks and chest. Waves thrashed the sides of the boat, lurching me onto the balls of my feet and whipping me back on my heels.

Golda and Fenrir stared out at a stewing sea. Small, glittering bubbles broke on the surface and steam thickened into a sheet of mist as it met the bitter air.

Falael dropped the anchor, and the water hissed as cold metal met a hot ocean.

"He's here," Falael said. "Beneath us."

Sigyn and I stepped next to Fenrir and peered over the edge of the boat. Something large slipped within the water and tangles of foam. A flash of pointed scales. A glint of yellow eyes that burned.

Jormungand.

I couldn't stop a frown from tugging at my lips.

"All we have to do is lift the spell," Fenrir said.

"Yes. I can't hardly wait..."

This would have all been exceedingly exciting were it

not for the nagging feeling that we were about to do something incredibly stupid. I hated that feeling. It really killed the buzz of danger.

Golda sucked in a breath thick with steam and salt.

"I've waited so long for this day," she said, keeping her eyes on the writhing pure muscle and bone beneath us. Enthusiasm pulled her features taut.

Sigyn's right eyebrow pushed up to her hairline.

"To meet the Midgard serpent?" Sigyn said. "Or, for something else?"

"You don't trust me, do you dear?" Golda said.

"Since you asked, not really."

A crooked smile cracked Golda's face.

"I'm just a fan of mythical beasties, is all," she said. "As I am a fan of reuniting families."

She faced me, framed by the clouds behind her collapsing in on themselves and blossoming again.

"Now, let's free your boy. I made you a promise and I *don't* break promises."

This time she didn't lie, which unnerved me more.

I started to question her, but she unzipped her alligator skin bag and pulled out a dagger. My mother's dagger, *Truth*.

My heart leapt.

The razor's edge sang and the bevel glistered in a straight line down to the biting tip. It was a beautiful blade of the strongest Dwarven steel and a hilt wrapped in the finest Elven leather. Nothing was sharper. Deadlier.

Perfect.

I ached seeing it again, the only link I had left to my mother. The ache cut deeper, knowing the blade was no longer mine. I'd given it away as payment to Golda five hundred years before for her to tell me how to protect Sigyn from the Destroyer...

...The fact the Destroyer turned out to be me was besides the point.

Instinctively, I reached out to touch the buttery leather hilt. To feel it mold again to my fingers. My palms.

Golda pulled it back and tightened her grip on the handle, and looked at it as if a dear, dear friend. The same way when I handed it to her all those centuries ago in that hut in the middle of a swamp.

"And just what part does *Truth* play in all this?"

Her expression stretched into a look of bewilderment, as if I'd told her hippopotamuses are spotted purple.

"*Truth*? Is that what you think this blade, this marvelous weapon, is named?"

"It's what my mother told me when she gave me this dagger before she..."

Before she died.

Golda cackled.

"So, you never knew?"

"Knew what?"

"It's name is *Lævateinn*," she said. "Destruction. And it's not so much a dagger as an instrument to channel and wield magic. Like a wand, if you will."

She stared at the blade harder. Hungrier.

My mother had always been a walking encyclopedia. It seemed odd she would make such a mistake in wrongly identifying this dagger, or wand, or whatever it truly was.

But, if a relic was ancient enough, things did get muddled and lost in the cracks.

Golda shuddered as if waking herself from a dream.

"Anyway, that's not worth concerning ourselves with right this moment. For now, it is how we will get the blood we need."

I sighed.

"So it is a blood spell after all. Thought as much," I said. "Because when is it not a blood spell?"

Sigyn crossed her arms.

"And exactly whose blood is it you need?"

Damn.

The muscles in my neck stiffened and I let out a frustrated sigh.

"Odin's," I said. "He's the one that cast the spell, only his blood can break it." I pinched the bridge of my nose. "That's going to be awfully hard to get given he isn't here. That is a shame, I would have quite enjoyed draining his every last drop of life into the sea."

Golda snickered again, this time deeper in the back of her throat.

"Oh, it's not his blood we need. It's yours."

"Mine?"

"You of all people should know nothing is stronger than the blood of family. Nothing can quite *tie one down* so adeptly. So permanently. Only your blood could imprison Jorg within the Bermuda Triangle forever."

"That's not possible. I took no part in this spell. I'd never have agreed to imprisoning him in essentially a cage. There must be another explanation—"

My skin turned clammy as the truth of what this explanation meant struck me hard.

oh...that bastard.

Golda nodded, a savage knowing shining through her eyes. She seized my arm and brushed her thumb over the thin scar on my wrist, where Odin and I had cut our flesh, clasped tight onto the other, and mixed our blood binding us together in an oath.

Then it all went to shit.

"Yes, that was a nice benefit of being your blood brother," she said. "Not only does Odin's blood flow through your veins." She paused, as if savoring the idea. "But yours through his. Odin knew how to make good use of this bond. How very fortunate for him when he learned he could trap your son using your blood gushing through his chambers and valves."

I ripped out of her grip and crushed my nails into my palms. Pain lanced each crescent. Yet again, I was betrayed, and it rubbed salt further into already festering wounds.

I've always tried to find alternatives, Odin's voice echoed, twisting my guts.

As long as the alternatives were convenient for him.

I ground my nails deeper, wanting to crush Odin's neck beneath my boot heel.

Burn them, Kill...

Sigyn touched my shoulder, jerking me out of black thoughts.

"Are you alright? You're rigid."

I cleared my throat and nodded.

"Let's just get Jorg out."

I rolled up my sleeve, exposing a web of pulsing veins ripe for blood letting.

"So, how much blood are we talking about? One bucket? Two buckets?"

Steel flared. A prick seared the side of my neck.

"Ow." I clapped my hand over the cut, rubbing out the sting.

Golda clasped *Truth*—sorry—*Lævateinn*, its tip wet with my blood.

"Willful waste makes woeful want." Golda winked.

She held out the blade over the simmering ocean. My blood trickled down the sharp edge, collecting into a quivering droplet on the tip. One firm shake and the red bead plummeted into the froth and foam.

I couldn't help my lips from twisting into a barbed smile.

Odin would be so pissed. At least there was one silver lining.

The ocean roughened. Bubbles burst and snapped and water spewed over the sides of the boat, speckling our faces. We all jumped back and held onto ropes and handles to keep our balance as *The Last Nail* tossed and pitched.

Thunder rumbled beneath the waves.

And the sea erupted.

A serpent surged out of the churning waves, all scales and strength and menace rising into a bloodied sky. Water rained down over our heads and shoulders as Jormungand coiled and stretched. Lengthened.

I craned back my neck, looking up at him. I'd forgotten just how big Jorg could grow if he wished to. He could swallow us whole and follow us down with the sun and the moon if he still felt peckish. Maybe Odin had a point keeping him tethered to one spot...

"He's magnificent!" Golda cried over the storm of water.

Magnificently short-tempered was more like it. And that was before Ragnarok whispered all its lovely calls for blood and death to him. I knew he heard it...

Yes. This promised to be quite the cheerful reunion.

The waves settled, and I stepped out to the edge of the boat. His yellow eyes hard as lightning shot to mine.

They pinched into slits.

He squirmed and tossed and twisted and disappeared within a blur of movement, shifting back into the form of a man.

Jorg stood in the center of the deck.

Water dripped off his wet hair and clothes as he took in the deck.

He cut a striking pose. Fierce and elegant. Beautiful. His cropped, straight bleached hair contrasted his black tunic of linen and leather. He always favored a bold look, and he pulled it off, much like me.

"Brother!" Fenrir ran to him and Jorg caught him in an embrace, burying his nose and chin in the Fenrir's knit scarf.

"It's good to see you again," Jorg said. His voice. Soft. Cold. Silken.

Jorg pushed away from Fenrir and smiled at him, and it softened his sharp cheekbones and pointed chin. He looked over Fenrir's shoulder at me.

His smile faded.

His eyes flickered between the yellow of the serpent and his usual green.

"Father."

"Jormungand."

I planted myself in front of Sigyn, Falael, and Golda, who beamed absolute stars. I wanted distance between him and them. There was a lean hunger to him I didn't quite like.

I was not one to be on edge, in fact, I loved the edge. But I could hear the eggshells crack beneath my feet as I walked towards him.

Fenrir stepped aside, letting Jorg and I stand face to face.

"At last you've found time to release me," he said. "Only took you what? Two millennia? I'm glad you could work it into your busy schedule of drinking and bedding anything with an orifice."

This was actually going far more pleasantly than I expected.

"It's slightly more complicated than what you think, but I'm here now, and it's time to come home—After we attend to one or two pressing matters first, that is."

I held out my hand to him.

I stretched it out further.

"Home." Yearning saturated the word. His fingers twitched towards mine. Then shadows of memories hollowed his cheeks and his fingers drew into a fist. "Why did you let them take me?"

I let my hand fall back to my side.

"Don't think for a moment I would have agreed had I known you'd be imprisoned."

His thin lips pulled back into a sneer.

"Because being banished is *so* much better?" he said. "Stop the charade. You were glad to be rid of me. I was something to be *endured*. My interests. My poetry. My art."

Not this again.

"You painted all the canvases black."

"You never understood me or the role of emotional expression!"

A rush of rage from him struck me hot and vicious. His eyes snapped to yellow again. Bitter. Lethal.

And I knew...Ragnarok had him. And it fed on his anger. As it did Hel's, Fenrir's, and my own.

But I had to get through to him. We needed him if we had any hope of ending this poison running through our veins.

"I don't have to understand you to love you."

The hard lines of his face eased. His muscles relaxed and his eyes that searched mine, desperate and hopeful, returned to green. They wanted to believe my words, and he could believe them.

Because they were true.

In a second, spite washed it all away and his eyes returned to those of the serpent.

"Love me?" he spat. "Is that the sentiment you had when you sent me away with Odin?"

"I'm not denying I made mistakes as a father, because I have, and I will ask for your forgiveness, but right now we have a rather large elephant we need to address first."

Jorg stretched his neck, and his bones snapped the length of his spine.

"Ragnarok?" he said. "I've had the loveliest visions of ash and flame. So grim. So *poetic*." He took in a breath, as if sucking in the awaiting death. "I am looking forward to finally bringing the Aesir to their knees. For once we have something we can all do together as a family."

I rubbed the back of my neck.

"About that," I said. "I—"

Fenrir stepped next to me, the wind pummeling his hair, ripping strands and strands out of his bun.

"We need you to tell us if you know a weakness of Surtr," Fenrir said, cutting me off.

Jorg laughed. That laugh. Sharp as broken glass.

"You always were the dear of our family, Fenrir," he said. "But the time has come. Can't you feel it? It calls to us. We are heartbeats away..."

He held out his arms, as if relishing the vibrations of Ragnarok I felt drumming into my own bones and sinew.

"Look," I said. "There's been a change of plans. We are going to stop Ragnarok."

His arms slackened at his sides.

"Stop it? I don't understand."

"Well, circumstances, changes of hearts, you know how it is. Could you stop looking at me like that?"

He breathed heavily. Like he wanted to strike me and scoop out my eyes with spoons.

He stalked towards me until our noses were an inch apart. He smelled of brackish water.

"You're the Destroyer. This is your destiny. This is *our* destiny."

"Sorry to disappoint," I said.

He ground his teeth and his jaw flexed.

"You've let me down more times than I can count," he said. "But this is the worst. You side with betrayers? With those who hunted us and locked us away? Those who have unleashed countless horrors?"

Sigyn pushed past me and Fenrir. Falael tried to pull her back, but she wrenched herself free. She walked to Jorg and glared up at him. He was a head taller than her, having inherited my height along with my impeccable fashion sense.

"Tell us what you know about Surtr," Sigyn demanded.

Jorg looked down at her and leaned in, closing the distance. Sigyn held her ground, betraying not a shiver or worry. His eyes flickered again, bouncing between green and yellow and back to green. To clarity.

"What are you?" he asked Sigyn. He winced and rubbed his temples.

Golda inched next to her.

"Answer Sigyn," she said. "And make sure you tell the *truth*."

He looked at Golda. His eyes snapped fully to yellow. To a want of blood.

He stepped back and straightened his lean shoulders.

"Gullveig gave us Ragnarok as a gift. A way to cleanse

the Nine Worlds of the evil the Aesir corrupted them with their bloodlust. With their treachery."

Fenrir started chuckling beneath his breath.

"What is so amusing, Brother?"

"Gullveig is a fiction," Fenrir said. "Mummy told you it was all rubbish. The ramblings of someone who had one too many blows to the head."

Laughter burst out of Jorg's gut now.

"You think that old man just told mad stories from a demented mind?" He wiped away a tear. "They were memories. Memories that slipped through a spell meant to make him forget what the Ancients never wanted remembered. Of a great woman the Aesir tore to shreds."

Falael scoffed.

"Great?" Falael said. "She wanted to murder entire nations. I don't think exterminating all peoples constitutes someone being 'great'."

Jorg shook his head and crossed his arms.

"No one ever understands," he said. "She tried to destroy them only because they were destroying what she swore to protect. What they swore to protect. It was for the greater good."

"Of course," I said. "Isn't it always."

Jorg threw me a dirty look and cleared his throat.

I feared we were in for a long monologue.

"Gullveig was hailed a hero by the Aesir," he said. "She was a great sorceress beloved of all. She helped Bor win his throne. She helped the gods make Asgard the strongest of all the Nine Worlds."

Jorg's hands curled into fists at his sides.

"But evil took root in them. And it spread. Gullveig knew there was no hope for the Aesir. For any realm. That's when she set out to cleanse the worlds and start again."

Falael skated his fingers over his lips, thinking. He straightened.

"Which led her to Surtr," Falael said.

Jorg nodded.

"Surtr was a solution. The cleansing balm she needed. She consumed Surtr. Drank it down. Armed with such raw, dark power she would extinguish the realms of their evil so that goodness would have a chance to flourish in a new world. A better world. Ragnarok would be a fresh start. Change. And she would have succeeded—"

"What stopped her?" Sigyn interrupted.

He turned and looked at me. He smiled. It made me chill. Because the smile was not his.

"Your mother," he said to me. "Laufey. She tethered Surtr to Gullveig's heart. She cut open her chest and ripped the still beating chambers out from between her ribs and trapped it within the tangled branches of a burning tree. Cursed and broken, Bor cast Gullveig out of Asgard and into a corner of the worlds fit only for devils and putrid things. And now Laufey's son is going to right this wrong."

I cocked my head.

"Beg your pardon?" I asked.

He took a step closer to me. A ravenous fervor flushed his cheeks.

"You are going to reunite what never should have been torn apart," he said. "The Destroyer's time has come to fulfill his destiny."

I was right that coming here was a bad idea. Just when I thought the day couldn't get any worse.

"This is just Ragnarok spouting nonsense in your ear," I said. "Let's talk this through."

He chuckled.

"What's there to talk through?" he said. "You are going to

wake Surtr from Gullveig's heart. And with your call, Surtr will rise. The worlds will burn at your hands. And when Surtr plunges its flaming sword into the heart of Vigridr... Gullveig's noble work will be complete. Ragnarok will be finished."

It took everything in me not to bury my face in my hands. Why did they always have to get so verbose when it came to talking about destiny?

"No," I said.

"No? *No?*" he spat. "It was horrible when I discovered the truth. To know my grandmother, my own flesh, subjected Gullveig to the same fate as me. As Fenrir. As Hel. Casting out what got in their way. What terrified them. We owe Gullveig Ragnarok. We owe it to ourselves and the future. Countless have suffered at Aesir whim. We cannot allow this evil to continue."

I crossed my arms and snorted.

"Because ending everything is the proper response?"

"Says the man that started it all."

He had me there.

"Trust me, I see the irony, but this needs to stop."

He furrowed his brow as if I were mad.

"What's wrong with wanting a better world?" he asked. "I thought you would understand most of all, having suffered the most at their hands."

My skin sizzled and my mouth filled with the acrid burn of venom. It blistered down my throat. Down my nostrils. I choked. Gagged. Drowning, drowning, drowning...always drowning. Darkness chewed at my edges.

Burn them. Kill them. Destroy them.

"I won't summon Surtr," I said, forcing the words through the venom. Through the horrors racing in my head.

"Have you gone soft?"

"Have you gone deaf? I'm afraid you're shit out of luck."

His mouth pulled into a dangerous smile.

"Am I?"

His smile pulled wider. His canines lengthened into pointed fangs. His neck stretched along with his torso and legs. Scales shot out of his skin that was no longer human.

I shoved Sigyn and Falael behind me. Golda clapped and hopped. Crazy old prune.

Jorg vanished into a haze of color and movement and dove back into the roiling sea.

The wind stopped. The waves stilled.

Calm descended.

The kind of calm that sank into your core and told you to run.

Falael bolted to the edge and looked over with Fenrir.

"Is he gone?" he asked.

This was bad. And not in the fun way.

The ocean growled. Heaved.

And I knew what Jorg was doing.

A crack thundered out of the water and cut through the sky. The water started to spin, launching us off our feet and throwing us against the deck. My hands and knees slapped the fiberglass.

"Does that answer your question?" I shot at Falael.

I pulled myself up and lunged at a railing.

"What's happening?" Sigyn asked, gripping a rope.

Deep waves swept over us, hot and suffocating. Drenching. *The Last Nail's* stern rocked to the left, slipping towards the center of the growing maelstrom, sucking and pulling in the sea, pulling in froth and foam, and soon, pulling in us.

That was the thing about the Bermuda Triangle. The veils between this world and the others were thin here. *Quite* thin. Paper. Tissue. You could easily pop between realms within its borders without even trying.

And Jorg was about to take us some place I knew we rather not go.

Another crash of ocean pounded our chests, forcing burning sea water up my nostrils and down my throat.

I spit out a mouthful of bitter salt.

"You just had to suggest releasing your brother!" I shouted at Fenrir, who hugged the base of a table. "*Oh, it's fine. There's nothing to worry about.*"

"How was I to know he went insane!"

A string of curses raced out of my mouth, colorful and detailed.

The ship groaned. Fiberglass split. The boat jerked us to the right. Water ran off our hair and streamed down our cheeks. We were jolted to the left, hard and unforgiving. Salt stung my eyes.

More curses followed.

Falael held onto the rope wound around his waist. Golda clutched a chrome bar, still cackling like a crazy woman.

The vortex roared, and we spun faster into its gaping mouth. *The Last Nail's* bow tilted up, our feet and bodies rising slowly off the deck as we neared a ninety-degree angle. Before us was sky, and below, a swirling darkness ready to eat us.

My fingertips burned holding on to the rail.

A yelp cut through my ears.

Sigyn flew past me, screaming and arms flailing trying to grab onto anything she could as she raced into the maelstrom.

No.

Falael struggled to undo his rope to save her. He wouldn't be fast enough.

The things I did for this woman.

I loosened my grip and slid down with her, head first and arms outstretched. I latched on to her fingers and wedged my dagger through the ship's deck. We jerked to a stop, only inches from the water's edge.

She looked up at me, relief blazing in her eyes.

The boat moaned and creaked and shivered.

I tightened my grip into iron on my dagger hilt. The sea boiled beneath us. Wanting us.

Scales writhed behind her. Jormungand burst out of the spinning water and coiled his tail around her waist.

I held onto her as tight as I could. White pain shot down my fingers, fighting against Jorg's pull.

You cannot have her.

Laughter struck me, bleeding from the air and the waves.

Sigyn slipped out of my grasp and disappeared into the black.

I let go and followed her.

20

A HEARTBEAT AWAY

I coughed out sea water from my lungs. My soaked clothes chilled my skin and my hair stuck to my forehead and cheeks.

Sigyn. He has Sigyn.

Taking in a heaving breath over the sear of salt water, I pushed into my palms. Dry grass scratched my hands as I hoisted myself up.

I have to get to her.

I wiped my mouth on my sleeve and blinked, clearing the bite of the ocean from my eyes. I scanned the rough landscape for any sign of them.

A barren field of rock and brown turf sharpened and stretched out towards a horizon broken by a single, black jagged mountain.

Hot air gusted around my shoulders and dried my hair and skin. Brimstone filled my every breath.

A lump settled in the base of my throat.

Vigridr.

He brought us to Vigridr.

Pop!

Fenrir, Falael, and Golda smacked in a flurry of elbows and knees against the parched turf next to me, hacking and choking up water.

Vibrations pulsed up my legs and down my fingertips. My chaos hummed as if Vigridr itself charged my element, sparked my blood, heated my sinew, and coaxed my fire, already tossing within my ribs, to come out and play.

I swallowed it down. Then pressed it down deeper.

"You feel it, don't you?" Jormungand's voice sliced through the still behind me. "Vigridr calls to you. Ragnarok calls."

I turned.

My stomach clenched.

Jorg stood back in his human form, his long fingers wound tight in Sigyn's mop of red curls. He wrenched back her head, pulling her neck taut, revealing all that vulnerable flesh he pressed the edge of a knife against.

I dropped my hands to my daggers at my hips, and steel rushed against leather as I pulled them out of their sheaths.

Jorg clucked his tongue and crushed the blade harder into her thrashing pulse. Falael lunged, but Fenrir and Golda held him back.

"Let her go," Falael said.

"I wouldn't do that if I were you," he said.

His eyes blazed yellow. Burned. Boiled. My son was gone, replaced by a monster only craving blood.

Sigyn struggled against Jorg, trying to stomp on his toes and kick his shins.

"Get off me, you bastard!"

"This one has fight in her." He tugged her hair again, making her hiss. "I see what Father likes about you."

I stalked to the right, keeping my distance. His gaze followed my every step. My palms pulsed against my hilts as

I calculated every move, every angle. He could not have her, and I also could not hurt Jorg. Otherwise I would have had a throwing knife already wedged between his eyes. But him being my son made things complicated...

"Release her," I warned.

Falael continued to hurl curses and threats at Jorg. I was glad they held him back. Now was not the time to let emotions best us.

I assessed whether to leap quickly or close in slowly. Evaluated what speed I'd need to reach him and rip his knife away. My muscles tightened with every passing second realizing he'd always slit her throat first.

"Finally, I have your attention," he said. "You just needed the proper motivation."

"Do not test me," I said.

"And don't you test me!" he shouted. "I'm tired of waiting. Waiting for you to ever follow through on *anything*. You want Ragnarok, you don't want Ragnarok. Back and forth, round and round, whatever you feel this second, whatever you change it to the next. And we are just supposed to accept. To go along with your excruciating moods. Your petty whims. You selfish prick. Not today. You started Ragnarok, and now you're going to finish it."

He motioned behind us.

A flash of light. A crack like lightning striking earth. The earth quaked.

We turned.

A crooked, dead tree no taller than myself stood encased in fire. Crackling and spitting flames coated gnarled and craggy branches and shot down the notched trunk.

I narrowed my eyes, peering through a knot of charred twigs. Something fleshy thumped snarled in brambles.

I stepped back.

It was a heart.

Wet and real.

The story had all been *real*. And I knew what he wanted.

"Your chaos, your element, makes you the only being in all the Nine Worlds capable of removing that heart from that tree," Jorg said. "Wake Surtr."

I lengthened and grounded my footing.

"I won't."

He bared his teeth.

"You can't keep putting this off," he said. "Ragnarok is happening. The worlds are already ripping apart at their seams. They are dissolving into ash. And your stalling just draws out the suffering of millions. They writhe in pain. Agony swallows them."

My palms started to sweat against my hilts.

"I already told you. No."

Jorg stiffened his arm, ready to pull the blade through Sigyn's neck.

"Not even for her?"

Sigyn gave a rasped laugh.

"You have lousy leverage," she said. "Why save my life just to see it ended in Ragnarok?"

He smiled, as if she asked exactly what he wanted.

"Ah, but there will be survivors of this final battle. The Elect. The chosen few will enjoy the new world Ragnarok will give them. *You* will give them. A land of beauty, peace—"

"Elect?" I interrupted.

I wanted to slap the smirk off his face.

"And once again, I have your attention," he said. "Sigyn can be one of them. The Elf, too, if it pleases you. You can spare them both from burning in wrath and woe. They can live without fear of bloodshed. Without fear of death," he said. "All you have to do is take out the heart, wake Surtr, and fulfill your destiny as the Destroyer."

Chaos stirred my insides, loving his words. I hung off of each one tugging at me to give in. To do it. To accept this was the only option.

I looked at Falael fighting to pull free of Fenrir's hold. Panic filled his usually calm eyes. Anger warped the smooth lines of his face, turning him into a pitiful creature.

But beneath all that churned fear.

Fear because what he had warned us all back in Alfheim had been right.

As much as I hated admitting it, our every decision, our every twist we took, every turn we made, shot us right into all Ragnarok wanted. What was ambiguous had become bitterly plain.

Each action led directly to this moment. It had all been inevitable.

Surtr will be woken, and it will be by your hand.

I turned back to the tree and faced my fate. Hot wind ripped at my hair. Tore at my clothes.

Sparks and cinders and ash.

All I wanted.

Now all I wanted to stop.

The heart pumped fresh and clean, as if carved out of Gullveig's chest seconds before. Need filled me. My chaos raged, pulling me towards its beckoning whispers.

A million threads unraveled in my mind, racing and weaving together into a web of ways. Of outs. The threads spiraled and twisted, running along different levels and through cogs and wheels and I followed each to its solution. Each ended in failure.

I pulled out more threads. Knitting them together. Knotting them into nets. Searching for loopholes. Possibilities.

This can't be how it ends.

I held out my hands inches from the white and blue blaze licking the bark, assessing. Determining.

This can't be how it ends.

My head throbbed as the threads tangled. *What ifs* and *maybes* pulled them taut to the point of snapping.

"There's no point in fighting anymore," Jorg said. "Wake Surtr."

I smiled.

I saw a way.

Bold. Brash. A chance.

One chance.

I smiled wider.

I shoved my arm into the entwined branches. The twigs caught on my sleeve and scratched across my knuckles. I reached even deeper towards the heart. The fire stormed up to the crook of my arm.

My skin prickled.

This was power.

Pure power. Violent. Unflinching. Merciless.

Dark.

And it was mine.

"Loki, no!" Sigyn shouted. "Don't do what he wants."

Fenrir released Falael, and both raced to stop me. A wall of fire burst out of the ground and circled around me and the tree. Surtr protected me. Protected itself.

They both jumped back, shielding their eyes from the light and the heat.

Golda remained planted in place, her face enthralled as if at the theater enjoying an acrobatic act.

I caught their gazes through the flames. Terror bled through their eyes.

But it was the only way. To save Sigyn. To save everyone. To stop Ragnarok.

"I know..." I said. "But you must trust me."

But why should they, knowing who I was? The God of Lies. The Trickster. The Destroyer. And I was going to fulfill my destiny.

Trust was a big ask.

I looked back at the heart.

And I took it, slick and cold beneath my touch.

My chaos boiled in my core as I grasped the heart harder, burning me into coal. My element liked what I felt shooting up my fingers. Up into my arms. My body. My soul. And it hungered for more. And Surtr promised me more. It promised me everything.

One chance.

I yanked the heart out of the tree.

A surge of power kicked me in the chest with each staccato pulse drumming against my palm. I hissed as everything in me blistered and crackled. Dark matter seethed down my veins to my elbow. It flooded my arteries. Spiraling. Tempting. Enthralling...

My muscles shook, wanting me to drop it.

I tightened my grip.

It whispered.

Murmurs, soft breaths, purrs.

I closed my eyes, and I listened.

It told me what to do.

Sparks popped and snapped around my shoulders. My torso. In my hair.

I guess at least I would get to see that thousand foot fire giant after all.

I opened my eyes, and I knew they were full of fire. Full of my chaos.

I rotated the wrist of my free hand and called my element out, kindling a single spark of my chaos within my palm. It hummed. Glowed. Catching it between my thumb and forefinger, I held it over the heart and forced it deep inside the valves and chambers.

"I, Loki, the God of Chaos, the Breaker of Worlds, the Destroyer..." I paused. "...do wake you."

I braced myself.

The heart only thumped like the pathetic lump of flesh it was. Nothing.

Nothing?

"I think it might be broken," I said.

The wall of fire circling me extinguished. The tree followed.

Then a hush.

Then a million voices babbling and shouting and screaming all at once.

The heart shattered.

Shards of raw element glinted like polished black stone as it writhed and starved.

Surtr.

Jorg's mouth opened as he stared at the cloud swarming like flies, and his arms fell slack at his sides. Sigyn slipped free and raced to Falael, who caught her in his embrace.

Fenrir stepped back from the roiling element, Sigyn and Falael doing the same.

Higher Surtr rose, twisting and snaking as it floated in the air over our heads.

Golda walked towards it.

"Don't go near it!" I shouted.

She spread out her arms.

Surtr shot right for her and swirled around her in a vortex of glittering tendrils. She opened her mouth and darkness entered her. Drove into her nostrils. Filled her. Her eyes burned black. Surtr filled her to the brim.

The fine lines covering Golda's skin smoothed. Her short hair lengthened, twisting into a thick braid of chestnut that fell past her hips now swathed in purple silks. Coal lined her eyes, and an absorbing fierceness infused into the square and youthful features of her face.

Golda was a consuming völva teeming with ancient secrets and lethal knowledge.

She gave a small belch, a shiver, and chuckled admiring her new set of sharpened fingernails so clear they resembled glass. She stroked her furs around her shoulders.

"What the—" Fenrir whispered.

Golda clapped her left hand over the center of her chest and stars filled her large eyes.

"You never quite get used to the rush of Surtr flowing in your veins," she said. "And to feel my heart beat again. It's true what they say. You only appreciate something when it's ripped out of you."

"*Your* heart?" Sigyn asked.

Her perfect, full lips pulled into a wry smile.

It hit me. What it all meant. Who she really was.

She was *so* dead for all this.

"She is Gullveig."

The blast of the Gjallarhorn shook the ground and rocked the air, and with it, rumbled the sounds of coming war.

The final sign of Ragnarok had come to pass.

21

STIFF UPPER LIP

Satisfaction twisted her mouth into a smile that made me want to crush her windpipe all the more.

"Sorry..." she squeezed the word, drawing it out. "I suppose I should have mentioned that, but I couldn't risk any more hiccups until after I was reunited with my heart. Until after I had my powers restored."

She closed her eyes and took in a breath, as if savoring the snap of energy I felt flooding out of her.

"It's been damn tedious organizing all this," she said. "Astral projection is a bitch when your powers have been cut to bare shreds. All those meetings you and I had...took me days to recover after each one."

Oh. She was doubly dead now.

"You're the spirit that's been yammering in my head all this time?"

Deviousness fluttered within her gaze.

"Honey, you don't know the half of it."

I had to hear this.

"Explain." I pointed my right dagger at that delicate spot between her collarbones.

Excitement brightened the lines of her face as she brushed it away.

She stepped a bare foot to the right and started circling me. Her purple gown and furs trailed behind her, snagging on the blanket of dead grass.

"It was me who created the prophecy of Ragnarok that drove you to the path I wanted," she said. "It was me who sent you those headaches and warnings all those centuries ago, so you'd finally seek me out. The one god I was most eager to meet."

"Why me?"

She chuckled, continuing to circle me. Every step she took split the earth beneath her toes.

"When I first took Surtr into me, I thought I could start Ragnarok on my own. I failed."

"Surtr's powers not what they are all cracked up to be?" I said. "Or, are you just too weak to wield it on your own?"

She stopped and leaned in to me. A second of hatred flashed in her black eyes as she stared me down.

"I'm the most powerful sorceress that has ever lived," she said. "I was the only one to ever steal an element. In making myself a god. I became darkness itself."

"Then why do you need me?"

Her anger weakened, a coyness taking root in its place.

"Because, I discovered there was more to Ragnarok than just a snap of the fingers. Dark matter is meaningless by itself. It needs to be ignited. Woken. Only chaos, pure change, can give it the spark it needs to explode."

She reached out and cupped my cheek. Heat crackled beneath her palm. I shoved her off me.

"Of course, after my failed attempt, your mother got suspicious."

I chuckled.

"I'm sure she saw you were nothing but rotten shark meat."

Her eyes narrowed.

"Laufey and Bor found out my plans for Ragnarok and stopped me. But not before I ensured your birth. The chaos I needed to finish my work." A smirk tightened her features, turning her beauty ugly. "The satisfaction when I told her what the child in her belly would become as she took out my heart...It was glorious."

The novelty wore off.

I lunged at her. She waved her hand and a punch of magic struck me like a brick wall in the stomach and threw me back.

I hit the ground hard, my joints and muscles burning as I tried to catch the breath she knocked out of me.

Golda stood over me and laughed.

"Love that rage in you!" she said. "Your chaos is perfect, as I've always told you. As I ensured it would be. I know the truth is painful, but once I drive my sword into that mountain, the heart of Vigridr, it will all be over."

She unsheathed *Lævateinn* from her hip and the steel sang.

Victory washed over her and she grinned as flames shot down the blade that lengthened into a sword.

Surtr's flaming sword.

I stood and squared my shoulders.

"That's why you wanted my mother's dagger," I said.

Her eyes snapped to mine and her expression hardened, as if I'd flung her an exceptionally rude insult.

"*My* dagger. *My* weapon. *My* wand," she corrected. "*Lævateinn* was mine, and Laufey stole it from me. It's how she tethered Surtr to my heart. It's how she cut my heart out of my body. *Lævateinn* was the only blade capable of such magic. Luckily for me, she gave the blade to you. Stupid bitch. I promised her one day you'd come to me and finish what I started. I guess she didn't believe me. But, as I told you, I *always* keep my promises."

The earth growled. Shards of rock quivered at our feet.

We all turned and looked out at the horizon.

Thousands of warriors marched towards us, coating the barren hills in black armor, spears, and horses. Skeletons, corpses, and all of Hel's battle hardened elite soldiers and all the dead of the worlds struck their shields with the hilts of their swords, filling the sky with thunder.

Leading the charge riding a fantastic white stallion was Hel.

I smiled.

Right on schedule.

Hel thrust out her right, skeletal arm covered in black chain mail and halted her army.

Leaving them behind, she galloped out to us. She tugged the reins, stopping her horse, and swung her leg over its back and dismounted in one elegant swoop.

Her hair was pulled back into a severe braid that matched her equally severe expression. It really showed off the two distinct halves of her face, that of dark angel and the other of death.

The grass crunched with every step she took towards us, and her tight leather armor snapped. Her metal breastplate caught the red light, its bursts of glare stinging my eyes.

A sensational thrill shot down to my toes.

Just where I wanted her.

She stopped. Dry wind blew clouds of brown dust through the space separating us.

"Hel! Wonderful to see you again." I brushed soot off my

shoulders. "And look! You've brought a few of your friends. Marvelous."

Her soldiers growled and drooled behind her in the distance. Her horse beat the dirt with its hoof, impatient for the final battle to begin. Poor beast. I knew what it suffered. I was quite impatient as well.

But all good things come to those who wait.

"As promised," she said, smoothing away a lock of hair from her perfect, living left cheekbone.

Her gaze trailed from me to Jorg. A smile tugged at the decaying corner of her mouth. She raced to him and embraced him.

Warmth twanged my heart seeing my children reunited again.

She pulled back and looked at Fenrir. She smiled wider.

"Fenrir," she said. "Why do you stay so far away? Come and give me a hug. I've waited long for this day to see you both again."

She took a step towards Fenrir. Jorg grabbed her wrist and stopped her.

"He sides with Father," Jorg said.

"And Father sides with us," she said, pulling her arm free.

Jorg chuckled.

"Well, it seems Father has changed his mind," he replied. "As always."

Hel snapped her gaze to mine. My insides turned frigid from the disappointment filling her eyes. She could always cut you to the bone with a single, demolishing look.

"You barter for my army and then don't even want it anymore?" she said. Cruelty settled in her features. "Typical you."

"I will not let you down." Golda stepped forward.

"And who are you?" Hel demanded.

Golda smiled. Vicious and wicked.

"I am Surtr. And I am the way. I am salvation."

Gods.

Hel threw me the dirtiest of looks, faced Golda, and beamed at her.

"Then I offer my legions to you," she said. "It will be an honor—"

"Where is lover boy?" I interrupted. "I thought you'd take this opportunity to show Balder off. You've not broken him already, have you?"

She sneered.

"You sent me Balder's soul. He is mine. He stays in Eljudnir."

Another fantastic rush swept between my shoulder blades and down my spine.

And it wasn't just from the lovely image of Balder chattering alone in the dank chill of her frigid palace. I'm sure that mist did nothing for the bounce in his hair he so adored.

"Quite right," I said. "Can't risk having that beautiful face scarred by some errant blade. Glad to see you take good care of your possessions."

Golda stretched her neck and shoulders.

"Odin nears," she said. "And so does reckoning. Prepare for battle."

The sky darkened, turning an even deeper shade of blood. Wind picked up and the stench of brimstone thickened.

Hel looked behind my shoulder at Fenrir.

"Join us, Fenrir," Hel said. "Don't make the same mistake as Father by being on the wrong side of this war. Please."

Fenrir stiffened from the entreaty filling that last word.

Fenrir stepped next to me. His jaw flexed and sweat glistened through the dirt smeared across his forehead.

He looked her in the eye.

"But I'm not on the wrong side," he said.

Hel scoffed.

"You really align yourself with the gods?" she spat. "This is our moment, Brother, and you so dishonor it?"

Fenrir squared his shoulders.

"I have no taste for blood. I hate war," he said. "But I will do what I must to stop you both from taking the lives you hunger for."

Sigyn stepped on my other side. Wind rippled through her hair and she lowered her chin. Her stance was firm and dripped determination.

"As will I," she said.

"And me," Falael followed, planting his heels beside her. His usually soft and welcoming expression hardened into steel and danger.

I was almost impressed with him.

Laughter burst out of Golda's lungs.

"Four against thousands," she said. "Have you not noticed how very outnumbered you are?"

Leather squealed as I squeezed my dagger hilts at my sides.

"Those are my favorite odds," I said.

Golda chucked and held out *Lævateinn* and started walking towards the mountain, the heart of Vigridr behind us.

Ash fell from the sky.

I stepped in front of her, blocking her path.

Her laughter ceased.

"Out of my way," she said. "We have a universe to

destroy, and the fun of you thinking you can stop it is wearing thin."

Sad she felt that way. Because for me, the fun was just beginning.

"I have to admit, I really thought you'd be larger," I said. "And a smidgeon more powerful."

Her nostrils flared.

Clumps of ash collected in our hair and on the tops of our shoulders.

"I'm the most powerful entity in existence!"

She made to pass me again. Fire crackled down *Lævateinn's* length to the lethal tip.

And again, I stepped in front of her.

"Well, for the *most powerful entity in existence*, it must be a great burden knowing all your power is wrapped up inside a bit of twitching flesh. How tragic it would be if someone were to rip your heart out again."

A fan of sparks sputtered around us.

"You speak nonsense." Her breath was hot on my skin. "You woke Surtr and now it flows free through my veins."

I smiled.

"True, I woke Surtr, but I didn't free Surtr from that heart of yours."

Her left eye twitched.

"What?"

"Freeing was never part of the deal. All you said was 'wake.' Surtr remains trapped inside your heart. It remains tethered, just as Mother intended. Pity when we forget to mention the specifics."

Her teeth flashed white and she tightened her grip on her sword, digging her pointed fingernails into the leather hilt.

"What have I to fear?" she said. "Especially when your

weapons cannot hurt me. Especially when soon your own element will scorch this battlefield to cinders."

She swung *Lævateinn* and pointed the tip directly over my chest. The fire consuming the steel warmed my cheeks, but it was nothing to the chaos and fire burning my insides, fighting me to set it loose.

"Your chaos wants out," she said. "It wants to unleash the destruction it was made for. You can't stop it, like you can't stop me."

Embers popped beneath my palms against my hilts. Cinders crinkled between my fingers.

I had to keep it in.

I didn't know if I could.

"When will you accept the truth?" she said. "There is only one way out of this. Death."

Golda's legs lengthened, her torso and arms followed. We all craned our necks following her, growing taller and taller. Her skin split and cracked, creating a web of molten fractures. Lava dripped off her shoulders and shins in heavy globs of hissing yellow. They pummeled the grass, scorching into the earth and saturating the air with smoke below her thirty-two foot frame.

Huh.

Impressive.

Not quite the thousand foot behemoth I hoped for, but maybe that was for the best.

"We are finished," Fenrir said.

We all stepped back. It seemed the reasonable thing to do, given the dropping coal and charred chunks falling off of Golda's elbows.

"Don't worry," I said. "I've been in stickier situations."

Sigyn threw me a look like I said I had a troupe of waltzing puppies.

"Stickier in which way?" she said.

Another rumble came from behind us. What now?

Golda smiled, sending another storm of fire pelting us and searing our clothes.

I turned.

Odin rode out ahead of a storm of gods and horses and legions and legions of warriors straight from Valhalla.

Thor rode by his side. As did Freya and Freyr. Njord, Tyr, Sif, Braggi...Even Skadi came wearing her best scowl and swung a morning star. All of the gods and goddesses.

Armor flashed and swords gleamed next to heavy battle axes and sleek bows already nocked with arrows. His army stretched to the horizon where the barren landscape met the sky.

Not days before I wanted to see all their skulls crushed and brains scattered across this field like scrambled eggs. And now, I was on their side.

Funny how life can be sometimes. Hilarious.

Odin stopped next to me along with Freya and Thor. White foam lined his horse, Sleipnir's, mouth. Freya unsheathed her sword and Thor's biceps threatened to burst out of his armor as his grip pulsed on Mjolnir's handle. They, and all the gods, looked up at Golda.

"Nice of you to finally join us," I said. "As you can see, things are going well."

"What in all that is holy did you do?" he asked me. Soot already collected in the dense whiskers of his beard.

"I know, I'm disappointed too. I thought Surtr would be bigger."

"Odin." Her breath gusted over us. Hot. Damning. "Son of Bor. I've waited for this day. Prepare your souls. Finally, all you gods will die and your evil will finally be stopped. Today is judgement."

Odin pushed out his broad chest and lengthened his body packed with muscle. He glared at her with fierce bravery, but I saw the truth. Beneath his armor, beneath his raw magnificence stood a five year old boy staring his death in the face.

Everything he gave his entire life to prevent.

He narrowed his gaze and brandished his great spear, the tip razor sharp.

"The battle isn't won yet," he growled.

Formidable a weapon as Gungnir was, it looked stupid next to Golda and her flaming sword. Like trying to jab an extremely irritated grizzly bear with a toothpick.

Golda laughed, and another roll of heat hit us.

Thor gripped Mjolnir.

Hel pulled out her long sword.

Both armies gripped their weapons, awaiting the order to charge.

"Let Ragnarok begin."

22

IT'S A BEAUTIFUL DAY IN VIGRIDR

S weat. Sulfur. Metal scraping metal.

Smoke stung my eyes. The tang of blood filled my lungs. Screams pounded my ears.

Screams of the dying. Screams of the winning.

And I loved every second as I cut and stabbed my way through Hel's legions.

It wasn't every day one had the chance to fight in the war of the literal apocalypse. In all my millennia of life, this was definitely a highlight.

Though the continual nagging pulse of my chaos threatening to burst out of me was a bit of a buzzkill.

And it kept growing stronger.

I swallowed it back down for the fifth time.

Sweat collected at my temples. Time ran thin, and I still had a fire giant to kill.

I stabbed a corpse in the face and leapt onto a boulder. I looked out over a clanging jumble of steel and bone as swords sliced open bowels, spears impaled guts, and arrows gouged eyes.

I squinted, trying to lessen the sting of smoke.

There!

Across the field, Golda butchered entire units of Valhalla warriors with a single thrust of her flaming sword, leaving lines of fire and gobs of searing flesh in its wake.

To her right, Frey led a second charge beside Njord, crashing their army through a wall of shields and spears.

To her left, a thousand bows groaned as Freya's unit nocked arrows and stretched back bowstrings. Freya shouted the order to fire.

A stream of arrows shot at Golda, turning the sky black with lines of wood and sharp points.

Each plinked off her and rained to the ground, immediately trampled into splinters beneath the heavy boots of the soldiers attacking her ankles and legs with swords and maces.

Not a scratch. Not even a tickle.

This might be harder than I thought, which suited me just fine.

It wouldn't be any fun if it were easy.

I jumped off the rock and rejoined Falael and Sigyn, who fought only feet away from me.

"Gargh!" a brutish soldier yelled behind me, striking his sword at my throat.

I spun around and locked blades with him, blocking his blow. He thought he could sneak up behind me, the dear.

I twisted my right arm with his muscular one. He tried to tug free. Not today, poor thing.

A firm yank and I pulled him against my chest and sank my blade in his neck, slicing through his trachea. He crumpled and his blood rushed between my fingers.

Cinders and ash crackled within the hot breeze.

Falael swung two swords, massacring a dozen warriors in a tempest of clean slices and artful precision. A flick of the wrist. A wave of the arm. Down fell eight more. He made slaughter an elegant dance.

Sigyn grunted as she blocked the sword of a gnarled soldier with half a face. She forced his arms up. She lunged, ramming her knife between his ribs. It brought a smile to my face, and a bit of a flush between my legs.

Vigridr quaked beneath my feet.

Clouds darkened and churned. The wind growled, riling up the drifting ash and embers choking the air.

Thor stomped across the field, striking heads clean off shoulders and shattering tibias and femurs with his hammer. Lightning sputtered over Mjolnir's blood-stained steel, and electricity sparked the atmosphere.

He jumped, face washed with glee, eyes white with his element of thunder, and lifted Mjolnir over his head. Three of Hel's warriors looked at him rising over their heads. Their eyes widened. They shoved and scrambled over each other, trying to get out of the way. It was too late. Thor hurtled towards them, swinging his hammer.

A storm of crunching skulls and squishing flesh rang out through the clang of swords and battle. Lightning bolts followed, cracking and splitting the earth.

Twenty streams of scorching blue and purples struck around me. A small axe whizzed towards my chest, thrown by a soldier missing a nose. I snatched it out of the air and hurtled it back through ricocheting lightning, cleaving it between his eyes.

Thor laughed fracturing hips and singeing hair, keeping the entire battle flashing in and out of whites and rifts of thunder. He leapt over Tyr, whacking his sword across the guts of the ones still standing.

Tyr caught sight of Fenrir punching a woman with a split lip and planting his boot into the chest of a man. Even now he couldn't bring himself to kill if it could be avoided. Fenrir glanced at Tyr. A second of acknowledgment. A flicker of a smile.

I dragged my left dagger through tendons and cut down branches of arteries with my right dagger.

I ignored the gnawing rage of my chaos thrashing my insides to come out.

Odin jumped next to me, his hair slick with blood and sweat and grime. If this had been any other time, I would have laughed at the piece of intestine stuck in his beard.

"You just had to summon Surtr," he barked over the cries of dying warriors. He swung his spear and dropped four men in a row, butchering them with a single blow.

"I think a thank you is in order," I said.

"How is that?"

I grabbed the arm of another racing me and flung him on his back and skewered my dagger in his chest. A second one rushed me to my left. He stopped. Blood dribbled out of his mouth. He fell to his knees, sliding off of Falael's blade who stood behind him.

Damn. He just had to butt in. Now I owed him a favor.

Another axe spun by. And an eyeball.

"I had to ensure Hel came to Vigridr." I threw a small knife into the liver of a soldier wielding a lance. I took out a second knife strapped beneath my pant leg. "Waking Surtr was the only way to save everyone."

"Why?"

I ducked, just missing a spinal column flying over my head. That was a failing of having an army of corpses. Not much held them together.

"If you haven't noticed, Hel is rather distracted and her entire army is here, leaving Balder alone back in the under-world. *Quite* alone," I said. "Not only that, but I ensured

Surtr remain tethered to that heart. It's a neatly wrapped little present we can—"

"Don't you dare say it..." Odin jabbed his spear into a woman's mouth and out the back. He retracted, spun, butted one in the chin and flayed open a third. Impressive.

"—take directly to Balder where he can crush Surtr. The way I see it, instead of taking Balder to Surtr, we take Surtr to Balder. We just have to cut the heart out of a smoldering lava monster with a mild temper."

A head flew past. The rest of the warrior followed as Thor catapulted him with a solid hit with Mjolnir.

"Is that all?"

"Yep," I said. "That should do the trick."

"And how do we accomplish this?" Sigyn cut her sword into the shoulder of a soldier. Blood sprayed out, drenching her face and soaking into her clothes.

I couldn't help being aroused even more. That woman always could make me go weak at the knees.

"I'm working on it." I wedged my blade into a warrior's forehead, scraping against thick bone. "The important thing now is to keep Golda away from the mountain. It will buy us the time we need until we can get her heart out and get it to Balder to defeat."

I wrenched my dagger out.

I cringed. My fire started to escape through my right fingertips and travel down the steel in a thin sheet of blue flames.

Not good.

I rammed my elbow into the nose of a snarling soldier as we fought our way towards Golda. Odin sent his ravens to alert Freya and Thor of the change in plans.

"This is madness," he said.

"Madness is all we have."

We split off. I jumped over a swing of a broad sword and felt the whoosh of a morning star brush my temple as I swerved, narrowly missing its deadly punch.

I hated how fatigue started to work on me.

Worse, I felt my hold on my chaos slip.

The closer we got, the more my chaos broke through my cracks. My fire raced out of my right hand. My knuckles glowed.

Fenrir's eyes flashed between his normal green and the gold of the wolf.

The wolf fought him with the same ferocity my chaos fought me.

Golda towered over the legions attacking her, slashing through hundreds with a single cut. Laughter boomed out of her lungs and lava dripped off her sides and doused the warriors below her, scalding them into charcoal.

My chaos lashed and snapped inside my ribs, loving how they all burned. Gorging on how they all died. I was no longer my element's master, it was mine, and it would destroy along with Surtr...

Time ran thinner.

My chaos would escape. Erupt. And when it did...

I knew what I had to do.

I ran towards Falael, bursts of lightning striking on all sides of me.

I wove around soldiers locked in steel. I dashed between rearing horses. The earth trembled as more lightning blazed. I lowered my head as Mjolnir flew clear across the battlefield and plowed down a group of twenty soldiers.

A warrior swung a mace at me. I slid beneath the spiked ball and stabbed her in the back of the leg. She fell, and I hacked into her sternum. Bits of skin and sinew flew into my hair.

Falael fought viciously to my right. A warrior raced behind him. He didn't notice.

I lunged and locked my arm around the soldier's left arm, and sliced my other blade through their throat, dropping them and saving Falael's life.

Good. We were even again. I hated owing anyone a favor.

He turned and looked at me, his mouth slightly open.

"I know, you're welcome." I flicked a thumb off my shoulder. "You need to take Sigyn and get out of here."

I stepped to the left and jabbed my dagger into the armpit of a warrior. Falael stepped to the right and sliced open a corpse.

We faced each other again. He pulled in heaving breaths and soot and blood smeared his cheeks and his once pristine sweater.

"No," he said. "We do this together."

I held out my right hand to him. The flames glazing my skin washed his face in yellow.

He understood.

"I can't control my element anymore," I said. "It's breaking out of me and...and I will not be the reason Sigyn or you lose your lives today."

A horse barreled towards us, leaping over gods and warriors. I grabbed the reins, stopping the beast and pulled the soldier off the saddle and snapped their neck.

I held out the reins to Falael.

"Take the horse and take her."

He shook his head

"She won't leave you."

I held his gaze.

"Falael...If you love her, you will take her away."

I held out the reins closer to his hands.

The corners of his mouth pulled taut.

Falael took the reins and mounted the horse.

Good.

Turning, I shoved warriors out of the way and raced towards Sigyn.

Sigyn pulled her sword out of the bowels of a man with clouded eyes. She spun and faced me, so close I could smell her breath over the brimstone.

Cinders spiraled around her. Lightning lit her face in quivering shades of white with each bolt pummeling the land around us. Blood sprinkled her cheeks and stained her chin. It only brightened her brown eyes.

Soot and sweat covered her lips and I hungered to taste them.

To kiss her one final time and lose ourselves within the cries of the dying and roar of battle.

I grabbed her wrist instead and pulled her towards Falael.

"What are you doing?" she tugged back.

"You need to go with Falael."

She dug her heels into the slick gore that had turned the dirt into mud.

"I'm staying. You need us."

Emotion pricked my insides. I wanted her to stay...

"I won't let you die because of me."

A stream of arrows whizzed past our ears and skimmed our sides. They struck at least thirty men that dropped around us.

She beat against my chest as I dragged her over their bodies.

My throat burned.

She cursed me as I hoisted her off her feet and up to Falael. He held her securely in front of him on the horse, avoiding her punches and slaps. He kicked the animal's sides.

The beast reared back and took off.

Everything in me tightened as they disappeared into the battle, leaving me behind to stop what I started.

I turned and looked at Golda. She continued stomping towards the mountain. She was only paces away from her mark that hungered for the pierce of her blade.

She kicked Odin's warriors and spit flames over their heads.

I started after her, cutting a hard right away from the throng of soldiers, trying not to think of Sigyn and how I'd likely never see her again.

A boiling rage blistered every inch of me at Golda.

She was responsible for all of this.

I ran through patches of dead grass, gaining on Golda.

I would get that heart. I would get it to Balder.

And I would end her.

I zagged left, back into the battle. Charging her, I was feet away from her heels...

I took out my dagger.

I just needed one solid leap. One firm thrust...

Fenrir screamed.

I stopped and looked out across the field.

Fenrir buckled over, grinding his fingers into his stomach. His shoulders popped out of their sockets. His back arched. His body thrashed as his muscles seized and convulsed. His clothes tore. His skin sprouted black hair. Thick hair.

His eyes glowed vibrant gold.

Shit.

The wolf had won.

And he kept growing.

And growing.

His frame blotted out the sun and drool dripped out of his jowls that could crush any man.

His eyes narrowed, and he sniffed the air. A deep growl shook in the back of his throat.

He turned his gaze, sharp and deadly, on Odin who fought against one of Hel's generals.

Cold sweat ran down my back.

In a second Fenrir leapt over the battling soldiers, pounding his paws into the turf, racing towards Odin. I followed, cutting down anyone that stood in my way.

Odin turned, he grounded his heels and held out his spear. I couldn't read his face, but I knew his insides churned. This was all he feared, and it looked right at him.

Fenrir roared, flinging Odin back and covering him in spittle. Odin grunted striking a rock and his spear flew out of his grip and landed in a pile of dead men, just beyond his reach.

A twist of pleasure rippled through my veins.

Fenrir lowered his muzzle and leaned in to Odin, his breath tussling his hair and clothes like a gust of wind. There it was! A spark of panic. A glint of terror in Odin's eye.

I drank it down like a bottle of fine wine.

A dark desire lit my blood and a smile tugged at my lips.

This was everything I wanted.

Odin was going to die.

And it would be beautiful.

Just.

But I wouldn't let Fenrir become the killer he swore to never be.

I had made him a promise. And I would keep it.

Fenrir opened his mouth. I rushed in front of Odin and put out my arms to Fenrir, stopping him.

"His life is mine," I warned. "You can't have him."

Fenrir snarled and snapped. Hot breath beat my cheeks with each indignant snort.

"Back away."

My eyes blazed with my fire now, reflecting back at me in Fenrir's golden irises.

I stepped towards him, staring him down. Not giving him an inch.

"Back away..."

Mjolnir zoomed in front of Fenrir's nose. His golden eyes followed the shining steel as it shot back to Thor's hand somewhere in the far distance. Fenrir took off at a run, chasing it, crunching corpses and warriors beneath his paws with every heavy step.

I guess Thor was in for a surprise.

And soon were we...

Golda was steps away from the mountains and the center of Vigridr. A firestorm hurtled smoldering rock and coal over Freya's archers.

I picked up Odin's spear and threw it to him. He caught it and started to speak. I'm sure it was going to be something disgustingly appreciative.

"Before you get any notions of mercy, I spared your life for Fenrir, not for you," I said. "Now, if you excuse me...I have a heart to rip out."

I took off, leaving him behind and stalked towards Golda, my daggers out and ready to slice into her chest.

My blood thundered in my ears.

Her toes touched the base of the mountains, stomping an entire unit of Valhalla's best into a warrior puree.

"Hey, you molten asshole!" I screamed. "I'm not finished with you yet!"

She turned her head and looked down at me. A crackling laughter surged out of her lungs.

"You still think you have a chance?"

"As long as I have breath I have a chance."

She laughed again, darts of embers falling from her lips.

"I told you you can't run from your fate. You want to burn them..."

My chaos stormed within my core, violent and starving. It hacked at my insides, splitting me open. Shredding my flesh.

She called to it, and it answered her.

I ground my teeth and took another step towards her...

My fire raced up both my arms.

Just a little longer...

"You want to *kill* them..."

Every muscle in my body jerked and spasmed as my blaze chewed my edges ragged. I grunted, choking down the spiral of fire seething to get out.

"You want to *destroy* them," she said.

Each word struck me. Hard. Relentless. Inescapable.

I fell to the earth. I ground my knees into the mud and blood. I clawed at the grass, pulling myself towards her.

"This is pathetic." Sparks floated in her breath. "Stop fighting your destiny."

Fire bled from my palms. Fire shot out the soles of my feet.

The grass ignited around me and a firestorm raced towards Odin's army. Flames gorged on their armor. On their lives. They screamed.

"There is no choice in Ragnarok."

There is always a choice.

My element stilled as Sigyn's voice fluttered like a cooling hush through my seething chaos. Fidelity soothed my broiling chambers. Hope drenched me in a serene truth.

Something in me shifted.

And I knew.

My legs shook as I stood. I lengthened and squared my shoulders, taking back my power. Standing firm. Unmovable.

Golda tilted her head, and confusion burned through the molten cracks in her charred skin.

"Ragnarok isn't a lack of choice," I said. "It's a lack of hope."

I sucked my fire back into myself, extinguishing the surrounding blaze. Holding out my hands, I burst a stream of flames directly at her chest.

She bellowed and fell back, a glorious and resounding crunch of rock and her own broiled skin ringing out.

I walked towards her, an absolute inferno spinning around me, casting her in fluttering reds and yellows. Embers whipped around my shoulders, and darts of light exploded beneath my every step.

I'd missed this. The power. The potential.

"This isn't possible," she said.

I laughed, my eyes brimming with fire.

"You of all beings should know you can't predict chaos."

I lifted my dagger and forced it down towards that beautiful spot over her heart.

She scrambled back and stood. She roared and aimed her sword at my head. I jumped to the right, letting her bury the molten blade deep in the soil and missing me completely.

She tugged at the hilt, trying to wrench it free from the earth.

I loved when little opportunities presented themselves.

I shot threads of fire at her, wrapping the burning chains around her arms and ankles.

She struggled, grasping at the cascade of flames coiling around her. She ripped at the glowing cords. Tore.

I drew the lines tighter and leapt on to her. She thrashed, trying to throw me off.

I gripped my dagger and drove it into her chest.

I struck something solid and white pain shot up my arm. My Dwarven steel blade shattered into jagged pieces of worthless metal.

Well, this was bad.

She snapped the chains tying her, sending tendrils of fire lashing all around. She grabbed me by the neck and my legs flailed as I struggled for breath.

"I told you, your weapons cannot harm me."

She flung me back, and I struck the dirt hard. I choked for air. My head swam, weighing at least five bags of sand. Through the shimmering black and white dots speckling my vision, I made out Fenrir chasing Odin across the battlefield.

Jormungand twisted his serpent's tail around Thor, repeatedly bashing him against a wall of rock.

Hel cornered Freya, preparing to bring her two swords down on her.

Men fought around me, sawing the air with their swords and striking the ground a breath from my elbow. An axe blade fell between my thighs, uncomfortably close to hitting something I would really rather not lose.

A soldier with a mouth full of rotting teeth stepped over me. He swung back his mace, aiming directly for my skull. This was going to hurt. But I definitely preferred that over the other thing.

He flinched. He looked down. A steel blade stuck through his stomach. His eye twitched, and he dropped to his knees that squelched in the mud.

Falael and Sigyn stood behind him. Falael's blade dripped with blood.

Damn. That was the second time that man saved my life today.

I took Sigyn's outstretched hand, and she yanked me back to my feet.

"I told you you needed us," she said.

23

FOLLOW THE LADY

"Never send me away like that again," Sigyn snapped, pointing her finger at my nose.

"Is this really the time?"

"We agreed to do this together."

Apparently it was.

"I assure you, I have this all under control."

The field quaked. Golda stormed towards us, spewing goblets of lava from every fissure and split in her skin. She screamed, and ribbons of fire flickered out of her open mouth.

I grabbed Sigyn and Falael's arms and dove us behind a boulder as a jet of fire spewed over our heads.

"Ok, maybe I could use a little help," I said. "She is feistier than I anticipated, and apparently when she said none of our weapons can hurt her, she meant it."

I tossed aside all that remained of my broken dagger, a hilt and a bit of jagged steel. Seeing such a good blade rendered into pathetic splinters physically hurt me.

"Then how will we cut out her heart?" Falael asked.

I peeked over the edge of the stone.

More units of Valhalla warriors attacked her heels and calves. Her solid muscles shredded their spears. She stomped two men flat and kicked the third through the sky, a screaming pile of metal and fear.

Those were the lucky ones. She swung *Lævateinn* through the torsos of the rest, leaving only pairs of legs standing like trees in its wake.

She set her gaze on the mountain, and dragged her sword behind her, letting its tip split through the earth.

I couldn't believe my mother thought that a suitable weapon to give a seven-year-old boy—this was for a nine-year-old, at least. But then, I never understood why she gave me a blade named *Truth*. The irony wasn't lost on me, given my proclivities for tricks and pranks. I always figured giving me that blade was because she wanted me to wield the truth, which was a capital joke.

I scratched my head. Something poked me with all this.

But if she knew this blade was called *Lævateinn*, why tell me it was called *Truth*? Why give it to me when she knew what it was capable of...When she knew what *I* was capable of...

...and what I'd become.

I smiled.

Was it so simple?

It wasn't about changing who I was, it was about affirming who I was.

A trickster.

"I think I know a weapon that will," I said.

Golda split a warrior in two down the middle.

"You must be kidding," Sigyn said.

"My mother gave me that blade for a reason. She called it the wrong name for a reason," I said. "Because truth is a double-edged sword, and the answer is staring us blatantly in the face."

Golda swiped her sword across another unit, threshing them down like a field of wheat.

"The answer being?" Sigyn asked.

"That truth requires a trick to have any meaning," Falael said.

"Precisely."

"That's all fine and good," Sigyn said. "But just how do we get it out of her grip?" Sigyn said.

I smiled.

It all unfolded beautifully before me.

"Leave it to me. It will be quick, so be prepared to act as soon as I do it."

"Do what?"

"It won't be hard."

I jumped out from behind the boulder and raced towards her. Sigyn and Falael followed close on my heels.

Golda reached the base of the mountain again, and all that separated us from oblivion was a single thrust into the heart of Vigridr.

We had seconds.

My boots slid through the mud. Darts of lightning sputtered and flashed.

I grabbed a bow off a dead soldier and nocked an arrow between my fingers.

Thunder ripped the sky. The battlefield groaned.

I pulled back the bowstring and aimed the arrow at Golda's smoldering forearms.

She swung her sword over her head.

Two seconds.

"Loki..." Sigyn said.

She flipped the sword down, pointing the sharp tip of the blade at the center.

"Anytime would be good."

One second.

She drove the flaming sword towards the mountain...

One chance.

I moved my aim to the tip of her sword and I released the arrow.

It flew in a beautiful arc through streams of lightning and orange sparks and struck Golda's *Lævateinn*.

The blade flung out of her grasp, spinning in swirls of yellows and hot blues and landed between us.

Golda growled, and we both ran for the blade.

I reached it first and grabbed the hilt with both hands and jerked it up. The sword was at least a foot taller than me, and my muscles strained from the weight of the steel.

Golda stepped in front of me, and I swiped the tip across her chest. She laughed and seized my wrists.

I glared into her eyes, wanting her to see my hatred. To understand how far I would go.

She smiled and squeezed, grinding her fingers into my tendons, turning my breaths into sharp staccatos. My bones flexed and threatened to snap. I hardened my gaze. She squeezed tighter, forcing a grunt out of my throat. Lances of white agony shuddered up my arms.

My fingers trembled and weakened. *Lævateinn* fell at her feet.

But I refused to lower my eyes from hers. I would not turn away first.

"Did you really think that would work?" she asked. Her breath stank of brimstone.

She threw me on my side, skidding me across dirt and flesh.

She picked up the sword.

My heart pounded.

"I'm glad you can have such a good view to watch the worlds burn," she said. "Ragnarok is now finished."

She lifted *Lævateinn* and plunged it into the mountain.

Rock split as she sank the steel all the way to the hilt.

Absolute glee stretched her mouth and face.

The battle continued to rage.

Thunder rumbled without pause.

Her eyes narrowed. She scratched her head.

I stood and brushed the dirt off my shoulders, wiped the blood from my mouth, and stepped towards her.

"Why isn't this working?" she asked.

She jiggled the sword in the rock, trying to get it to blow.

"Perhaps had you paid closer attention, you would have noticed."

"Noticed what?"

"Noticed that."

I snapped my fingers, dissolving the illusion I'd cast of her sword from her hand. She clawed at the air and turned just in time to take in Falael plunging the real *Lævateinn* into her chest.

She gasped for breath and sank to her knees.

Falael cut the blade down her broiling skin, thousands of embers bursting out of her. He took out the blade, and Sigyn reached into the cavity, the fire skating over her flesh not burning even a hair on her wrist.

She wrenched back her arm and tore out Golda's beating heart.

Golda wavered and looked at the gaping hole in her chest.

"Clever," she said, her words dry and forced. "Very

clever, but not clever enough. You really think ripping it out sufficient?"

Golda stood and lurched forward. Sigyn and Falael stepped back.

The wind picked up.

Sigyn's fingers pulsed with every pump of Golda's heart in her palm.

"Only Balder can defeat me now Loki has ignited Surtr. Only Balder's element is contrary to my own. Only order can still entropy. Only light can smother darkness. And you'll never make it to him in time." Golda took another step. This one stronger. "This is Ragnarok. This is the end. There is no hope."

Sigyn's eyes fluttered. The muscles in her neck stiffened and corded. She listened, but not to Golda.

Surtr spoke to her as it had spoken to me. Telling her. Whispering. Chanting.

Sigyn snapped her gaze to Golda's.

"You know," Sigyn said.

"Know what?"

She squeezed the heart, her grip twitching with the rhythm of its pulse.

Golda jerked, as if punched in the gut. Her eyes widened, and she scratched at her chest.

"What's happening?" Golda asked, panic drenching her voice.

Sigyn took a step forward, straightening her stance.

"You know Surtr isn't inevitable. It's only the illusion of inevitability, an illusion you fed."

She clutched the heart harder, making it convulse beneath her knuckles.

"Stop!"

A perfect and divine anger radiated from Sigyn, coating

her skin in a pale blue that shimmered.

"You took away their faith," she said. "You took away their choice."

Sigyn took another step.

Golda squirmed.

"You made Loki think he lost control of his chaos."

And another step. She dug her nails deeper into the heart.

Golda clawed at her chest. Choked for air.

"You made Fenrir believe the wolf his master."

Golda fell to her knees at Sigyn's feet.

"You used Surtr to strip their hope, making it all seem inevitable, making *you* seem inevitable, but you forgot one thing."

Sigyn's eyes flashed blue, her light and element swathing all of us in its vibrance. In her absolute power.

"What?" Golda shielded her face.

A small smile fluttered across Sigyn's lips and her eyes glowed. Burned.

"I *am* hope."

Sigyn thrust her fingers into the heart's chambers.

Golda screamed as Surtr splintered and cracked within her heart. Glittering shards sprung out of the valves and wet flesh. They spun and floated up Sigyn's arms and sank into her skin, making her veins run black.

Her energy grew stronger. She radiated fidelity, dissolving the darkness in her light. Her hope feasted on Surtr.

And I realized.

We all did.

Balder wasn't the only one with a contrasting element that could stop Surtr.

Sigyn sucked the last shards into her. Drained the heart

dry, taking Surtr in and tucking the dark energy away in her bones and marrow, wrapping it in her peace. Smothering it in her hope.

The red sky turned blue and a warm sun cleared the clouds of ash and smoke.

Golda cried out as she dropped into the dead grass. She writhed and twisted, aging thirty years and returning to her normal form of a woman.

The charred crust peeled off her healed skin. Blonde hair hung over her solid shoulders. The coal rimming her eyes ran down her hollow cheeks and her red lipstick smeared her mouth and square chin.

She was no longer Surtr, she was no longer the beautiful enchantress, but the pathetic, middle-aged witch left to rot in a swamp.

She crawled towards Sigyn, digging her split fingernails into the dirt.

Sunlight warmed our skin. The dead grass beneath Sigyn's feet turned green. Became alive.

"Stop!" she croaked. "You're ruining everything."

"No," Sigyn said. "I'm giving everything a second chance."

Blue light exploded out of Sigyn.

The pulse of peace lapped over me, coating me in warmth. In tranquility. We stood on the edge of a bright tomorrow, full of joy.

Color spread across the field, racing towards the horizon, a wash of color and blossoming wild flowers.

A valley of death was now lush with life and full of potential.

Sigyn's fidelity sucked back into herself. She straightened and glanced at us, her eyes warm, but fatigued.

"You were right," she said. "That wasn't so hard."

24

A BITTERSWEET SUNSET

The battle ended as all battles end.

The victors celebrated. Singing rose out of the lungs of Odin's warriors and the more vocally talented gods. Mead splashed down knuckles in explosions of toasts, and as the toasts continued into the night, the singing grew louder. And more off key.

The losers slunk off into shadows, returning to the underworld with Hel. Jorg escaped with her. It was probably for the best. There was a lot of dust needing settled. Not everyone could take nearly being destroyed in their stride. Or understanding that sometimes powerful, dark energies occasionally take over your mind and make you do crazy things.

In the end, it was best to agree that Ragnarok had just been one big, complicated, massive misunderstanding.

But someone had to pay, and unlike the rest of us, Golda had no excuses.

Odin took her heart, freshly squeezed of every last drop of Surtr, and stuffed it into his satchel. One should never waste a good bargaining chip.

Golda hurled curses and threats as Tyr clapped her in steel shackles. Her curses grew darker. More vivid. Detailed...

But what more could she do?

A chill sparked each vertebrae of my spine.

Actually, I didn't want to think about that now.

Now was just to enjoy the fact we survived the impossible.

The inevitable.

Sigyn and Falael spoke with Fenrir, comparing close calls and near misses. He was once again himself, rugged and gentle, looking as if he'd just returned from a fine afternoon of birding in a misty forest.

Warmth coated my heart, watching Sigyn laugh as Fenrir mimed Thor's face when he stood before him holding Mjolnir in his jaws. How Thor shed buckets of tears when he swallowed it down. How Thor wasn't fast enough when Mjolnir came back up...

"Yes, when his lip gives that little tremble...sublime!" I said, stepping next to them.

"I doubt Thor will ever forgive me," Fenrir said.

"Trust me, Thor's suffered his fair amount of shame at the hands of our family, I dare say he's used to it by now," I said. "You've made me proud."

Fenrir gave me a big grin, like the kind he used to give me when he was a child and I'd surprise him with a basket of Asgardian strawberries.

And now to turn this conversation dreadfully gooey...

"I..." I rubbed the back of my neck. Why were these two words always so hard for me to say? "I want to thank you. For coming back. For helping me. I couldn't have done this without you all."

I turned to Falael. Even covered in mud and the blood of

battle, he still looked like a scrumptious amuse-bouche I wanted to shove into my mouth.

"You saved my neck back there with that sword of yours," I said. "As much as it pains me to say this, you've won the rarest of prizes of all...me in your debt."

I held out my hand to him. He chuckled beneath his breath and his eyes danced along with his smile.

"I think it is we who are in yours."

He took my hand, and we shook.

I might have made my grip a touch firmer than his. I know...

"What will you do now?" Falael asked me.

I ran my fingers through my hair, brushing out the knots and dried globs of corpse flesh.

"I really want to experience these *bars* I saw back in Midgard. They looked like exquisite things. I wouldn't mind spending a fantastic week, or month, where I don't remember a thing."

Sigyn's arms slackened at her sides.

"You're leaving us?"

I shrugged.

"With the worlds saved, there's not much else left to do," I said. "But, if you ever need me, I will always be here for you." I looked at Falael. "Both of you."

"As will we," Sigyn said.

My gaze settled on hers.

A thousand strings tangled in my chest and yanked taut, threatening to slice me into pieces. But this was the only way I could make her happy.

"It's time I go," I said, forcing the words to be strong though each wanted to break. "That rum won't drink itself."

Sadness washed over her eyes. I swallowed down hot sand and turned away.

I walked towards the setting sun, and though each step tightened and frayed every shred of myself, it was all quite simple.

I wasn't the one she needed.

"I swear, if you toss one more curse at me," Tyr groaned over Golda's string of profanities and hexes.

He shoved her into a small cart with iron bars and slammed the door shut and huffed away.

Oh. I really shouldn't...

But I never could pass up an opportunity to rub noses in failure.

I walked up to the cart and looked at her between the bars. She rolled her eyes and sat cross legged in the straw in the middle. Dirt and blood smeared her white clothes.

"Haven't you ruined my day enough already?" she said, picking a twig out of her hair tangled with mud.

I brandished *Lævateinn*, now returned to the deadliest, most beautiful dagger I ever beheld. And it was mine again.

Her eyes widened and fixated on the blade. She stretched her arm out towards it, but stopped an inch from the iron bars, careful not to touch them.

I smiled.

"I suppose my mother wasn't such a *stupid bitch* after all," I said. "It's because of her your heart is safely out of that vile chest of yours again. It was quite cunning what she did, calling *Lævateinn* by the wrong name and all."

She retracted her hand, and she scoffed.

"Too bad her resourcefulness didn't keep her from getting herself blown up in Vanaheim," she said. "What was it they found of her? A foot?"

I squeezed my hilt.

It had been a hand.

Bile burned my throat.

That day.

If only Mother had taken me with her, maybe...But I had been a child. What could I have done?

Golda's lips twisted into a smile bleeding with meanness.

"You want to kill me," she said, almost as if a dare. "Go ahead. Try."

I did. But I wouldn't.

Sheathing the blade, I gripped the iron bars and leaned in. I laughed darkly.

"And deprive the gods of their fun?" I said. "Odin has all kinds of tortures waiting for you back in Asgard, and trust me, I know how very unpleasant the gods' wrath can be. I wouldn't want you to miss that for anything."

Her face stiffened, and I enjoyed the delicious flicker of fear behind her makeup smeared eyes.

"I thought you'd understand," she said. "More than any of them."

"Why? Because of the chip on my shoulder you ensured?"

She smirked.

"Because we both trusted the gods," she said. "We both loved them."

"And what do you know of love?"

Pain settled in the lines around her mouth. She grew smaller. Fragile.

"She promised me..." her voice hitched. "I didn't ask to be set on this path."

"I didn't ask for this path either," I said. "But at least I chose to walk away from it."

I pushed off the bars, turned and started off towards the sunset.

"You think you've stopped Ragnarok," she called after me. "That you've won. But Yggdrasil's roots remain shaken."

I rolled my eyes and kept walking, shooting up my right hand and extending a certain finger that told her exactly what I thought.

25

DO NOT DISTURB

Midgard

Coronado, California

Thanks to Sigyn, the worlds had stitched themselves nicely back together. Of course, the humans on Midgard shirked off the whole Ragnarok ordeal with a myriad of reasons and theories ranging from government conspiracies to hoaxes to global warming, or that the earth simply just had a bad day. It happens.

I stretched on a cushioned lounge chair on my private deck and pulled in breaths of salt from the Pacific ocean. Opting for a three-room beach front cottage at the Hotel Del was definitely the right choice.

Excessive?

Most definitely.

But I never did anything less than excessive. And after everything, I more than deserved a bit of pampering.

The sun soaked into my skin as I laid out in a pair of red

bathing trunks and looked out at the rugged California coast. I shot back the last swallow of twenty-year old scotch and followed it with a drag of a cigarette. It was a lovely melange of tobacco, smoke, and peat moss.

Three solid knocks rapped at the door.

Right on schedule.

I had utterly decimated the packed mini bar within twenty-minutes. I drained those lovely little bottles of vodka and gin one after the next, chasing that bliss of not giving a damn.

I ordered up a bottle of whiskey. That lasted about an hour.

Living in the haze of alcohol helped me continue to convince myself I was ok.

To not think of *her*.

And there I went. Thinking of her again.

The deck was warm and rough beneath my bare feet. I walked through the wide open French doors into the living room of soft beiges and teals and dark wood floors.

I took off my aviator sunglasses and opened the door, already tasting the oak and vanilla of the bourbon I had the concierge send me.

My stomach plummeted into the depths of disappointment.

It was not my bourbon.

It was Odin.

"One of the benefits of being banished from Asgard I thought was the promise of never having to see any of you again," I said.

He smirked, crinkling the fine lines around his one eye.

"Can I come in?"

"If you appreciate your health, you'll stay outside."

"It's not for human ears."

I sighed.

"Two minutes."

He walked into the living room, and pushed his hand through his hair that fell perpetually in front of his black eyepatch.

He stood beside the couch stuffed with satin pillows. The marble countertops of the kitchen gleamed behind his solid frame.

I crossed my arms and leaned against the fireplace.

The ocean breeze tumbled around us both, rippling his blue, buttoned down linen shirt and dark khaki pants. Despite his best efforts to never try for anything past basic, he still had that rustic edge to him, as if he belonged to the sea or the forest.

"Hel has returned Balder," he said. "Amazing how accommodating one becomes after losing a war."

I frowned. I didn't think he could possibly make this surprise visit any worse. I quite liked the idea of Balder remaining in Hel until he grew a nice coat of mildew.

"Thirty seconds remain," I said. "Best spit out what truly brought you here, because I know it wasn't just to tell me that."

He dug his hand into his pocket and pulled out a golden apple and sat it on the coffee table next to a stack of magazines all about the joys of California living.

My arms fell slack at my sides.

"Is that..."

"Yes," he said. "Direct from Idunn's orchard."

I picked up the apple, my fingers gliding over the supple skin. The golden peel gleamed in the sunlight.

Such a fruit could cure any ailment of a god.

Including the ravages of five centuries of snake venom...

I met his gaze that softened and filled with wishes.

"We can never erase what happened between us," he said. "But maybe, this can be a start."

I kept staring at the fruit, barely hearing the shuffle of his footsteps headed back towards the door.

I cleared my throat.

"Don't think I've forgotten about me killing you," I said.

He turned and faced me. Calm. Accepting.

"And are you?"

I walked towards him. The sage on his clothes woke a dense web of memories. Good memories and bad. And my own wishes for it to have all been different.

"Recent events have made me feel somewhat merciful," I said. "So, no. I won't kill you. But I never want to see you again."

His lips thinned, but he nodded.

"I think that's best for us both."

He pulled on the door handle and opened the door.

A question crept out of the pockets of my mind. A terrifying question I'd locked away and wanted to keep hidden in shadows forever.

But I had to know.

"Will…"

"Will what?"

I swallowed down my fear of the answer.

"Will there be ramifications for what Sigyn did?" I said. "Will there be a price for her defeating Surtr?"

He froze.

"Elements cannot be destroyed, only transferred…" I said.

He pressed his mouth flat and his jaw flexed beneath his short beard.

"I'm afraid only time will tell," he said.

I didn't like that answer.

He walked through the door and closed it shut behind him.

I rubbed my eyes, shoving the thought back into the darkness, silencing that nagging thrum of *what if*...

I returned to the living room. The ocean waves breaking on the beach rumbled through the open French doors along with the rattling squawks of seagulls.

I held up the golden apple.

I sucked in a breath as my reflection looked back at me.

And I let my illusion fade.

My stomach twisted at what stared back. A man I didn't know. Couldn't recognize.

Didn't want to admit was me.

Thick bands of pink scars crisscrossed my chest. Long cords of marled flesh wrapped around my arms and down my legs. As for my face...well, calling it a face was a bit of a stretch.

It would take decades of my skin and sinew slowly knitting itself back together for me to resemble myself once again.

...If I didn't have the apple.

I lifted it to my lips and the scent of sweetness should have filled my nose had I had a nose.

I took a bite, the flesh giving a firm snap.

Honey and fruit and an exquisite crisp tartness filled my mouth, sending a delightful tingle down my spine. Warmth spread through my veins, relaxing my muscles.

I took another bite. And then another.

I devoured the fruit, licking the juice from my knuckles.

My knuckles that were now healed. Normal. Perfect. Just as my hands. And my arms...

I looked at the mirror hanging over the fireplace.

The scars faded into perfect skin. My hair grew in thick waves just past my shoulders, red and vibrant.

I reached up and touched my cheeks. My chin. My lips.

My nose. My perfect, pointed nose.

I was back to my old, devilishly handsome self.

Another set of knocks hit the door, breaking me from admiring myself.

I walked to the door.

"Don't make me change my mind about killing you," I said, whipping open the door.

My heart stopped.

Sigyn.

26

TOMORROW

"Hello," Sigyn said.

Cold shock froze me, and for two seconds, I forgot every word I'd ever known.

"Come in," I pushed out.

I stood to the side and let her walk in. A seersucker dress of white and blue stripes hugged her waist, and the afternoon sun outlined her in an aura of gold.

I hurried past her and went into the kitchen and took out a tumbler from the cabinet. She planted herself in the center of the French doors and stared straight outside at the Pacific.

"I thought you'd be back in Alfheim by now," I said.

I fumbled with a bottle of tonic water and poured it into the glass. I had to offer her something. Do something. Anything.

Her lips pulled into a thoughtful smile, though she kept rubbing her thumbs and forefingers against each other.

"I was, actually," she replied. "And then, I decided that's not where I wanted to be."

I twisted a slice of lemon into the tonic water. Gin. Where was the bloody gin?

"Is everything ok?" I asked.

I opened the freezer. I searched for ice. Any ice.

"I suppose that all depends on the answer I get."

I started to question her, but she slipped through the French doors and walked out onto the patio.

I grabbed the tumbler of tonic water and followed.

Wind raced over the Pacific and fluttered through her hair. She leaned over the railing and stared out at a sea that blazed blue.

If only...

I shook away such blissful thoughts and sat the glass next to her on a teak table.

"Why have you come back?" I asked, standing beside her. "Where's Falafel?"

She kept her gaze on the glittering horizon.

"After we left Vigridr, he had a talk with me about you and I. Very frank. About what he noticed."

"And what did he notice?"

She picked at her nails.

"He told me I'm true to others to a fault, but that I needed to be true to myself," she said. "I asked him what he meant. He said he saw my heart didn't truly lie with him, because it's ever only belonged to you."

She turned and looked at me, her cheeks flushed and lips pink.

My heart hammered my ribs.

"When I said what I did in Vienna, I was afraid. I was afraid to be with you because I was really afraid of losing you again."

She reached out and touched my hand. She grazed my fingertips.

"You won't lose me," I said.

I squeezed her shoulders, showing her I was here. I'd always be here.

"But I had," she said. "I found you only to lose you again to the gods and that cave. The thought of it happening again...I couldn't survive losing you a third time."

She inched closer to me and laid her hands on my chest. The bracelet I'd given her in Vienna dangled on her wrist, reflecting flashes of sunlight.

"But I realized, I couldn't survive without you more."

"What are you saying?" I asked, my skin burning where she touched.

"I want to be with you," she said. "If it's only for a breath, or for a thousand years, I want to be yours."

If only...

No. This wasn't that simple.

I cupped her face and rubbed my thumbs over her glowing cheeks. Wanting to savor this moment, to pretend, even though I knew.

"I love you, Sigyn. And I want you more than anything," I said. "But I want your happiness more, and that means not being with me."

"I don't understand."

"I am chaos, Sigyn," I said. "Calm is not in my nature. And although I'd do anything for you, give anything for you, you will not have a moment of peace with me. Falael can give you the stability your fidelity needs." I paused. "You deserve the better man."

She smiled sweetly, as if I were a fool.

"You're right, I do."

She embraced me and our lips met in a kiss.

In all my millennia of life, no kiss ever compared to that one we shared.

Pure.

Beautiful.

True.

Our mouths moved tenderly together, and she tasted of that salvation I remembered.

We pulled apart, and I leaned my forehead against hers.

I smiled and plunged my hands in her hair, winding her curls around my fingers. Remembering how I had done the same on that stormy night in Basel when we first came together.

A familiar longing lit in me.

It was more than longing.

It was necessity.

To be held. To be hers.

To be freed.

Whole.

"Will you have me?" she whispered.

I laughed gently in the crook of her neck, holding her tighter. Breathing her in. Rosemary. Saffron.

"You are all I want."

I took her lips again, and our kiss deepened with hunger. Her mouth parted, and I entered her, flicking her tongue with mine.

I skated my hands along the dips and curves of her sides,

desire pricking my depths with every inch of her I memorized.

The thunder of the ocean dulled into a faint growl.

She broke our kiss and pulled me into the bedroom of soft beige accented with glass teal lamps and dark wood furniture. A storm of ripping seams and popping buttons followed. She tore at my trunks, and I cursed the zipper of her dress. Could women's garments ever be less complicated?

Her cheeks flushed, she tugged me against her naked body, and I wanted to melt cradled in her soft curves.

A gust of salt and sea blew in, flapping curtains and white sheets and magazines on side tables. Life breathed around us, electric with promise.

I wrapped my arms around her waist and she trailed hot kisses down my neck. I fought for air as she concentrated on the delicate flesh of my collarbone that sizzled with every brush of her lips.

She ran her hand down my chest, down the ridges of my stomach, and down to...I shivered at the slice of pleasure cutting into me. Splitting me into a million pieces.

But this was a two player game.

One I was quite adept in.

I picked her up and threw her on the massive bed, the springs giving a nice creak beneath her.

She gave a coy smile and her eyes sparkled as she lay naked on layers of cotton sheets and covers, her hair spreading out around her like a halo.

I joined her and took her right breast in my mouth and skated my fingers over her hips before resting them between her legs.

She quivered and sucked in a shivery breath as I kept slow. Loving her. Worshiping her.

Sigyn arched her back, rising to meet me.

"How much longer are you going to make me wait?" she said, digging her fingernails into my scalp.

I gave a wicked smile, leaning in closer to her, letting her lips almost graze mine.

"You always were impatient."

And I was not a so-so lover.

I kissed her, hard and ravenous, weaving our tongues together. She moaned and writhed beneath me as I continued to work her. We sucked in each other's breath and she scraped my bottom lip with her teeth. And when she whimpered with release into my mouth, it nearly undid me.

I pulled back, loving how dark her eyes grew.

"Impatient?" she breathed. "I'd say five hundred years is long enough to wait."

I laughed and she flipped me on my back and straddled my hips between her thighs. My blood pounded hotter.

"I'd say you're right," I said.

I gripped her hips and she squeezed my shoulders, sliding me into her. Hot velvet stretched around me. And then she rocked, taking me in deeper.

I pressed my head back into the feather pillows falling into the ecstasy washing over me, wiping away what parts of my mind remained.

"You don't need to hide your pain beneath your illusions. I want to see you as you truly are," she breathed.

"You do see me as I truly am."

Her brow knit together.

"I don't understand...the scars..."

I reached up and cupped her cheek in my hand, my perfect, healed hand.

"I have no need for illusions anymore."

"But how?"

I smiled.

"Idunn's apples."

It was all that needed to be said as knowing filled her features.

She laced her fingers between mine and we held each other's gazes, moving together gently. Rhythmically. Matching the waves crashing outside. Rising and ebbing.

One roll of pleasure receding only to be followed by the next.

And we were free.

Free from the horror.

From the loss.

The grief.

It all melted between us. Splintered.

There were no more ghosts

There was only us.

There would only ever be us.

And for once, we had all our tomorrows.

We collapsed, and our souls blended together, chaos and fidelity, as one.

Tangled in the sheets we curled into each other's arms and held each other, our skin drenched with sweat and the scent of the other.

Sigyn laid her head on my chest, and I combed my fingers through her hair, watching how she rose and fell with my breath.

She tilted her chin up, and I looked into her eyes.

They glittered black and endless and threatened to suck me in.

I blinked.

"Is something wrong?" she asked, nestling deeper beneath my arm.

Confusion filled her perfectly normal, perfectly brown eyes.

Time will tell...

I shook Odin's voice and the ice along with it away. It was just the whiskey.

Yes. That's all it was.

That's all I would let it be.

I smiled, pulling her tighter against me, dissolving any

worry. Because there was none worth having.

We had each other now, and that's all that mattered. We had our tomorrows.

"No," I said. "Nothing is wrong."

Time will tell...

I caressed her skin, and I was happy.

"And what now?" she asked.

My lips pulled into a smile.

"We live."

EXCERPT FROM "THAT GOOD MISCHIEF"

THE NINE WORLDS RISING BOOK 3

Sigyn thrust her dagger between my ribs.

A punch of steel. A flash of white heat tearing muscle.

"I didn't want to do this," she said.

I know.

But that didn't make this any easier.

Blood spilled inside me, flowed warm over my stomach, filled my chambers and empty spaces.

I tasted copper on my tongue. Hot silk coated my lips and trickled down my chin.

Sigyn yanked out the blade, her skin taut over her rigid knuckles.

Pain followed, deep and searing and splitting.

The world shifted and blurred. I reached out to her...

I wavered. My knees buckled.

I fell.

My head struck hard earth, sending dirt and rot and damp into my nose that burned with blood coursing out my nostrils.

I choked on iron and stretched my fingers towards Odin standing over me, a tangle of roots and shadow behind him.

Help me.

But that wasn't how this worked.

His mouth moved quickly, chanting a guttural and ancient language brimming with dark magic.

His words drowned in the ringing that battered my eardrums.

Cold raced through me as fast as blood raced out of me.

I crushed my hand against the jagged gash in my flesh, trying to stop my blood from emptying. Trying to stitch my torn sinew back together. Trying to survive.

I must survive.

Sweat coated my skin.

The wound wasn't healing itself.

Damn.

I'd already forgotten.

Of course it wasn't healing itself.

I wasn't a god anymore.

I was mortal.

I pulled in thin breaths that kept growing thinner.

So, this was dying.

* * *

Three Weeks Earlier

Midgard

Los Angeles, California

To be continued...

* * *

That Good Mischief
(The Nine Worlds Rising Book 3)
is available on Amazon

THANK YOU!

I sincerely hope you enjoyed reading this book as much as I enjoyed writing it. If you did, I would greatly appreciate a short review on Amazon or your favorite book website, such as Goodreads or Bookbub! Reviews are crucial for any author, and even just a line or two can make a huge difference.

ALSO BY LYRA WOLF

The Nine Worlds Rising

Novellas

Lies, Knives, and Apples — *Free for **newsletter subscribers**!*

Novels

Truth and Other Lies (Book 1)

The Order of Chaos (Book 2)

That Good Mischief (Book 3)

Untitled (Book 4)

Untitled (Book 5)

Untitled (Book 6)

ACKNOWLEDGMENTS

The person I must thank first is my friend, Hannah. You always provide me with encouragement, always help me untangle knotted-up story threads, and always push me to make my characters hurt to their fullest potential. I don't know what I'd do without your stinging questions, like "but what if you made it worse?" or "why is this scene not more naked?" You are my dastardly muse, the destroyer of my happiness, and I love you for it. Thank you.

To my husband, who kept me fed, watered, and even occasionally succeeded in luring me out of my editing cave of despair with homemade chocolate cakes...I'd definitely have a lot less cake in my life if it weren't for you. I'd also have a lot less support. Thank you for all you do for me.

To my mother, who once asked me if there has to be so much blood and "spilled bowels" in this book. Yes, yes there does. Thank you for your continued fostering of my dreams and passions, even if my passions might churn your stomach due to all the blood spillage.

To my dad, who encouraged me to add even MORE blood. You get it.

To Cait, who gave me so much incredible support, encouragement, and unlocked more of my evil side than I knew I had in me.

To my friends, near and far, who helped in more ways than they can ever know, either by geeking out with me over Norse mythology, or cheering me on to do the thing, thank you!

Finally, a seriously big thank you to you, the reader. It is because of you, I keep going. It is because of you, I wake up excited to get to the keyboard and find out what happens next to Loki. And it is because of you, I write this story at all. This is all for you.

ABOUT THE AUTHOR

Lyra Wolf is a Swiss-American author of fantasy and mythic fiction.

Raised in Indiana, home to a billion corn mazes, she now lives in Central Florida, home to a billion mosquitoes. She enjoys drinking espresso, wandering through old city streets, and being tragically drawn to 18th century rogues.

When Lyra isn't fulfilling the wishes of her overly demanding Chihuahua, you can find her writing about other worlds and the complicated people who live there.

Lyra has earned a B.A. in History and M.A. in English.

* * *

Sign up for the **Lyra Wolf Pack VIP Newsletter** for exclusive content, updates, and other delicious goodies.
Sign up Here

You can connect with Lyra on her website, or by following her on social media!

lyrawolf.com

Made in the USA
Middletown, DE
07 November 2021